Shifter 6:
The New Breed

By
Jaden Sinclair

Published by
Melange Books, LLC
White Bear Lake, MN 55110
www.melange-books.com

Shifter 6: The New Breed
Jaden Sinclair, © 2010, 2011
ISBN 978-1-61235-032-5

Names, characters, and incidents depicted in this book are products of the author's imagination or are used fictitiously. Any resemblance to actual events, locales, organizations, or persons, living or dead, is entirely coincidental and beyond the intent of the author or the publisher. No part of this book may be reproduced or transmitted in any form or by any means, electronic or mechanical, including photocopying, recording, or by any information storage and retrieval system, without permission in writing from the publisher.

Credits

Editor: Nancy Schumacher
Copy Editor: Taylor Evans
Format Editor: Mae Powers
Cover Artist: Caroline Andrus

Shifter 6: The New Breed
Jaden Sinclair

Kane is a one of a kind shifter. He's more animal than man. Tortured all his life, beaten and experimented on. He has very little tolerance for anyone, except for his twin sister.

Jada Leonard is a woman who never followed anyone's rules but her own, but those rules change when she is caught spying and taking information. To save her life she is forced into hiding and forced to follow rules.

Like a match to gas, these two ignite a fire of passion. Both are strong willed and both refuse to bend. Will Kane give in to his instincts and take what belongs to him? Or will Jada be the one to make the new breed bow down, showing him that he's more than just an animal inside?

www.jadensinclair.com

* * * *

To Ms. V for giving me one hell of a
line to use in this book. You rock lady!

Shifter 6: The New Breed
Jaden Sinclair

Prologue

    Kane lay on his back, on the cold steel bed chained and naked. He opened and closed his fists, strained against the chains, but the damn things wouldn't give. Not when he was pumped full of drugs which kept him in a weakened state. But no amount of drugs could steal the burn he felt in his veins right now.
    He could see the full moon from a dirty, cracked window and deep down Kane knew it had to do with why he was feeling this way. He didn't know what it was, but he knew it had to be because of the moon. That much he'd figured out on his own.
    "I'm worried about you."
    Kane strained again when he heard his sister in his head. Sasha was scared and he lay helpless on this slab.
    "Every month you suffer like this, but this time it's the worst ever."
    "I'll be fine," he answered her. "It never lasts too long before it goes away."
    "But what if it's something big? What if they decide to destroy you?"
    He heard the desperation and hated that he was pinned down, unable to go to her like she needed. She was his twin, born eight years after him. Kane had known in those first eight years of his life that something was missing, and he wasn't talking about a parent or the knowledge of what he was. Sasha had been missing and he was only complete after she was born. And even though they were now forbidden to be close, and he couldn't hold her at night to keep her safe and warm from the horrors of this life, he was whole. But now something else was missing.
    "Blood count is different, and I can't figure out why." One of the men taking blood and shooting him up with other stuff looked up from his work when Josh came up next to Kane.
    "Is that it?" Josh asked.

"For now, yes." The man picked up another syringe and got closer to Kane. "After I check over his sperm, I'll let you know."

"You do that." Josh turned and walked away.

Kane snarled at the guards who parted his legs and he growled at the doctor right before he pushed the needle into the heavy sac between his legs. He didn't feel a thing, like he knew he should have, thanks to the burn in his body, but it still didn't stop the rage at having something else taken from him.

"I'm going to kill you," Kane said to the doctor, his voice low and vicious. "I'll enjoy watching you bleed to death at my feet."

The man's face paled and the syringe dropped to the floor. Clearly, Kane could scare this one.

Kane, don't, please. Sasha begged in his head, but Kane couldn't control himself.

He strained against the chains and began to change; at least he let his face change. A wolf snout replaced his human nose. His mouth opened for a snarl that turned into one hell of an animal growl. Fur began to cover his nakedness. The sight caused everyone around him to take a step back.

"That's enough, Kane."

Someone shot him with a stun gun. Fifty thousand volts hit him in the side, stopping his change and sent pain all through his body. Kane yelled and stiffened up, the chains preventing him from curling up. For longer than necessary, the volts kept coming until he almost passed out.

"Now play nice, Kane." Jason leaned over the table, smiling at him. "I would hate for the good doctor to damage something down there. You might want to use it one of these days."

Breathing hard, Kane tried to twist from his bonds. He wanted to be free right now, so he could wrap his hands around that son-of-a-bitch's neck. Nothing at this point in his life would give him more pleasure then to squeeze the life from his cold eyes.

"Fuck you," Kane hissed before he spit in Jason's face.

Jason stood back and wiped his face with his hand. "And here I was afraid that you were going to be too good. When the doc is done," he spoke to the guards, but kept his eyes on Kane. "Take him out back. Been a while since he was in the chair."

Normally Kane would shake at the mention of the chair. Jason had put it together for nothing more than torture. After a beating by the guards, he was whacked repeatedly by a ball on a rope until his *whole groin was black and blue. The last time he was in the chair he couldn't stand or piss comfortably for at least a week afterward.*

"*Enjoy it while it lasts, you prick!*" *Kane yelled at Jason when he turned and walked away from him.* "*Your time is coming.*"

Kane jolted awake from the same nightmare he had now for a week straight. Sweat covered his whole body and his groin throbbed in pain from the memory. They only had been free now for four weeks, but it didn't mean that the painful time he spent in the lab was going away yet. His body still ached each night; he had a very difficult time sleeping in a bed, wearing warm clothes and just being able to walk away to the outside without anything or anyone stopping him.

The first week of their freedom, Kane spent it with Sasha. He held her each and every night tightly in a corner of the room that was given to them. The family didn't try to pressure him away from her, they only worked on them both to use the bed instead of the floor. By week two Kane gave in and shared a bed with Sasha. Once he was healed enough, his father, and that was still a very strange thing to say, took him and Sasha away from the city to a cabin home in the mountains. Kane loved it on sight.

Drake treated them both as if they were humans, or shifters, which is what they were called—like him. It took a little time getting used to it, but he still wasn't, yet. Drake Draeger was his father and not too much older than Kane. Too weird if you asked him.

Drake had been kidnapped when he was almost one. His grandfather experimented on him, took what he needed to make Kane, and was planning to dispose of the boy before his father managed to rescue him. They thought that everything Martin had taken was destroyed, but they were wrong. Kane was created and tortured his whole life and Drake didn't even know he existed.

Drake kept telling Kane that it was all in the past. He was free now and he could do what ever he wanted. Kane didn't believe him at first, not until the day he took Sasha from the house to go looking in the woods alone and no one stopped them. That shocked him.

However, no matter how good they were treated, or how they were accepted, Kane still couldn't shake off the nightmares. His body was still healing, and Drake and Carrick made damn sure his wounds were well treated. Sasha was kept warm, fed and taught to read and write. She was happy, and that made him happy. What might give him peace would be to get rid of these damn dreams.

Kane got out of his bed, dressed, and groaned when he saw the time. Three in the morning, another night with only four hours of sleep. Not wanting to disturb everyone, Kane left the house. He went to the woods, to the small cabin he'd found when he and Sasha went walking a few days ago. He loved the woods. It was peaceful and quiet, just the way he liked.

He walked silently out of the house towards the woods. Deeply hidden was the small cabin he felt drawn to right off. Kane went to the porch and sighed, watching the sunrise. It was one of many he'd watched. Each time he saw the golden sky the knowledge that he was finally free hit him. Standing in the cool morning air each day proved that.

It had been a month since his last beating. He still had trouble believing it was all finally over, thanks to the continuing nightmares. Sasha and he were no longer caged up. He could do what he wanted with or without her, and, there wasn't anyone around to stop him, or that he needed to worry about hurting her.

But that wasn't where his mind was taking him. No, now Kane was thinking about his father, Drake Draeger. It was all so strange to him knowing not only that he had a father, but also that the man was near his own age.

They had someone that cared if they ate, or if they were cold. Someone that gave a damn. Not someone that used him for his own sick needs. It was still something he was having a bit of difficulty getting use to.

One of the strange things about all of this was that Kane knew the moment he opened his eyes that Drake was his father. He felt it, and once he was well enough to understand a few things about himself, other things made sense.

He was a shifter. Part wolf, part human. He was also stronger than most. His senses were more acute and his mind was sharper. He learned that how he communicated with Sasha using his mind was a way to seduce and tempt his mate, whenever the time came for him to find her. And he was going to *have* to find her he was told. Only she could tame the raging hunger in his body and soul. In the short amount of time, he'd been free, he learned so much about himself and what he was that Kane was finding it very difficult to digest it all.

Werewolf. Him. A beast inside his soul that raged and demanded. It sure did explain a lot, but still left him with unanswered questions.

Sasha was different compared to him. She didn't have any of that wolf thing that Drake told him. She was all human but for this unique birthmark on her shoulder. It matched the mark a shifter left on his mate's shoulder after he claimed her. She was also able to communicate with him using her mind, but couldn't do that with anyone else. Drake explained that it was a special treat twins shared, and he could also do it with his brother, Brock.

"Thought I would find you out here." Drake strolled silently up and Kane couldn't stop himself from stiffening. It still took him some time to get used to someone walking up to him that didn't intend to hurt him in some way. "Each morning you're on these rotten steps. I'm starting to think you like this place."

"It's quiet here," Kane remarked.

He watched Drake, saw each movement the man made. It was another thing Drake had pointed out this awareness in the shifters. They watched everything as though everyone was a potential threat. In Kane's case, he *did* treat everyone as a threat. He was shocked at how fast Sasha warmed up to Drake. She trusted him, and *she* didn't trust anyone.

Kane looked like Drake in his facial features. The fist time he ever got to see what he looked like, Drake was standing next to him, and he saw it. Kane thought he had black eyes but he didn't. His were blue, like Drake's, in a way. When Drake was in a good mood, they would turn a slight shade of blue. Drake thought it had something to do with the way he was treated and his moods. Kane had thick, sandy blonde hair with streaks of black that touched his shoulders, and his whole complexion had turned a dark tan since he was spending so much time outside. His lips were full, teeth white and straight, but the rest of his profile was dark. At night against the moonlight and stars, he came off as lethal.

The rest of his body, well that was something that even shocked Kane. After his very first shower, alone and under his control, Kane looked his body over in the mirror.

His height was around six-seven and he was like a brick wall of muscles, wide, broad shoulders tapering down to a powerful chest. Since they weren't allowed to eat like they needed to, Kane was underweight, but that didn't take away too much from the power in his body. Narrow waist, thick and long legs. In fact, when he saw the thickness of a tree his own leg came to mind. Even his hands and feet had a strong, powerful look. And the flesh that hung between his legs had a dominating look to it. Thick and hard, Kane measured it because it fascinated him, and made him wonder why those girls that he was forced to perform on seemed to enjoy it so much. In its hard form, he was close to ten inches, and limp it was about seven.

Drake caught him doing this and it quickly turned into a sexual conversation. Even though his body might not be a virgin Kane's mind was. He never got any pleasure out of the act and after Drake gave him a book, *The Joy of Sex,* he still didn't think he was going to get any. Sex wasn't something he thought very important. Drake only told him that when the time came he'd change his mind.

"What brings you out here so early?" Kane asked Drake.

"Oh, I went in to check on Sasha." He held his hand up, silencing Kane before he could panic. "She's still sleeping and your little place on the floor was gone. When are you going to use the bed?"

"I still feel like this is all a dream and that any moment it's going to be over."

Drake nodded. "I can understand that. You've had one hell of a life." He brought out of his pocket the tub of cream and fresh bandages. "Time to put more medicine on them."

Kane turned his back and pulled his shirt over his head. It was still very difficult for him to give this kind of trust to Drake, or anyone else for that matter.

"I heard Cole tell his brother on the phone the other day that he was going to start looking for that girl," Kane remarked when Drake pulled the large bandage off his back. "The one that was there the night you came."

"Yeah, Chase thinks she needs protecting and can't find her."

Kane held back a hiss when the cream touched the one wound that was still open. It stung, but was nothing like the pain he had experienced before. "Do you?"

"Guess that depends on what she has that they want." Drake pressed a fresh bandage on and Kane pulled his shirt over his head once more. "There are some secrets that people are willing to kill to keep."

Kane nodded. "Must be something very good then."

"How're the boys doing?" Drake asked.

Kane turned around and frowned at him. Drake rolled his eyes and pointed between his legs. "Oh, um still tender," Kane answered.

"You know I think when someone uses the term blue balls I'm going to have a whole new idea in my head," Drake sighed. "But don't worry too much. I'm sure you'll be able to use the whole package again."

"I don't have any interest in using it." Kane frowned.

"Kane, sex isn't as bad as what you were meant to think it was." Drake sighed again. "You're pretty much a rape victim, and one day you will be able to have a mate and live a normal life. I promise you."

"I've never gotten anything out of it." Kane shrugged. "The one and only time I ever came was when Sasha's life was threatened and when I thought I could smell something different. It was the only time that sex was close to pleasurable." He crossed his arms over his chest. "I don't think I can have a normal anything."

"It's going to take time, Kane," Again Drake sighed. "Right now you're healing. Don't think about sex, a mate, or anything except for getting yourself healthy. You both are under weight. You've been beaten *severely*, and you won't sleep in a bed. As far as I'm concerned you having any kind of sex is the farthest thing from my mind. But..." Again, he stopped Kane from speaking with a finger up in the air. "If you think there is something wrong with you then the only way to test it is very simple. Experiment on your own body. If things go right, then we know you're just fine."

Kane cocked his head to one side, eyes locked on Drake. "Can I ask something from you?"

"Sure," Drake shrugged.

"Can I have this cabin?"

"Will you sleep in a bed?" Drake grinned.

Kane didn't stop the smile that started to form on his lips. He didn't have much to smile about, but standing here with his father and the way he asked the question, Kane couldn't *not* smile at him.

"Only if I can pick it out. The one upstairs is too damn hard."

Drake laughed and slapped him on the shoulder. "Come on. Let's wake Cole up and go to town. We're going to need a shit load of supplies if we're going to get this damn place livable."

"Is Chase going to come home soon?" Kane cocked his head to the side as he walked with Drake back to the house. "I can see it in Cole's eyes that he is missed."

"When the time is right he will," Drake nodded. "Chase needs to be his own man and this is the way he's going to do it."

"I don't understand."

"I think what Chase is wanting is to get out from his big brother's shadow, and I know just what he's feeling. When you're the youngest, you feel different. Chase is out there exploring, discovering himself. When he feels the time is right, he'll come home."

"And that camper thing is his home?"

Drake nodded. "Yep."

"But you think he left for something else."

Drake stopped walking and Kane followed suit. "Kane, you're listening to your instincts better than most who know nothing." He smiled and said, "Yeah. I think Chase left for a different reason. I think he left because of a girl."

"This girl he's looking for?" Kane didn't understand. He couldn't comprehend why someone would go looking for a girl the way Cole and Chase were doing.

"No, not that one." Drake shook his head. "Someone else, but not sure who yet. Come on, I'll let you wake Cole up, and I'll tell Carrick we're heading to town."

Kane smiled, "Can I pounce on him?"

Drake laughed, "Just don't break the bed again. Carrick's still pissed about that."

Chapter One
Three years later

Jada Leonard paced her hotel room, thinking and waiting. She was waiting for the pizza that she'd ordered and thinking about her next move. Not to mention hiding from *two* groups of people it seemed.

One wanted to protect her. She snorted at that idea. No one wanted to protect her. She was on her own and liked it that way. The other group of people, well that was a different matter. If she had to put her finger on it, then Jada would say they wanted her dead. And she wasn't stupid about the why. She *knew* why. She took something important and they wanted it back. Tough! She wasn't going to give them jack shit! They could kiss her ass.

"Where the hell is that damn delivery guy," she mumbled as she started to pace the room, her stomach grumbling. Jada sat back down at the desk, checked her email, and frowned. Chase was emailing her again. The message was the same. Where are you? She rolled her eyes and replied again, none of your damn business. She didn't want him in this mess. Chase was safe away from her and those two that were in the lab were safely hidden away from the nuts that held them in cages. As long as she stayed on the run, then she would be just fine too.

She hit send, shut her computer down, and packed it away. Instead of in the morning, Jada decided that she would leave after she ate. Already she had stayed too long as it was and she didn't need to draw any attention to herself. The last time she stayed too long in one place she almost got caught. Sure as hell, she wasn't going to let that happen again.

She jumped when she heard a knock on the door. "Finally," she groaned, storming over to the door and yanking it open. Big mistake. "Cole!" she gasped, backing away.

"You are one hard ass girl to find." Cole walked into her room, slamming the door closed. "Real hard."

Jada kept backing up until she couldn't back up anymore. "Wh…what are you doing here?"

Normally she wasn't the kind of girl to get scared, but the cold expression in his brown eyes had her toeing a thin line. Cole wasn't like Chase. To her, Cole was a harder man who took what ever he was doing very seriously, and right now, it appeared that business was her.

Cole Sexton and his brother Chase looked a lot like each other. Both had brown hair, but Chase's tended to be a bit lighter. Both stood about six foot five and both had dark brown eyes. But like she thought before, Cole was more serious than Chase and it showed by his mouth. Chase has a fun grin on his lips most of the time were Cole's was thinner, at least to her.

"I think I should be asking you that question." He looked around her room and she slowly made her way to her things on the bed. "Get that thought right out of your damn head." She stopped, peering up at him. Jada didn't hear him come closer to her. "You're not running any more."

"Cole why don't you take my advice and—" another knock on the door and she stopped speaking and he tensed up. "Chill out," she rolled her eyes and brushed past him. "I ordered pizza."

However, pizza wasn't what greeted her when she opened the door again, but a gun.

Two men pushed forward and she backed up, raising her hands over her head. One man closed the door. "What's up boys?" she asked, putting a smile on her face. "Car break down or something?"

"Where is it?" the one with the gun asked, cocking it back.

"You know, asking questions that aren't specific with a gun pointed at one's face tend to create this amnesia effect." She pointed a finger at him from in the air. "And right now I don't know what the hell you're talking about."

"Excuse me." Cole tapped the guy lingering in the back on the shoulder. Neither saw him hiding in the corner behind the open door. Cole grabbed the guy, by the front of his jacket and head butted him so hard it knocked him out.

Jada used the distraction to kick the one with the gun right between his legs as hard as she could. He yelled, dropped the gun, and collapsed to his knees, holding himself. She took a step back and kicked him in the face, turned and grabbed her things on the bed and made a dash for the door. Cole stopped her by grabbing her arms.

"And where the hell do you *think* you're going now?" he demanded.

"Piss off, Cole!" She tried to yank her arm free, but he wasn't giving so she kicked him as hard as she could in the leg. "I have to get the hell out of here before more of those assholes show up."

He hissed before chuckling at her. He actually laughed at her while he yanked her bags from her hand and forced her out the door, still holding onto her arm.

"What the hell are you doing?" She tried again to get him to let her go and grab her stuff. "Cole I need to get out of here."

"And you will." He stopped next to a jeep, opened the passenger side door, and tossed her things into the back seat. "Get in."

"No!" Her voice was a bit high pitched and strained.

"Jada," Cole let her name draw out on a sigh. "I don't have the patience for this shit right now. I've been searching for your ass for two weeks now. Celine is going to be home for a long weekend and I would *like* to be there. Not out here searching for your sorry ass. Now get your ass in this jeep, or I'm going to force you in and cuff you. "

She narrowed her eyes on him and put one hand on her hip. "You wouldn't."

Cole cocked his head to one side and his eyes narrowed on her. In fact, she could have sworn that they had a shimmer in them. Almost as if he enjoyed the challenge, she gave him.

He bent to the side, opened the glove compartment, and pulled out a set of cuffs. When she saw them she started to fight, but she might as well go back and fight those two guys in the hotel room passed out alone. Nothing she did fazed Cole.

He picked her up, cuffed one wrist, and had her sitting in the seat, putting the other on before she landed any hard blows to him.

Cole leaned in real close to her ear and whispered, "You should learn right now. Never challenge any of us. We take them personal and will take the challenge." He backed up, closed the door, and went around the jeep to the driver side. Starting the engine, he turned his head and smiled at her. "Now be a good girl. I would hate to have to tape your mouth shut."

* * * *

The sun was coming up eight hours later and Jada gripped the handle tightly over her head in the jeep as she bounced around in her seat thanks to Cole hitting every pothole he could find. He didn't let her free until they were in the middle of nowhere and she had very little chance of running away. When he pulled into a gas station, he let her at least go to the bathroom alone, but when she wasn't fast enough he came walking in as if he owned the place. All of this meant she was going to have to bide her time and try to get away later on when his guard was down. Hopefully, that wouldn't be too long. She hated waiting.

Three years. That was how long she had been on her own, hiding, and she has been doing one hell of a job, until last night. Sure, she had half-expected Chase to be looking for her, but not Cole, and she sure as hell didn't think that Drake was involved in it.

The first time she heard that Chase was looking for her, she made the mistake of calling him with the hopes that she could get him to back off. That backfired on her. She never thought that Chase would get his brother to track her down when he couldn't seem to find her. Once she found out that Chase wasn't home with his brother, but out on his own, Jada made extra sure to stay on the go. When Cole almost caught up with her the first time she broke contact with Chase all together for six months. But a third time was not a charm for her. Cole caught her.

"How long are you going to sulk?" Cole asked her. It was about the eighth time he had tried to speak to her since he walked in on her in the bathroom. "Never got the impression that you were the quiet type."

She kept her mouth shut. There was no way in *hell* she was going to give him the satisfaction of speaking after he forced her to leave. And it was definitely force. Cuffed her to the damn car on her ass!

"Jada?" Cole tried again, only to be cut off.

"Don't talk, Cole," she finally said, keeping her eyes forward on the road but her hand up in his face. "It only reminds me more of how much of an asshole you are."

Cole took a deep breath. "I am trying to apologize here. Give me a damn break."

"The only thing I want to break right now is your fucking neck," she snapped. "And you're only apologizing because you're afraid your damn girl is going to cut you off for the weekend once she finds out you cuffed me to your damn jeep!"

"You are not going to put this shit all on my shoulders," he said. "What the hell did you expect? You've run from me twice. There wasn't going to be a third. And I'm not afraid of Celine."

"Ohhhhhh," she waved her hands in the air. "That's a great excuse for cuffing me to your damn jeep. Fuck you!"

"I believe that the last time you called Chase he told you that you needed protection." He kept glancing at her, but she didn't look at him. "He warned you that I was coming and that you were *not* going to run again."

"You hand cuffed me, you dick!" she yelled, finally turning and looking at him. "And I swear by God if I would have known how much of a prick you guys were I would have told you to go fuck yourself. This is the thanks I get."

"You were *told* to stop!" he yelled back. "Chase explained to you that things have changed. For Christ sakes they caught you right before we went in to get Kane and Sasha."

She raised her hand up in his face again. "Stuff it. I don't want to talk to you right now." She turned back around in her seat, crossing her arms over her chest.

"Too damn bad!" he snapped. My brother risked his damn life for you so you are going to listen to what I've got to say. Like it or not, I don't give a shit."

"Eat shit and die," she said through her teeth.

Cole skidded to a stop in front of a large log home, where two people were lounging on a wrap around porch. A blonde girl and one huge ass guy stood up when she got out. She didn't really look at them, but something about the big guy looked familiar to her. She just couldn't place him.

"Jada, we're not done," Cole said when she got out of the jeep.

"Yes, we are," Jada snapped back. I would rather have teeth pulled without drugs than try to have a normal conversation with you!" She yanked her two large bags from the back seat and looked him up and down. "Can you even have a normal conversation?"

"You're acting like a spoiled brat." Cole growled, pointing his finger at her. "And that damn mouth of yours is going to get you into a lot of trouble one day."

She rolled her eyes at him. "Like I haven't heard that one before."

"Hello, Jada." A woman came out with a smile. "I'm Carrick, Drake's wife."

Jada stopped and smiled sweetly at her. "You in charge of this zoo?"

She laughed, "Some what."

"Be careful, Carrick," Cole said from behind her. "She has a very bitter yet charming personality."

"How would you like my fist down your charming personality?" Jada kept her voice sweet and turned with a smile to him. Cole walked up to the porch and shook hands with the other man leaning against a support beam. Again, she was hit with that nagging feeling that she had seen him before, but she shook it off. She was too pissed to think about who she did or didn't know. Shaking her head, she walked up to the porch, "Who the hell are you? The Incredible Hulk on steroids?" Jada cocked her head to one side, looking him up and down.

"Jada, you remember..." Cole began.

"Don't give a shit," Jada sang back while she walked into the house with her bags. But she still heard the comments from the porch.

"Lovely girl."

"You have no idea," Cole chuckled. "Stay away from that one, she bites real hard."

"So do I."

Jada closed the door looked over her shoulder and quickly made her way to the back of the house. She smiled when she saw the door, but the smile vanished when she went through it and someone grabbed her arm, turned, and dragged right back inside. This time the grip on her arm was a lot tighter than the one Cole had on her.

She kept her mouth shut, and it probably was the best thing she could do. A big ass guy practically dragged her back into the house and into the front room. His steps were so wide that she was almost jogging to keep up with him. He pushed her to the stairs, pulled her all the way up into a bedroom, and shoved her inside.

"You need to lighten up on the red meat," she said, turning around to face him. "Hear it tends to bring out aggression if you eat too much." He said nothing. "Drake right?" she pointed her finger at him then snapped the fingers. "Long time no see. How've you been?"

He cocked his head to one side, arms crossed over his chest. She supposed by the look he gave her, the cold emotionless eyes were supposed to have her trembling or something.

They didn't.

"No more running," he said. "No more hiding."

"Says who?" She crossed her arms over her chest also and narrowed her eyes, giving him the same "I don't give a shit" look. "You're not my boss."

He snickered then stormed up to her. Jada jumped back. "For now, I am. You'd be dead if it wasn't for me sending Cole out to get your ass."

"Am I supposed to thank you for that?" She moved around him, putting more distance between them. "I don't recall asking for anyone's help. I do just find on my own."

"Yeah, I can see that." He scratched his chin. "Two sent to get your ass, one had a gun." Her jaw dropped open. "He called me while you were in the bathroom."

"You can't keep me here." She dashed towards the doorway and slammed into one large ass chest that was solid muscle. Jada slowly took two steps back and looked up.

Kane! That was the guy. He was fucking huge. Something she knew for a fact wasn't so the last time she saw him. The three years of freedom had done wonders for him and he appeared stronger than what she remembered. He was still tall, but the rest of him looked like it had grown another person. Those shoulders and chest took up just about the whole span of the doorway, leaving maybe an inch of space on both sides. One of his legs was thicker than hers put together. The term big was an understatement. Kane was a fucking giant.

"Call your pet off, Drake." Her mouth went dry when she looked up at his face.

Deep, cool blue eyes stared down at her without any emotion. Full lips didn't thin out, smile or grin in the normal smart-ass manner that she was getting very used to with these guys. Not even an eyebrow went up. No, Kane was as cold as a blizzard, and that alone had her taking another step back. Distance between her and this guy was a wise move. Her gut screamed to stay as far away from cave boy as she could get and stay that way. Because if Kane decided to do something or wanted something, nothing was going to stand in his way. It was just a vibe she felt.

"He isn't my pet, Jada." Drake sighed behind her. He came up close and silent. "He's my son, remember."

"Okay!" She raised her hands up and moved to the side of the room away from them both. But the way Kane followed her with his eyes gave her the chills. "I should have told you."

"You think?" the sarcasm came off Drake in waves.

"What do you want, an apology?" she smarted off, casting Kane a quick glance before facing Drake. "I'm sorry. Now can I go?"

"How long?" Kane spoke and boy did his voice affect her in ways she didn't like. He had a vibration in his tone that traveled all the way down her spine to gather between her legs.

"So he can talk," she said as she turned to Kane and looked him up and down boldly. "Didn't think he knew how."

"How long, Jada!" Drake raised his voice and she turned her attention back to him.

"How long what?" she yelled.

"Did you know?" Kane said.

She turned to him and pointed her finger back and forth quickly. "About you two?" Drake nodded. "A while."

"Months, years?" Drake sighed. "I want to know how long you have held onto this information."

"Why, so you can do some funky ass punishment?" She turned back to Drake and one eyebrow of his went up. She rolled her eyes and sighed, "I've know only a few weeks before you found out, okay."

"You fucked up, girl." Drake ran a hand in his hair and she glanced at Kane. He was still blocking her way out. Drake chuckled, "Oh, lose that thought. This time I'm going to have you watched *all* the time."

She frowned. "What?"

"You're in the woods now with a bunch of animals." Drake smiled at her and slid his hands into the pockets of his jeans. "We all have very good tracking senses and Kane is even better. His sense of smell is a hell of a lot better than the rest of us. So is his eye sight and hearing." She turned and faced Kane. He was still just standing there staring at her with those cold ass eyes of his. "Say hello to your personal escort, baby."

Jada shook her head, "No fucking way! I am not going to have King Kong here on my ass twenty-four-seven."

"He's also fast," Drake added, acting as if she hadn't said anything. "You run, he'll catch you and bring you right back here. If he does, then I'm going to lock you in the house. Let you get a taste of what being locked up is like."

Drake turned and walked towards the doorway, but stopped when she spoke. "You can't do this, Drake. You can't keep me here. It's fucking kidnapping!"

"Would you rather be dead?" He faced her again. "Because it's either here or in the ground, Jada. Which would you prefer?"

"I was doing just fine on my own."

"Oh yeah, I know." He chuckled without humor. "That gun to your head should have been enough to tell you that you were anything but fine. But what has me curious the most is why."

She sighed, leaned on one foot, and glared at him. "Why what?"

"I want to know why those men were there." He turned his whole body towards her and those damn cold eyes of his stared her down. She could tell right then where Kane had inherited them. "What were they after? What do you have?"

"Maybe they wanted to know where those two were," she indicated with a nod in Kane's direction. "Ever thought about that?"

"Bullshit!" both hands went to his hips. He stared her down and after some tense seconds, she lowered her eyes. "What the hell did you take?" he demanded. "Because I'm betting that's what this is all about. You have something that belongs to them and Stan wants it back."

"Nothing."

"You're lying to me." He pointed his finger at her. "I can smell it."

"What I have or know is on a need to know basis, and right now you definitely *don't* need to know."

"There it is," he whispered, stepping closer.

"What?" she took a step back and bumped right up against the desk that was in the room.

"That attitude. The very thing that is going to get you into soooo much trouble." His voice turned into a low purr. "You want to keep secrets? Fine." Drake shrugged. "You keep your secrets. But just keep in mind that I will find out what it is they were after, one way, or another." He turned his back on her and went back to the door. "The bathroom next to you is free. Carrick and I have our own, and Sasha has the other room with its own bathroom. Kane sometimes sleeps in the room next to yours and sometimes in his own place, so keep that in mind when you start thinking about running again. Don't trash this room."

"Drake!" she yelled, and when she went towards the door, Kane moved to the side, blocking her. "Shit," she mumbled.

"You should have told him," Kane said. "He's doing this to keep you alive. Stan doesn't mess around. If he wants you dead, then you're dead."

"Why don't you take your big badass self advice back down stairs where you belong?" Jada snapped at him. She was pissed off about this whole situation and didn't like being babysat by Kane, either. "Before my foot ends up so far up your ass you will taste the leather for weeks and Drake will have to dig out what's left." She knew she was being rude, but now she didn't care. She wasn't going to tell him or anyone else for that matter what she took or why they were after her.

Kane growled.

"Save it, Tarzan." She put her hand up to him. "The growling shit doesn't work with me. You have to keep an eye on me, fine. Do it from a long distance so I don't have to see your barbarian ass."

"They're right about you." He took a step inside the room, closing the door. "You do have a mouth that is going to get you into a whole lot of trouble," he finished calmly.

She rolled her eyes and turned her back on him, going to the desk to unpack her cameras. "Please. Like I've not heard that one before." Jada stiffened when she felt him behind her. She didn't hear him move, but she sure as hell felt the body heat that came off him.

He sniffed her. His face brushed the back of her head, moving her hair. He didn't wrap his arms around her, but he did press up against her body, his hands flattened on the desk, boxing her in.

"I've picked this scent up before," he remarked in her ear, his voice low with a rumble to it. "Now that I've experienced it, your scent reminds me of the wind after it's been raining. Not the kind that I would ever forget and I can easily track."

He grabbed her arm, forcing her to turn around, and he picked her up sitting her down on the desk. Jada gasped when he leaned into her again, forcing her legs apart to stand between them. His blue eyes darkened and she could have sworn his body heat became hotter.

"Tell me something, Princess," the words rolled off his tongue with a purr, giving her the chills. "Did you like watching me in the lab?"

"Not really," she sighed with a roll of her eyes. "You didn't really stand up to my expectations."

He didn't smile but she did see a slight curve to his lips for a brief second.

"You know you really need to learn what boundaries are." She pushed at his chest, and boy it was as hard as it appeared. And what a surprise, he didn't budge. "I don't like people in my personal space."

He cocked his head to the side and those eyes roamed over her body. Just that simple action had her feeling as if he was undressing her. "Is that so?"

"Yeah, that's so," she told him matter of factly. "You're not going to intimidate me Kane."

"You should learn more about us," he told her. Jada held her breath when he leaned in, his face next to hers and his hot breath brushed over her ear and neck.

"Challenges are something that we can *never* walk away from.

Ever!"

* * * *

He pushed away, turned, and left the room, leaving her sitting on the desk. He had to get out and he had to do it right now! Something came over him when he was close to her and he wasn't sure about it.

Jada was a very small woman compared to him. She stood maybe five-five, but he thought it was more like five-three. She was petite in height, with a frame that was slightly plump and he liked that. She wasn't fat by a long shot though, yet did fill out her clothes nicely and the fullness of her breasts had his hands itching to cup them. Her hair was soft and dark brown, reaching to the middle of her back and cut to layer around her face.

She had sea green eyes that held fire in them. Fire that he wanted to burn in, and that confused him majorly. With her soft facial features, and full lips, Jada was a knock out. And that damn mouth of hers was nothing but trouble. Sex wasn't something he ever thought about, but being that close to her. His senses drowning in her scent, he had the strong urge to have her under him with his body locked inside hers.

Drake was on the front porch, talking to Cole when Kane came down the stairs. He turned and headed for the back door, not wanting to talk to them. Instead, he went outside and spotted Sasha. She loved the outside and hated any kind of conflicts or fighting.

They had been free for three years now and she was still in a state of shell shock. She spoke very little, and kept to herself more than what he liked. Kane wanted to see her smiling, hear her laughing, and see life in her blue eyes. So far, all he got was her in his arms and a few smiles. Not enough. Drake wanted her to see someone. Something called a therapist, but Kane didn't like that idea. He didn't want anyone to know about them and he sure as hell didn't want people to know what happened to them. Luck seemed to finally shift to them when he saw her curled up on Drake's lap one night.

Kane came into the house late to check on her. He couldn't seem to pull himself away from the night and when he did go to the house and saw his sister in Drake's arms he almost lost it. No one but him could touch her, but when he saw her sleeping, saw that Drake was holding her like a child and nothing else he knew then that he could trust the man completely. She had a nightmare. One of many, but Kane wasn't there to take the demons away. Drake was. After that night, she changed some with Drake and Carrick.

Sasha opened up to them and both treated her like a daughter. Carrick started fixing her hair in the mornings, Drake gave her hugs, and light kisses on the top of her head. With constant small signs of affection from the two of them, his sister blossomed in a way he never imagined she would.

Drake also gave him affection, but it wasn't like Sasha's. Sure Carrick kissed him on the cheek and the first time that happened he was stunned. Any kind of contact that didn't involve pain was new. However, Kane did give Drake the benefit of the doubt. When he woke up himself from his first nightmare, involving the lab Drake was there for him. It was the very first time Kane cried, and Drake held him through it all. It was the first step towards healing for each of them.

Last year his grandparents and one set of Uncle and Aunt came to visit for the summer. Sasha surprised him by instantly bonding with Sidney and Jaclyn Draeger, and they surprised him even more by teaching Sasha things that he never would have thought to teach her. Cooking. They also taught him reading and writing, and Stefan took up the role of working with him to control the raging beast he had inside. With Dedrick's help, he was able to control his change.

Kane was still amazed at times, over how much they didn't know about this world they were born into. Most of everything he did was on pure instinct only. It was what kept him and his sister alive. One of the most interesting things that he learned about himself was what happened to him during the full moon. He burned from the inside out. Stefan explained it better than Drake had.

They called it a heat cycle. Raw, burning sexual need raced in his veins. The longer a male shifter went without his mate the stronger his desires would get, usually after he reached the age of twenty. Sometimes it was younger. Once his animal caught the scent of his mate, and then his heat would be almost ten times stronger than it had been previously. Kane wasn't sure if he could handle it being worse than it already was, yet each month it felt stronger than it had been the month before. Something was very different, but he couldn't put his finger on it.

Sasha was sitting on a blanket on the ground, staring out at the water. It was early October and the days were cool and cooler at night. It didn't bother Kane that much, but for Sasha she was miserable. She didn't like the cold and still couldn't handle it, but she loved being outdoors.

Kane was twenty-nine, Sasha eighteen, and Drake was thirty-one. It was weird to have a father around your own age, but they were dealing with it.

He went right up to Sasha, knelt down behind her, and leaned across her back to look over her shoulder. He saw her grin right before she snuggled back, resting against him. Kane touched her hair before wrapping his arms around her, hugging her.

"You're shivering," he stated.

"It's getting colder," she sighed.

"It will snow before we know it."

"So what's she like?"

Kane sighed loudly and dropped down on his back. Sasha giggled and turned over, resting her chin on his chest. For months, they all had been on the hunt to find Miss Jada Leonard, and she heard all the talk about it.

That wasn't what had his mind drifting. Kane's mind went back to the night he picked up that scent. After his first talk with Drake and learning what masturbation was about, Kane experienced his first wet dream and boy was it a hot one. It was as if his mind was refreshing his senses with what it picked up in the lab, giving him one hell of an erection that lasted for hours.

Never had he thought about sex as good or being pleasurable. It was an act required of him so his sister would get a blanket and extra food. He *never* got anything from it, and could count on one finger how many times he'd orgasmed. It just wasn't something he cared about, but when the dreams came it all changed.

He started waking up in the middle of the night with a very painful erection. For weeks, this went on before he finally had to go talk to Drake about it. They discovered that the drugs that were forced on him repressed his natural sexual desire and that they had to be coming back. Painful erections were something that the young went through, but since he never had the opportunity to experience anything natural his body was making up for it now. And boy if they weren't painful, too. Thankfully, that pain shit only lasted for a very short time, but the sexual need and release he was starting to feel didn't go away. Not even with the masturbation.

"Kane?"

Sasha's voice pulled him out of his thoughts and he groaned, "She has a mouth that won't quit. And Drake wants me to keep an eye on her. He thinks she's going to try to run again."

"What do you think?"

Kane touched her cheek. "She'll run."

"Will you catch her then?" She turned her head spilling blonde hair over her shoulder onto his chest, and her blue eyes were wide. He couldn't express what he felt just being this close to his sister. Maybe love, if it existed.

"Probably." He touched her face and hair before putting his arms under his head. "She has something that they are willing to kill her for."

Sasha lowered her chin to his chest. "I think she was in the lab the night you started to act funny."

"Probably. She's in danger." He kept his voice even when he spoke. The last thing he wanted was for his sister to pick something up that might worry her when he talked about Jada. "How are you doing?"

She gave him a quick grin before turning back around and using him as a pillow. "I like it here. The water is so calm and the sky so blue. I never thought the outdoors would be so nice."

"But if you stay outside all the time, you're going to get sick." He sat up, and then got to his feet, taking her with him. "Time to go back inside."

She nodded and picked her blanket up. "I should go help Carrick with dinner anyway. She's going to show me how to do chicken tonight."

Sasha loved to cook and Carrick loved to have her in the kitchen. It was one of the rare times Kane saw her flushed and very happy.

Dinner was tense and very quiet. Carrick and Sasha put out a big spread of fried chicken. It was good, but Kane couldn't get into this food as he normally did. No his attention was on trying to keep his body under control and his dick down. Hard to do when his senses were overwhelmed with the scent of Jada sitting across from him.

He wasn't supposed to be having these thoughts or struggling with the idea of touching her. However, when his thoughts were filled with nothing but her scent it was damn hard. He *knew* that it was her in the lab. Knew that she was taking pictures of what he'd been forced to do, but did she know that he came because of her. He would bet his life that she had no idea, and he was going to keep that information to himself.

Kane was very thankful when supper was over and he could leave without drawing attention to himself. He went back to his own little place, the small cabin in the woods that he'd requested from Drake. It was his own to do with as he wished. So far, he put a new porch on, with Cole's help. He kept it very simple, with just a bed, sofa, and small table with two chairs. Later on Cole had him put this bar up across the space between front room and bedroom. There were also leather straps for him to strap his ankles to and work out. Cole told him it helped sometime with the heat. It did and then some. Kane worked out every night before he went to bed, making himself larger than he'd been three years ago.

He stripped as soon as he closed the front door and walked into his small bathroom. He took a quick cool shower and then went to bed with one stiff erection.

"Shit," he groaned, rubbing his face. "This is going to be hell. I just know it." As his eyes slid shut, Kane was helpless and closed his hand around his cock. If he wanted to get any sleep, he was going to have to take care of this need, at least for the moment.

Chapter Two

Kane watched the sunrise like he always did from his porch. He sipped at his coffee, with his chair tipped and his feet resting on the railing. The way the air smelled it was hard to imagine that it was going to snow soon. It was hard to believe that his body was still tense and his damn dick slightly hard. He swore that he relieved that need enough last night, it was the main reason he didn't get much sleep. Damn cock was hard as a rock, and it was thickening even more the second his nose picked up a particular scent that didn't belong in the woods.

Jada. Kane groaned softly, put his chair down on all fours, and was about to stand up when she jumped out from the side of the cabin, startling him. What was left of his coffee spilled down the front of his shirt, burning his chest.

"Damn it," he growled, glaring at her, "Do you always sneak up on people?"

Jada strolled up on his porch, smiling down at him in a cocky way, "Are you always so jumpy? And I thought you were supposed to be the best, and here I snuck up on you!"

"What are you doing out here?" He couldn't keep the growl from his voice when he stood up and brushed the warm liquid on the front of his shirt. He also gave her a quick glare, which was a mistake.

Jada had her hair pulled up in a tail at the back of her neck. Jeans, boots and a gray sweatshirt hugged her body and a camera hung around her neck. Her jeans curved over her hips perfectly, giving him a few nasty thoughts. Like what did her skin taste like or what would she feel like under him? Hell, Kane even had a picture of watching his cock sinking into her, which had the damn piece of flesh throbbing back to life. *So this is what sexual wanting feels like.*

He hated that feeling. Hated to be reminded that there was life down there that he couldn't control. And Kane was all about control now. He spent three years learning how to control *everything* on his body. In the blink of an eye, it was all slipping away from him thanks to this girl standing before him.

"Sunrise gives the greatest pictures and landscapes sell like crazy." She looked at the front door, pretty much ignoring him. "So this is your house. Um, sort of pictured you in a cave."

She went inside and he didn't stop the growl of aggravation from slipping out. Kane quickly went after her, forcing himself not to close the door. If he closed the door, it would only add to the temptation. He was asked to keep an eye on her, not *fuck* her. *Now, from where did that thought come?*

"Typical." She swung around, facing him. "Kind of suspected your place would be a mess. Housekeeping not on the list of things to learn?" She smiled sweetly at him and cocked her head to one side.

One eyebrow went up. Kane wasn't a spot free kind of guy, but his home wasn't a mess. He didn't have a lot of things to make a mess. "Why are you here?"

She crossed her arms over her chest and those damn sexy green eyes of hers narrowed on him. *Sexy eyes? Have you lost your mind?* "Pictures. It's what I do for money. I decided that I would come out here and tell you in person that I really don't need a babysitter, at least not you. What's that for?" She pointed to the metal bar situated in the tall doorway.

"I work out on that." He glanced over to where she pointed at the push up, weight bar Drake had helped him put in the door way. Grinning, he realized even in Drake's house all the doorways were tall. Even with his height they were all around seven feet in height or higher, like the one here in the cabin. So, that made it where he didn't have to always duck his head every time he entered this room.

He moved past her into his room and pulled the wet shirt over his head. Tugging on a fresh one, he went back in and cocked his head to the side at her. "And yes, you do."

"Huh?"

"Need a babysitter."

"No I don't, and if I did it sure as hell wouldn't be you."

Kane frowned. "What's wrong with me?"

"You, I don't trust." She pointed her finger at him before turning and slumping down on the sofa. "Damn this thing is wide enough you could almost sleep on it."

"I used to." He moved to stand in front of her and Jada snapped a picture off, blinding him for a few seconds. "What the hell was that for?" He rubbed his eyes, waiting for the spots to go away.

"Needed to check my settings."

She was messing with her camera when he lowered his hand from his face. She was sitting Indian style, head lowered and face all sober. She really did take her picture shooting serious.

"Have a look." Jada turned the camera around so he could see.

Kane lowered himself down on the sofa next to her and peeked over her shoulder. He never saw a picture of himself before.

"It would be better if you smiled."

"How'd you do that?" He touched the small screen, amazed since he thought pictures came out on paper.

"It's a digital camera. I've several of them. I upload the chip to my computer and print out the ones I think are good." She turned her head to him and his heart started pounding.

Kane couldn't stop himself from inhaling deeply and closing his eyes. She smelled so damn good. He wanted to wrap himself around her and take her scent in all night long.

"What are *you* doing?"

Her voice snapped him out of his trance, but it didn't cause him to back away from her. He was still close. Close enough that if he stuck his tongue out, he could touch her lips. "You're scared of me," he stated, his voice purring softly. "It has changed your scent."

He heard her breathing hitch. "Am not." She gasped, eyes lowering to his mouth. "And stop smelling me."

"I can smell it," he whispered. He couldn't help himself from reaching out to touch her, but Jada stopped that by rolling away off the sofa.

"You need to work on those boundaries, wolf boy." She snorted, "And knock that shit off."

Kane took another deep breath and grinned at her for the first time. "And you need to work on your emotions. I can smell everything and your scent is changing."

"Then your nose is off, because nothing on me has changed." She backed up to the door and he forced himself to stay put, even though it was very tempting to follow her and box her in.

She didn't leave as he thought she would. Instead, she headed for his room.

"Where're you going?" he asked with a frown.

"Bathroom."

Kane was up and heading in that direction to stop her, but she made it before him. The new door he put on slammed in his face.

"Shit," he mumbled.

He closed his eyes and backed up to the bed, sitting down on the edge and waited. His gut twisted in a knot just thinking about her finding the book he left in there. How could he be so stupid as to leave it in the bathroom? But then, he didn't have hardly any company. Not even Sasha came out here anymore.

He heard a flush, water running and stood up. The door opened and his gut dropped. Jada had the *Joy of Sex* book in her hand opened to the last page he was reading. Oral sex.

"So this is what you read when you're alone in the bathroom." Her head lowered to the book. "Who are you planning on trying this stuff out on? A blow-up doll?"

Kane growled and snatched the book out of her hands. Her head came up, her eyes opened wide. He took one big step forward and she took two back, touching the wall with her back. He tossed the book onto the bed. Then he put both of his hands up against the wall, boxing her in.

"You're very nosy, Princess." The words vibrated as he spoke. "That's why you're in the trouble you are in now."

"You know, I get that a lot." Again, she pointed that finger at him. "But who ever said I was in trouble?"

Kane had a picture in his head of taking her finger and sucking it into his mouth. "You wouldn't be here unless you weren't." He cocked his head to the side, making sure that she got the full effect of his eyes roaming over her body. "How about I try the oral out on you, since you're so interested." He licked his lips. "I bet you would taste real good, like you smell."

"Not on your life!" she laughed out her answer, but her laughter quickly died down with his none smiling face. "I think it's time for me I left."

But he wasn't ready for her to leave and ended up doing something that he was going to kick his own ass for later. Kane leaned way down and kissed Jada.

The calm that he fought so hard to keep just shattered into pieces. He moved his mouth over hers, sucking, and devouring her mouth. With some force, he pushed his tongue into her mouth and moaned at the taste.

Kane moved his hands from the wall to cup her rear, crushing her close while he deepened the kiss. He tried to eat her up with his mouth, sucked her tongue between his lips, and pressed both of their bodies back into the wall.

He thrust his tongue in and out of her mouth, kneading her ass. Kane felt his control slipping and didn't even want to bring it back in. This was his first kiss. First touch of another that he engaged in willingly and boy if he wasn't enjoying it.

Then it all came crashing to an end with a hard knee to his groin.

He dropped to the ground, holding himself. Three years had gone by since he last felt any kind of pain between his legs, and now he was experiencing it all over again. Only this pain was different. This wasn't the same kind he had with the chair. No, this time the pain was different, sickening, because he was hard as stone when it happened.

"Now I owe you," he groaned, pushing the sickness back. Kane didn't need to be sick on the floor. Not right now.

"Call it even," she said. He glanced at her. Jada was backing away from him towards the door and he was helpless to stop her. "Stay away from me, Kane. I mean it or the next time it won't be my knee to your nuts." She turned and ran from the cabin.

It took about five minutes or so before he could move, and that was only to turn and rest his face in the bed covers. The sickness he felt went away, but the throbbing remained. Kane had experience a lot of pain in his life, but this was a new one for him. And it lasted! How the hell could a knee cause this much pain?

When he was finally able to stand up he winced, and wobbled to the wall, leaning back, breathing hard. As soon as the pain dulled, he moved from the bedroom to the front room. His place was so small that the kitchen space and front room combined into one room. Kane was talking to Cole about adding a room to it, making the place three rooms instead of two and half.

His kitchen space had a wood burning stove and a small fridge. He kept very little food in the place since he still spent a lot of his time at Drake's with Sasha. He also had a small table with two chairs pushed up against the wall next to the window. Most of the space he filled up with the large sofa that he kept facing the fireplace. Kane wasn't lying when he told Jada that he slept a lot on it. Even Sasha slept on it when she came out right after he moved in.

It was soft, very wide, and red. Now, with a beer in his hand, it was comfort.

Kane lowered himself down on the soft cushions and sighed. He twisted the top off his beer, tossed it into the dead fire, and took a big drink.

Kissing Jada wasn't one of the brightest moves he ever made, and why the hell he did it was beyond him. He was almost tempted to talk to Drake about it, but figured that it wouldn't be a very good idea. It was bad enough that he'd kissed her. He didn't need everyone else to know about it. After all, it was just a kiss. Not like he fucked her.

Finishing his beer, he left the cabin and went to look in on Sasha. He heard Carrick in the kitchen when he walked in the front door. He didn't bother telling her that he was here, just turned, and took the stairs two at a time. He was still tender in his movements and had to avoid walking in long strides. Before he went to his sister, he stopped at Jada's door and cracked it open. What a surprise, she wasn't there.

Sasha's bedroom door was cracked open. She always left it open just a touch. It was part of her no trust, but needed to trust. She didn't want to lock him out, but needed to have her own personal space.

But what had Kane at ease each time he saw his sister was how she no longer had to worry about being bothered or cold. She was able to get the kind of rest she needed. There wasn't anyone around to keep her awake with fear. She could sleep as long as she needed and there was food when she was hungry.

The first few days after he was healed enough to move she slept in his arms. They were both scared and not too sure about the family that they seemed to have inherited. Everyone wanted to help them, teach them, and care for them. But they also seemed to understand how the two of them didn't trust anyone or anything.

Somehow, Sidney Draeger got Sasha out of his arms. Thinking about it now, Kane realized that they were like animals boxed in. He was on the floor in the corner, his back throbbing to a point that he thought he was going to pass out from the pain. The beating he endured to his groin didn't help matters either. In his arms was Sasha, trembling from the cold and her fear. Sidney had the kindest eyes and Sasha could tell right off that she wasn't going to hurt them. When she left his arms and went to Sidney, Kane lost it all. He broke down for the first time and Drake along with Stefan was there to help him pick up those pieces. It was the first time in his life that he was held from comfort and not because he couldn't walk.

The first step to his new life was made that day, and he would never forget it. His twin trusted where he could not, and it saved them both. Because of that, he was now able to stand in this room, looking down at her not as an animal but as a man.

Sasha was taking a nap and sleeping deeply on her back, one arm hanging over the side of the bed and the covers pushed down to her knees. He went over to her and pulled the covers back up to her chin. She might not like to be cold, but she always forgot when she was sleeping that she had blankets. Warm blankets every night and between him and Drake they made sure she stayed warm. He smiled and touched her cheek. Yes, it was because of her that he was now a man, not an animal. But what kind of man was he? What kind of man would kiss a girl that he didn't know, as Kane had?

"Hey," Drake whispered from the doorway.

Kane jumped and turned around. Drake indicated with a nod to come out into the hallway. Leaving Sasha's side, he left the room and closed the door quietly.

"Where's Jada?" Drake asked.

"Not sure," Kane answered, keeping his voice even and his face normal. The inner voice that he was starting to hear told him that now wasn't the time to tell Drake something happened. "She snuck up on me at my place, but left. I think she is out taking pictures."

"Yeah, Chase mentioned she is some kind of photographer or something." His eyes narrowed on him and Kane became uncomfortable. "Something wrong?"

Yeah my nuts hurt. "No. Why would something be wrong?"

"You just act like something's' bothering you."

"I'm fine."

Drake nodded, "Okay, if you say so." He patted Kane on the shoulder and turned. "I'm going to get something to eat before your sister wakes up. I swear she eats more than Celine."

The corner of Kane's lip when up at the comment. He'd seen first hand how Celine ate when she was home for a weekend. He also saw how Sasha ate, and the two of them were a lot alike.

Shaking his head, he walked away from the door and followed Drake down stairs. The man did have a point. You wanted to eat, better get it fast.

* * * *

Jada took her last picture of Cole's house. Her memory chip was full and her mind somewhere else. She should be thinking about the landscapes she took, the few stills and how she was going to sell them. Instead, her mind was on Kane and that damn kiss.

Why the hell did he kiss her? She wasn't doing anything but teasing him about what he was reading in the bathroom. How did that say, kiss me? And why were her damn lips still tingling from it? *Because you liked it!*

"Oh shut up," she said to herself.

However, that wasn't what pissed her off the most. No, what had her gritting her teeth together and staying away from the house was the simple fact that she *did* enjoy it. She wanted more of it, which of course was crazy. Kane was an animal. One she had no business playing with or poking at.

So why couldn't she keep her mouth shut when he was around her? That question kept going around in her mind, distracting her from everything else.

"Now I don't think I've ever seen you this distracted before."

Jada turned, twirled around, and took a deep breath. "Damn it, Cole, don't *do* that."

"Do what?" he chuckled.

"Sneak up on me."

"Thought it was impossible to sneak up on you." He came up, went behind her to glance over her shoulder. "Nice. You should frame that one and let me give it to Celine. I'll pay you for it."

"Yeah, well just because it looks good here doesn't mean it's going to be a good one once I've downloaded it to the computer." She flicked back to some of the other pictures. Some were of the woods, the cabin, few animals like a deer and some birds.

"So where's Kane?" he asked.

"How the hell should I know?" She stepped away from him and pulled the memory chip from her camera.

"Isn't he supposed to be keeping an eye on you?"

She stopped what she was doing and glared at him. Cole sounded like he was enjoying the fact that she had a tail on her.

"How's Chase doing?" She hoped that the change of subject would shut him up. No such luck.

"Oh no," he shook his head. "You don't get to change the subject. What's going on?"

"You know, I've noticed that you're limping." She pointed at his leg. "Did my little kick hurt you more than what you're trying to let on?"

"I'm not limping—"

"Just plain limp?" She blinked her eyes at him several times before turning her back on him and walking away.

Cole laughed, "Oh that's low. Very low!" he yelled.

Jada smiled, shook her head, and waved to him without looking back. She put another chip into her camera and headed for the woods once again.

She walked in a daze. Her mind couldn't stop thinking about that damn kiss, the feel of his lips upon hers, the smell of him close and his hands on her ass. She stopped to yell at herself and she ended up groaning instead. She was lost in the woods.

"Great." She slapped her hand on her leg and looked around.

There was no trail, no markers, nothing that might tell her where the hell she was or how far away from the house, she might be. What she did hear surprised her.

Water.

Jada followed her ears to the sound of water and came out of some thick brush to a spring that she would never have suspected to be out here.

It was a beautiful spot with wild flowers that were still blooming despite the weather change. Steam came off the water and when she touched it, she was surprised to find it warm.

She never saw anything like this. The spring appeared to be cut out of stone. A perfect circle of stones went around the water and a few flat larger stones were on the side.

Jada took pictures. She snapped many, some with birds flying by, others with different angles. She kept snapping until her second and last chip was full. Then she got one crazy ass idea. She was going to take a swim in the water.

She found a spot that she was sure would be safe for her camera. Bending over she unlaced her boots, pulled her socks off then she unzipped and unbuttoned her jeans, wiggling them down her legs. Sweatshirt came off next, and then she reached behind her to unclasp her bra. With only her panties on, Jada moved over to the side and started a slow walk into the water.

She stilled when a flock of birds took flight. They made so much noise it had her wondering for a split second if someone was watching her or not.

* * * *

And someone was. Kane hunched down behind a thick span of brush, his eyes glued to Jada. He couldn't take his eyes from her as she stripped down to nothing but a pair of pink low to the hip panties. And they were lace, damn her. He could see right through them!

He saw just about everything Miss Jada had. Each bit of skin he viewed had his mouth watering to taste. Kane was certain that this wasn't what Drake had in mind when he said keep an eye on her though.

When the jeans slid down her legs, Kane couldn't stop his thoughts from racing in his brain. She was short compared to him, but those legs of hers looked damned long to him and just about right to go around his waist. He even felt a slight twist at his hips. It was almost as if his body was coming to life in other places, besides his dick, with each piece of skin that came into view. It was almost as if his body knew which of her parts went where.

Hips knew that legs wrapped around them, and his hand itched with the knowledge that there was a body to touch. That was what he felt like at this time. His mouth opened when she turned to place her jeans on top of the boots and he saw her rounded stomach. Jada wasn't pale white, nor was she golden brown, but she did have a slight tan. When her bra came off, he was very surprised that there weren't any tan lines.

He moved when her breasts came into view, startling some birds. Kane quickly hunched down further so she wouldn't see him and didn't move again until he heard her splash into the water. He peered over again and she was under the water. When she came back up, hands going to her wet hair, full frontal view for him, Kane lost his breath.

Water trailed over her breasts, nipples hard points catching drop after drop. What little bit of hardness he had in his jeans expanded by ten. He was steel between his legs and it throbbed in demand.

He wanted, and something told him that was very dangerous.

Kane had things denied him all his life. He wasn't about to go back to that and tell himself no when he wanted something. But the something that was in that water, having a great time was the something he shouldn't be wanting. Drake asked him to keep an eye on her. That was it. Touching, tasting, and fucking weren't on that to do list.

He frowned. Fucking. Where the hell did that one come in? *Your throbbing dick!* He suppressed a groan at the thought and had to bite his lip when her hands went over her chest, wanting to cup her breasts.

When she started her way out of the water, he turned on his heels and left. He couldn't stand to watch her dress. Not after he had the pleasure of seeing her undress. For now, he wanted to hold onto the image of her wet and nothing else.

* * * *

Jada sat in front of her computer doing a check to make sure her small printer was working and calibrated correctly. So far, there was a small glitch in her system and she couldn't seem to find it. She had a shit load of photos to upload, a few she wanted to print out, and her damn equipment wasn't working properly.

"Dammit!" she snapped, pushing away from the desk. She stopped herself from going into a rant with Sasha standing in the doorway staring at her. "Oh, hey."

"What are you doing?" She was shy. Jada could hear it in the soft way she spoke and the manner in which she held back from coming in.

Jada glanced over her shoulder at her computer. "Oh, trying to get my printer to work with my computer. Have a lot of photos I want to upload and print out."

"What do you mean?" She frowned.

"Come in." Jada sauntered over to the bed. After she unpacked her things, she moved the desk over in front of the window, next to the bed. Sasha came in and sat down and Jada turned the computer so she could see the screen and put one of the memory chips in. "See." She pointed to the screen, showing the girl a bunch of photos.

"Wow," Sasha breathed out. "This is so neat."

Jada smiled and turned in her seat to one of the bags next to the desk. She dug inside and brought out a smaller camera, one that she used to use years ago. Making sure it was working nicely she put a memory stick into it and handed it to Sasha.

"Here. You go and take a bunch of photos and then come back up here and we'll check them out."

Sasha shook her head, her blue eyes got big and she looked like she was about to panic, "No, I can't take that."

"Sure you can." Jada smiled at her. "I want to see what you see. Who knows? Maybe a few of your photos might be worth some money."

She lit up like a Christmas tree. Sasha stood up, cradled the camera as if it was made of glass, and headed to the door. She stopped because Kane was standing in the doorway watching the two of them. The expression he had on his face, and the darkness in his blue eyes had Jada feeling one hell of a chill go down her spine.

"Look!" Sasha breathed out in front of him.

Kane's eyes slowly moved from Jada to Sasha. He smiled and kissed her on top of the head. "Dinner's ready."

Sasha nodded and left. Jada tried to put on a good front smiled and rubbed her hands together. Anything but think about his kiss.

"Something wrong?" she asked when all he did was stand there staring at her. "I get this strange feeling that you're trying to undress me with your eyes or something." If she wasn't mistaken the corner of his mouth moved just a bit.

"Maybe I am," he stated.

"Okay, that's it," she snapped, shaking her head and waving her hands in front of her. "You are *not* going to be babysitting me or anything else. Period! Not after the crap you pulled today."

She moved with the intention of brushing past him and going down to have a talk with Drake. What she didn't expect was for Kane to grab her arm, to stop her.

"The crap *I* did today?" He leaned down close to her, lowering his voice, "How about next time you take a towel," he whispered in her ear. "I'd hate for you to get a cold after a swim."

Mortification hit with the realization that he was in the woods watching her take a swim. When the birds took flight, it was because of him.

"You bastard," she said between her teeth right before she slapped him as hard as she could in the face.

Kane let go of her and Jada ran away from him, down the stairs and right out the front door. There was no way in hell she was going to stay there and try to face him after he just pretty much confessed that he saw her taking a swim naked. Where she was going to go, she had no idea.

According to Drake, Kane was fast, but she wasn't expecting him to be as fast as what she was hearing behind her now. The way he was catching up with her made it seem like she never had a head start. That they both took off running together at the same time.

"Jada!" Kane yelled.

Jada pushed herself faster and harder, mostly out of anger. He saw her. Dammit, saw her swimming without her clothes on and she didn't even know it. What kind of man would hide and watch like that. *Well wait a sec, he* isn't *a man you dipshit!*

"Dammit, Jada, stop!" he bellowed.

He grabbed her, one thick arm going around her waist and plucking her right off her feet. Jada screamed and kicked her legs out wildly. He was still moving, slowing down with her in his arm, but he lost his footing and they both went down to the ground.

Kane quickly rolled, pinning her down, wrists over her head, body between her legs." You ran," he stated.

"No shit I ran," Jada panted. Her side burned and she was too tired to fight him to get him to let her go.

"You knew that if you ran I would come after you. So why did you run?"

Jada looked at Kane as if he'd lost his mind. "You have got to be kidding me!" She shook her head and licked her lip. "You spied on me!' she yelled in his face. "You were watching me take a swim for Christ sakes!"

"I was asked to keep an eye on you." He kept his voice even, but if she wasn't mistaken, then she was feeling something stiffen up against her, and that she didn't need now. "And I did what was asked of me."

"Yeah, dip shit," her voice rose in disbelief. "That didn't mean while I was naked. You could have told me you were there."

He grinned. For the second time since she'd been at the house he smiled. "I could have, but then I would have missed the show."

"You really are delusional, fur brain," she told him through her teeth. "I'm not a show for your sick entertainment."

"But isn't entertainment a show?" Now the grin broke out in a big smile. "I know I was very entertained."

Jada sighed loudly and squirmed. She tried like hell to put on the, *I don't give a shit act.* "You can get off of me now."

* * * *

Oh, this feels too damn good. "Are you going to run again?"

"Away from you?" He nodded and she snorted, "Damn right I am, every chance I can get now. You need to stay the hell away from me. Period." She squirmed more under him, struggling to get out of his hold.

Kane broke out in another big smile. "Is that a challenge I hear in your voice?" He licked his lips, roaming his eyes over as much of her body as he could, just for the affect of making her uncomfortable. "I thought I told you about challenging me."

"Go to hell, Kane, because that is the only place you're going and it's alone."

Kane narrowed his eyes on her. "Oh, really." He stood up fast, yanking her to her feet, keeping a hold of her wrists. With another yank and bending over, he slung her up and over his shoulder.

"What the hell are you doing?" Jada yelled, hitting his back and kicking out with her legs.

Kane shifted her a bit over his shoulder, turned, and started the walk back to the house. "I'm taking you back to the house."

"You can't do this!" she screamed, landing blows to his lower back.

Kane kept his mouth shut and his hands on the back of her legs. The urge to touch her ass and give her a couple of good swats were strong, but he fought it back.

"Listen to me, you large lump of shit." She twisted on his shoulder. "Put me down right now!"

"Lump of shit?" Kane shook his head. "That's a new one." It didn't take Kane long to walk back up to the house. He put Jada down roughly on the porch, right in front of the door. "In. Now!" he hissed.

"No."

Kane took a deep breath, letting it out slowly. *Control. I need some serious control here or I'm going to do something stupid for sure.* "Here's the deal, Princess." He grinned when she gritted her teeth. "You can go inside, sit down at the table and eat dinner and be a good little girl, or I can take you inside, let Drake know what just happened, and he can deal with you how ever he wants. That's the only choice you have at the moment."

He knew he had her when her eyes narrowed on him.

"I'm going to take that as a deal." He reached behind her and opened the door. Then he turned her around and shoved her inside, giving her a swat on her ass, which earned him a nasty little glare from her.

"Anything wrong?" Drake asked, waiting for them.

"Nope, nothing wrong." Kane stood behind Jada and nudged her back.

"Everything is fine," she said through her teeth. "But he's a damn perv."

He let her go into the kitchen and stood in the front room with Drake.

"Care to explain that one to me?" Drake asked.

Kane slid his hands into his pockets and faced Drake, eye to eye. "Not really, no."

"I didn't think so," Drake sighed.

Kane gave him a big smile, "I'm starved. Let's eat."

"When you smile, I know something is seriously going on." Drake turned towards the kitchen. "Something I'm pretty sure I'm not going to like one bit."

Chapter Three

He couldn't sleep. No matter how many push-ups or chin-ups he did, he couldn't still the burn in his body. Kane left his small cabin and went to check on Sasha. It was late, and he knew that the whole house would be sleeping, which was fine with him. He didn't want to have to answer any questions like why he was there so late. But he wasn't that lucky.

Drake was also awake, sitting on the sofa drinking a beer and staring at nothing. He handed a beer to Kane the minute he opened the front door.

"What're you doing up so late?" Kane closed the door and went up to him, taking the beer and sitting down in a chair.

"Should be asking you the same question," Drake remarked. "Something's wrong."

Kane glanced around the room, anywhere but at Drake. He felt as if he was letting the man down and he did not want to do that. Not after all that they had done for him and Sasha. He knew that if things kept going the way they were then he was going to do something very stupid. Something he couldn't take back. "Kane?"

He took a deep breath, let it out, and rubbed his face before he let his eyes land on Drake. "I don't think I can keep an eye on Jada after all."

"Why?" Drake crossed his arms over his chest and leaned forward towards him. "What's going on between you two?"

Kane shook his head and rested back in the chair, looking up. "That's just it, I don't know and I don't think it's wise for me to be the one to keep an eye on her."

"Kane you are the only one that I see that she can't run from." Drake sighed. "She's gotten away from Cole twice and stayed hidden for three damn years. I trust you."

"But I don't trust myself," he said through his teeth. "I don't feel like I have control where she's concerned. It's her scent, Drake. I can't explain it."

"Why don't you tell me what's really going on? I know for a fact that something happened before dinner. Something you two are keeping to yourselves." Drake narrowed his eyes on Kane, which forced Kane to lower his eyes.

Should I tell him? Kane stood up and started pacing. He wanted to tell Drake, have it all explained to him, but couldn't get his mouth to work. Talking or trusting, neither one was one of his strong suits. He kept things to himself, always had.

"Do you remember that first time you talked to me about sex and what I could expect once my body was free of all the drugs?" he asked.

"Yeah, I remember," Drake said.

"Well it wasn't too long after our talk that I experienced my first real erection."

"And I got you that book to help explain sex to you," Drake added. "What's this have to do with—?"

"I can't stop thinking about her," Kane blurted out before he could stop himself. He stopped pacing, grimaced, and mouthed fuck. "I mean thinking about touching and tasting her body. I want to have her scent wrap around me while I sink into her. Hell, I just want her." He groaned.

"Shit," Drake sighed.

"I don't know what to do here, Drake." He finally turned and faced him. There was no point in trying to act as if he didn't say it. "And before you suggest that she stay somewhere else, I've been thinking about that. I don't think it will work."

"I don't know what to say." Drake blinked several times before he stood up. "But thinking about her doesn't mean—"

"Drake, I want to fuck her." Kane spoke slowly so that Drake would understand it. "And I've never wanted to do that with *anyone* in my life."

"Okay, so we might have a problem after all."

"Yeah, and I sure could use a solution to it."

Drake stood up and paced a couple times then stopped and waved his hand in the air, "Okay let's think about this for a few seconds. Jada is an attractive girl, and so far, in the past few years you've been without a woman. I'm going to take a guess here and just say that it's nothing more than your sexual drive coming back." Kane frowned, not understanding what the hell he was talking about. Drake rolled his eyes. "I mean you just need to get laid is all. I bet once you do that then everything will be fine between you and her."

"Get laid?"

"Yeah, you know. Have sex with someone. But do it with someone *else*." He put one hand on his hip and the other at his jaw. "Maybe have Cole take you to town before he leaves for the weekend.

Go to the bar and pick some girl up. Fuck the shit out of her and you should be good as gold."

"Just like that?" Kane couldn't believe what he was hearing. If Drake was right, and if he could do this, then he wouldn't let him down and he felt better in the same breath.

"Yeah, just like that," Drake nodded. "I think that's all you need really. And since Jada is the only single girl here it's normal in a sense that she could be the one your needs are pointing to."

"And what if that doesn't work?" Kane felt sick in his stomach at the idea of touching another, or rubbing against some other skin besides the one he saw at the water.

Drake looked him dead in the eye. "Then we'll cross that bridge when or if it happens. For now, talk to Cole about taking you to town. Not healthy for a shifter to go so long without some kind of release."

Kane nodded because it was the only thing he could do.

"I'm going to bed." Drake rubbed the back of his neck. "I suggest you do the same. You look tired."

Kane finished his beer and had another before he headed upstairs to look in on Sasha. Jada gave her a camera and she had been walking around the yard taking pictures after dinner. Carrick took the camera and ended up snapping a shot of them together, and then Jada told her she would frame it for her. That made Sasha's night.

When he got to the top floor, he didn't go to Sasha's door right off. Instead, he headed for Jada's and peeked inside.

She was on her side, covers a mess. It seemed like she had been tossing and turning, and by the way she was breathing she wasn't in a deep sleep. She was dressed in shorts and a snug shirt. The sheet was between her legs and the bare skin he saw had the same affect on him as when he saw her naked.

Maybe Drake was right. Maybe he did need to get laid and this was his body's way of telling him that. He closed the door and went into Sasha's room. She was sleeping deeply, her chest rising and falling slowly. On her desk was the camera and he picked it up. He flipped through the shots that she took. Everything was of the new found family they had. There was Drake hugging Carrick. Carrick cooking, Drake chopping wood. She even managed to get a close up of Kane smiling, the wind blowing his hair. He stopped though at a photo of Jada. Sasha got it when Jada was turning around from taking a shot herself, her hair up in the air. It was perfect.

"What am I going to do?" he whispered to himself, sitting down at the desk, staring at the picture. "What the hell am I going to do?"

* * * *

Jada hung her head under the hot water, eyes closed waiting for her muscles to relax. She slept like shit last night and if she wasn't mistaken then she thought she heard someone peek into her room. She had a feeling that it was Kane and when she turned over to see, the door was closing.

Something was going on with him. Something that she was pretty damn sure she wasn't going to like.

She turned the water off, stepped out, and wrapped a towel around herself. She grabbed her brush, picked up the dryer and went to work on her hair. Before it was completely dry she stopped, dressed in clean panties and a long t-shirt and left the bathroom with the towel slung over her shoulder.

Opening her bedroom door, she came to a dead stop. Kane was sitting on her bed, correction he was lounging across the bed resting his back up against the wall. On his lap was her scrapbook and that pissed her off. She'd hidden it well, which meant that he was snooping around her room while she was in the shower.

"What the hell are you doing in my room?" She was short with him, but that tended to happen when first you didn't sleep much the night before and second the guy who was supposed to be keeping an eye on you so you didn't run ended up being a peeping Tom.

"Morning, Jada," he sighed. "No I didn't sleep well, and since it is before the sun is up I'm going to take a guess and say that you didn't sleep well, either."

She slammed the door closed before she thought about it. When she turned to open it, Kane snickered at her and she stopped. She turned back around and rushed up to him, taking her scrapbook away.

"Still don't trust me?" he stated.

"What the hell do you think?" She slammed it down on the desk before facing him. "What gives you the right to go through my things?"

He linked his fingers together over his stomach. "I could ask you the same question." She frowned and he cocked his head to one side. "You read my book in the bathroom."

"Your sex book was in the open. That," she pointed to her book. "I had put up."

"So who's Chris?" The way he said the name almost sounded like he was jealous, but Jada knew better. She also knew that she wasn't going to talk about him either.

"None of your damn business. Now leave." She pointed at the door.

"Was he a boyfriend?"

"No." She couldn't keep the bitterness from her voice. The last person she wanted to talk about was Chris.

"Come on little girl. Time to learn how to ride that bike I got you."

Jada looked up at Chris. He was perfect in her young eyes and everything their grandfather wanted in an heir. Every time he looked at her, his green eyes sparkled. Chris was what she needed, what she craved but never got from the man who called himself grandfather.

She was ten and for the past six months, the bike that Chris bought for her sat in the basement untouched. She was too scared to learn how to ride it, and every time Chris mentioned teaching her, her granddad found something else for him to do. The man didn't like Jada and he made sure she knew it.

"Grandpa won't let you," she whispered.

"He's gone and will never know," he took her hand, pulling her along. "Come on. Can't go through life without knowing."

"Jada?" Kane whistled and she lowered her head.

Chris. How could she forget about Chris? "What?"

"Who is he?" Kane spoke very slowly.

Jada rubbed her forehead. "Don't you think it's a little early to be giving me shit."

"Has to be a past lover then." The words sounded like a growl, but she knew she had to be mistaken. There was nothing between them or any reason for Kane to growl about a past lover, if she had one.

Jada held her mouth shut and ground her teeth together. She leaned against the desk, pushing back her anger. "Why don't you just leave?"

* * * *

Kane scooted from the bed and came up right behind her, placing his hands on the desk next to hers, blocking her in as he had the first day they met. She jumped and pushed back against him, but he didn't move.

"I thought we had talked about the space thing," she said through her teeth.

"We didn't talk about shit," he said. "You talked, I half listened."

He put his lips right up to her ear and spoke low. "Who is he, Jada?"

"No one you need to know about. Now back off, you're too damn close."

He closed his eyes and took a deep breath. "It bothers you, doesn't it?" He sighed. "It bothers me also, but I can't seem to stop myself. Your scent is addictive. Maybe we need to change the rules to this game before it changes for us."

She snorted, "Nothing's going to happen. I'm going to leave soon. And for your information the only rules I follow are mine."

He felt a domination hit when she said she was going to leave soon. Kane didn't like the idea of her leaving before he had a handle on her. Drake trusted him to take charge of her, to keep her safe, and he was going to do that no matter what his damn dick wanted to do.

She turned her head to the side and elbowed him causing Kane to react. He moved a hand under her hair, fisting the silk at the back of her head. This stilled her from moving. "That's the problem, Jada." He spoke low and right in her ear, pressing closer. It was a sweet torture, one that he never thought to experience in his life. Hell he didn't think he would have to control himself from not coming in his jeans just being pressed up against her. "Your rules suck."

She turned her head as much as she could and smiled. "Kane, there are three things you need to know, and I'm only going to tell you about them once. I'll even go slowly so you can understand it. You're not feeding me, supporting me and you sure as hell ain't fucking me. So as far as I'm concerned you don't get a say in anything I do or the rules I make. Period! So why don't you go find yourself someone else to rub your little dick on."

Kane growled soft and low. He pulled hard on her hair, pressing as close as he could get, grinding his dick against her ass. He was hard and throbbing. Defiance was a turn on just like a dare to some were. It was like a challenge, one he was sure he would give in to if she kept her shit up. In fact, he knew it. That inner voice of his was screaming that one more and she was a goner. So should he tell her that?

"Don't bet on the last one there, Princess," he let the words rumble and moved his hips **so** she got the full affect of his hardness on her ass. "I can always change *that* rule in a heartbeat. After all, an animal *never* asks permission for shit. They take."

He turned her around, but he didn't back up. She was so short compared to his height she had to crane her neck to look up at him.

"If you're trying to intimidate me, try harder. All you're doing right now is boring me. I have better things to do with my time than play mouse to your cat."

"The cat always eats the mouse." He gripped her hips, picked her up, and sat her down on the desk, coming between her legs. "Is that what you want, Princess. To be eaten?"

"By you?" she laughed. "What the hell do you know about sex, Kane? You were told when to eat, sleep and if I recall right, then you were even ordered to fuck." She narrowed her eyes on him. "You can't call reading a book and laying on your back experience." A tick started in his cheek, yet Jada didn't pick up on the hint.

"You're going to keep pushing, Princess," Kane stated in a soft, controlled, yet dangerous voice. "And push until I push back. I promise you one thing, darling, when I push back nobody will be able to save you."

"In your fucking dreams, wolf boy," she smirked. "I'd bet my last dollar you don't even know how to use your dick without drugs attached to it." She cocked her head to the side. "Tell me something, do you even know how to use it? Or are you afraid of your own dick?"

Kane felt something change then. Jada pushed against him and tried to get off the desk, but he stopped her by grabbing the front of her shirt with both hands. Yanking her back Kane kissed her. He couldn't help himself. She pushed too far and with that mouth of hers being so sharp he just had to do something.

When she tried to pull away from him, Kane growled and moved one of his hands to the back of her head, holding her in place. He deepened the kiss. If someone was to come in and see them they would think Kane was trying to eat her alive. In a sense, that was just what he was trying to do. His tongue plunged deep into her mouth, mating against her own, tasting her again. He wanted to devour her with his mouth and do so much more with his body.

He bent her back, fisted his free hand into her shirt and pulled it up enough so she wasn't sitting on it, then he moved his hand under it and touched her skin for the first time. Kane moaned into her mouth, sliding his fingers down her back and into her panties and cupped her ass.

He moved his other hand down to her ass and pulled her even closer. Kane read many things about sex. Knew a lot of different positions and wondered about a few. One of the positions was anal sex. He didn't understand why a man would want to do that until he touched her butt and parted the cheeks. One finger he used to tease the opening and just that small touch gave him a new pounding to his dick and had pre-come coming out of the tip. He was so close that Kane knew if he pushed a finger inside her, he was going to come in his jeans.

He somehow managed to pull that animal of his back in and slowly let the kiss go. If he didn't then there was a good chance he might take things further than what either one of them could expect. His last move when he pulled back was to lick at her bottom lip, before sucking on it one last time. "Still want to push me, Princess?" he rumbled. "Because I can keep going."

His answer was a fist into his face and a push at his chest. Kane rubbed his jaw and she jumped from the desk, grabbed her shoes and dirty jeans from the floor, and ran from the room. The need to chase her down and finish what was just started between them was strong. But he didn't.

Instead, he opened the scrapbook again and flipped to the page that he was about to read before she came in and he closed it. A yellow newspaper clipping was glued to the page.

Christopher James Leonard died October twelfth at one thirty in the morning following a fatal car crash.

Leonard. Kane frowned and ran a finger over the name. It was Jada's last name. Chris was related to her, not a lover.

Mr. Leonard was only twenty-two and had slipped into a coma after a drunk driver hit his car head on. His cousin, Jada Leonard, was also in the car and suffered injuries as well. It is unknown at this time what state Ms. Leonard is in, but it is known that she, as well as Mr. Leonard, has been in a coma for two weeks before Mr. Leonard died.

James Leonard, grandfather and guardian to both has refused to comment at this time. Services will be held at the end of the week for Christopher Leonard.

Kane couldn't believe what he was reading. Jada was in a serious car crash with her cousin, he died, and she was in a coma.

"Hey, what are you doing?" He jumped and turned his head to Drake.

"Did you know this?" Kane frowned, his attention going back to the news clipping.

"Know what?" Drake came into the room and looked at what

Kane was reading. A few seconds after he read it, he whispered, "Damn."

"Hey, um, Drake?" Carrick stood in the doorway, the cordless phone in her hand. "Cole just called. He said Jada is over there, upset and wants to talk to you alone but over there, and he's trying to pack up to head to your parent's place for the weekend."

Drake frowned at Kane, "What'd you do?" he whispered harshly.

"You don't want to know," Kane answered him under his breath.

* * * *

"Kane isn't a man, Cole. He's a fucking animal off his leash."

Drake heard Jada yelling before he walked into the front door of Cole's house. "Careful, Jada," Drake warned in a growl, his strides quickly bringing him into the argument in the front room. "You don't want to say something that you can't take back."

"Up yours, Drake." She turned her anger on him, eyes narrowing.

"Where's Kane?" Cole asked.

"Outside." Drake kept his eyes on Jada. Something clearly was going on and he had this strange feeling that he didn't really want to know, but needed to. "Does someone want to tell me what the hell is going on?"

"Kane," Cole sighed. "Apparently he's crossed some line."

"Some line!" Jada huffed. "He's done more than just cross some damn line. I'm not going back there."

Drake narrowed his eyes on her. "So far the only thing I can see is that he keeps *you* in line and that pisses you off." He pointed his finger at her.

"He doesn't keep me in line, you over grown prick." Her hands fisted at her sides, that was how pissed she seemed. "*He's* getting out of line. What are you going to do if he decides to do that mating shit with me? Then what?"

Drake shook his head. "That's not going to happen." *He hoped.*

"How the hell do you know?" she said through her teeth.

"Because if by a small twist of fate, if it was possible, then he would have done it already," he told her in frustration. "And he hasn't. He hasn't touched you, stripped you and I know for a fact fucked you. We *know*, Jada, when our mates are around."

"Yeah, you were real quick to discover yours." She crossed her arms over her chest, leaned on one foot, and looked him up and down. "How long was she locked in that room before you figured it out?" Jada smiled. "Chase told me the story."

"Don't go there, Jada," he warned. "Kane stays on your ass and that's final. If you want him off, then I suggest you think about telling me what it was that you took that is so important to Stan. Or did you forget that he was still out there hunting your ass down?"

"You're an asshole, Drake."

Drake laughed and extended his arms. "Tell me something I don't already know."

"Put that fucker on a leash, Drake or..."

"Fuck, Jada, he isn't a dog," Drake yelled at her. "Stop treating him like one."

"Then teach him some goddamn manners," she yelled back. "He has one shitty personality."

"And you have such a *sweet* one," he snarled back. Drake could feel his temper rising and with each second he fought with her the higher it went. "Stop acting like a bitch that isn't getting her damn way. Kane is keeping an eye on you and I don't give a fuck if you like it or not. You need protection and that's it. End of story!" he yelled at the top of his lungs.

Jada's eyes narrowed and her lips thinned out. "You want to see bitch? Fine. I'll show you bitch. He touches me again and I'll have him tasting his own nuts." She turned her back and went to the kitchen and out the back door, slamming it.

"This isn't good, Drake," Cole said. Drake rubbed his face and nodded in agreement. "If Kane is touching her, what's to stop him from going that extra step?"

"What do you want me to do?" Drake sighed. "He's just like us."

"But he isn't," Cole remarked. "Kane is still more animal than man. He's still learning how to control himself. What if she does turn out to be his mate and none of us knows about it. Who's going to stop him from taking her?"

"Cole, nothing stops us from taking our mates," Drake groaned. He was feeling the frustration of trying to teach Kane their ways, earn Sasha's trust, and now he had this shit. "You should know by experience just as I do. When we know, we know and we take."

"And if he is taking any liberties with her, then there's a damn good chance she's his!" Cole also seemed a bit strained. "Jesus, Drake, don't you remember him telling us about this scent that he picked up. Sasha even told us that he changed one night and it was when she was up there taking her damn pictures. I'll bet anything that—"

"Don't say it, Cole." Drake held up his hand, silencing Cole. "Please. I don't need to think about this right now. We have other problems to deal with."

"Drake, *this* is a problem that needs to be dealt with!" Cole's face flushed. "What are you going to do when he does mate and mark her? You need to think about that, because in case you haven't met Jada, she has a temper on her. Kane marks her as his, one hell of a fight is going to break out between them, and I don't think your eyes are open enough to deal with it."

* * * *

Kane forced Jada back to Drake's house by dragging her the entire way with a gentle but firm grip on her arm. She locked herself in her room, packed a few things into a bag, and when everyone went to sleep, she snuck down for some food. There was no way in hell she was going to stay one more night in this loony bin with Kane just itching to do God only knows what to her next. At midnight, she made her move, opened the bedroom window, and started the big plan of escape.

She smiled at the thought of giving Kane the slip, the dipshit. She hoped Drake ripped him a new one for letting her slip through his fingers.

She tossed her bag out, watching as it landed with a light thud and waited a few moments to make sure no one heard that before she made her move since she knew Kane had great hearing but she wasn't too sure about the others. She didn't think they did and so far, it looked like Kane was being a good little boy and staying in his hole in the woods. She had a feeling Drake and Kane didn't think she would climb out of the window to get away so soon. Dumb asses!

She couldn't stop smiling as she climbed down. Lucky for her there was a trellis that reached all the way up the side of the house, far enough away from her window for them to think she wouldn't try to climb out. Priceless. Guess it was a good thing Chase didn't know everything about her, like how great she was at climbing stuff. She was pretty sure now if he did, he would have told them.

Jada couldn't believe her luck. She was halfway down, no Drake and no Kane. Couldn't get any better than that, unless she had the keys to the truck. Now what she didn't expect was someone to be waiting for her after all.

Strong hands went around her waist, plucked her off the side of the wall, and put her back on her feet. Then hard hands roughly swung her around to face none other than Kane.

"I was wondering how long it was going to take you to try that again," he sighed with his hands on his hips. "Must say I wasn't expecting you to do it again tonight."

Jada glared up at him. She couldn't believe her luck. How in the hell was he able to know she was trying to run away? For christsakes, she didn't think up the plan until just a few hours ago.

"What the fuck are you doing here?" she snapped. "You should be asleep like the rest of them."

"And miss all this fun?" he said in a calm voice. "I started to think that you staying in your room without coming down to rip me a new one was not your style." He cocked his head to one side, crossing his arms over his chest, those damn blue eyes of his going up and down her body. "And I was right."

"Thinking isn't a strong suit for you." She smiled. "So get a new hobby and get the fuck out of my way." She tried to brush past him, but he stopped her and pushed her back where she stood.

"Not this time." Kane looked down at her and it gave her the chills. "This time you're going to answer to me for your actions and running."

"Really?" Jada bent over and picked her bag up. "I wouldn't hold my breath if I was you." She sighed and straightened up. "I really would like to stay and chat, well really I wouldn't. I'm getting the hell out of here and away from you. Try to stop me and I will bring you down hard."

"Can't let you." Kane made a move to grab her, but Jada jumped back.

"Back off, canine, or I will neuter you myself!" Jada yelled angrily. "I have had enough of your shit and you touching me. Go back to the cage where you belong and leave me the hell alone."

* * * *

"That is it!" Kane felt something inside him suddenly snap. A challenge that could *not* be left unchecked. His hand shot out and grabbed Jada by her arm. "I have taken enough shit from you, and enough abuse from that mouth of yours. You want to push, then, Princess, it's time I pushed back so you will remember it the next time you open your mouth."

Jada tried to yank her arm free. "Get the fuck off!" He heard the desperation, the fright in her voice but ignored it.

"I don't think so." He was calm, almost too calm. "It's high time someone does something about your mouth, and your attitude."

"Too bad you're not that *something*," she told him with gritted teeth. She tried to yank her arm free, along with digging her feet into the ground when he turned and started to walk away from the house towards the woods.

"Let's find out." He yanked her to him hard, catching Jada before she stumbled and fell. "Shall we? Because I'm dying to show you just what I *can* do."

Chapter Four

Kane half-dragged, half-carried Jada away from the house in the direction of his cabin. He didn't have a plan, but with each step he took and the fighting from her, a plan was quickly forming in his head. Something that had to do with her being tied up and at *his* mercy for a change.

"Put me down, you fucking animal!" she yelled.

"Keep it up," Kane remarked dryly. "That talk only gets you deeper and deeper in trouble."

"You need a leash," she went on. "Someone needs to put a damn leash on you and put you back in that cage!"

Kane grimaced each time Jada called him an animal, but he did so with a hidden smile. There was just something about her calling him that, which didn't really bother him that much. He knew if it were someone else telling him to go back to a cage, he would be pissed. But not her. No, Jada seemed to make it sound different, and he didn't understand why.

"And someone needs to show you what happens to smart mouth girls."

"Get your goddamn hands off of me!" She screamed, continuing to struggle while trying to yank her arm free as he walked away from the house towards the woods.

Kane grunted at her. "Oh, my hands are going to be on you." He stopped, gave her a good yank close, and lowered his face to hers. "Maybe even all *over* you."

"Not on your life, wolf boy," she said through her teeth. "I wouldn't touch you if you had the last dick on earth."

Kane knew from what Drake told him that he was one of the tallest shifters out there, and since he spent pretty much all of his life in a cage, he could be one mean ass one. He usually didn't have the patience for shit like this. It seemed that every time Jada started to smart off or fight him something inside came to life. Whether it was anger or lust, Kane didn't know. And he couldn't decide if he wanted to beat her ass or screw her. He was leaning towards the fucking, but pushed that thought aside.

"I think you have no idea what this wolf can do," he informed her, nose to nose. "But you're about to." He pushed her away just enough to turn and start the walk again.

"I don't give a damn what you think you can do," she said. "I'm not going to be bullied by you anymore!"

"I wasn't bulling you," he told her in his dry voice.

"The hell you aren't! Look at you now." Jada tugged on her arm, but he wasn't letting her go. "You're acting all alpha, and it's very boring."

"I'm not alpha. Do you even know what that means?" Kane stopped and turned back to her. They were in the woods, but not close to his cabin yet. Jada managed to twist her arm so he had to let her go for fear of breaking her arm.

"I know enough." She took a step back and he was instantly on guard. "Just like I know that there's no way you're getting me to your little cabin. You want a toy, go to the store."

He took one step towards her and she backed up. "Never said you were a toy, but I am going to play."

"Not on your life!" Jada raised a finger then pointed it at him. "You are not going to touch me."

"Wanna bet?"

He reached for her and Jada kicked. She connected with his knee hard enough that it did give him pause. She turned and ran, heading back to the house. Kane growled and took off after her. He wasn't afraid of Drake protecting her, Carrick maybe, but not Drake. What he didn't want was for her to have the protection of the house. If she got back there then his game would be over for who knew how long. And he definitely was going to play with her, just as he said. In fact, he was looking forward to it.

He lunged at her, tackling her to the ground. But Jada didn't give up easily. He flipped her over to her back and she began kicking at him. A couple of her hits landed in his gut, knocking the wind out of him, but it didn't stop him. Kane took hold of her ankles, flipped her back over to her stomach, and pinned her arms behind her. Using one hand, he unfastened his belt, pulled it from the loops, and tied her wrists together.

"Knock it off," he growled. "You're not going anywhere."

"Let me go right now, you bastard." She squirmed under him and he had to chuckle.

"Nope," he stood up, pulling her up not very gently by her arms. "We have some things to discuss."

He practically dragged her back into the woods and once his

cabin came into view, she dropped down. Kane suspected that she did that in the hopes of stalling him, but it didn't work. He turned her so she was facing him, smiled, and picked her up, carrying her all the way inside. Using his foot, he closed the door, and shifted her so he could slide the bolt lock across the door.

Holding her with one arm, he grabbed one of his table chairs and dragged it over to his work out bar. He placed the chair under it, set her down, turned her away and let one of her wrists go so he could put her wrist in one of the leather straps he used to hold his ankles. That was a mistake.

Jada slapped him hard across the face and made a dash for the door. Since he still had a hold on the belt and it was still wrapped around his wrist, she didn't get too far before he gave her a hard yank and she came right back, slamming into him.

"Let go, Kane." Jada's voice was low and if he wasn't mistaken it shook a bit. "This isn't a game."

Kane had to fight for his patience right now. It had been three years since anyone laid a hand on him in violence and being slapped surely fell into that category. That wasn't why he had to fight for in the sense of control. Now Kane had to fight to *not* put her over his knee and beat her butt until it was a nice shade of pink. The image of her bare ass under his hand seemed to give his cock instant life and it throbbed like a bitch.

"I don't think so, Princess," he spoke soft and low with a slight rasp. "It's time we come to an understanding right now, and you don't leave until I'm ready for you to leave."

"Oh, I know all I need to know," she jerked in his hands, trying to pull out of his grasp. "You're an asshole."

He chuckled, "Oh, I'm sure you're going to be calling me worse than that before we're through."

Kane picked her up and placed her standing on the chair. He grunted as he struggled with her and fought to miss the slaps directed at his face. Humor was a thing Kane never had much of, but for some strange reason Jada brought a little bit out of him right now. He loved the challenge and loved the fighting. Made things interesting.

"Kane, I mean it!" she yelled in his face. "Don't you dare tie me up."

"Or what?" he asked her coolly. He met her fire green eyes with a stare that was anything but calm. "Are you challenging *me*, Jada?"

Since he was so tall and she was short, all he had to do was reach up over his head to touch the bar. He forced one wrist up, shoved it into the leather, and pulled the adjustable strap tight. It wasn't easy taking slaps to his neck and one wild kick before he did this with her other wrist too. Though the chair was finely crafted and sturdy, it wobbled when she fought. Thankfully it didn't topple over as he finally secured her other wrist.

"You goddamn bastard!" she screamed, and kicked out at him. "You no good dirty, caged animal!"

He licked his lips and took a step back, looking her up and down. Kane had to grab her legs to stop the kicking. "That mouth is going to get you into trouble, Princess. So much trouble."

Drake had taken Kane and Sasha to a private doctor for a check up. Kane knew something was wrong with him. He had no sexual desires, no erections, nothing. She explained to him that with all the drugs pumped into his system for him to perform when they wanted him to, it was no wonder he couldn't experience the normal sexual demands of a shifter of his age. That males like him were sex machines and once his body was completely free of those drugs his body would wake up. That one day he would want to do the normal things like kiss, touch another person freely, and want a female for pleasure. The erections came, and he learned how to deal with it. He needed to learn to handle what he was feeling now, besides having Jada this close to his body he found he wanted to touch so much more of her. He wanted to feel *everything* with her.

"No wonder you had to live in a cage!" she said. "You never learned manners! And to think I risked my own skin to save yours!" She tried to yank her arms free. "They should have left you there."

Kane made a tsking sound as he went over to the table and brought the other chair close, setting it in front of her. He walked around her, looking her body up and down, "I don't think you will ever learn." Kane finished his walk and stopped to lean against the doorframe with his arms crossed over his chest. He cocked his head to one side when he saw her swallow hard. "Now what should I do about that mouth of yours? It's a question I keep asking myself over and over again, but can't seem to come up with the right answer."

"Go to hell, Kane," she again tried to kick out at him. "And I suggest you run real fast because when I get out of this I plan on making a girl out of you the hard way."

"Is that so?" he grinned. "And how would a little girl like you take me on?" Kane kept his voice calm and his stance relaxed, but he was anything but calm and relaxed.

"There is nothing *little* about me, you damn animal!" She was huffing now in her anger. "I could take you on any day."

Kane had a smile on his face but drew his brows together and looked her up and down. He really did enjoy how tough she tried to act. "You can't take on shit. I can smell your innocence all through the house just as I can smell how scared you are right now. You are a babe waiting for the right man to pluck you from the vine." He cocked one eyebrow up at her. "The sharp tongue, and kick ass attitude doesn't work with me." He tapped a finger on his lip. "But what has me wondering the most is how you have managed to keep that sweet scent of yours. It's almost the same as Sasha in that it's as fresh as a rainstorm scent." He tilted his head to the side. "Are you still innocent, little Jada?"

"None of your damn business," she snapped back, looking around the room, avoiding his eyes.

"True, but I'm going to find out." He pushed away from the doorframe and paced around her. "I just don't understand why some guy hasn't tamed your ass by now, but then getting to know you like I have, I'm starting to get it."

"Not likely," she mumbled.

He smiled. "You can cause any hard-on to deflate in a heartbeat, but it has the opposite effect on me, sweetheart. I'm stone."

"Well I do have to say I am impressed, Kane," she smarted off. "I didn't think you could get it up, without the drugs, that is. I bet you don't even know what to do with that tool you think you have between you legs." She gave him a crude smile. "And I have said it before. Thinking isn't your strong suit."

A tick started on his left cheek again. He knew that she had seen him in the lab several times being forced to fuck women. It was either that or Sasha that was going to get fucked and Kane was going to do everything he could then to make sure his sister was never hurt. No man, beast, or creature was going to touch Sasha ever! Plain and simple.

"You keep talking that talk, little girl, then I *am* going to show you all about my *tool*," he growled.

"Oh, please," she sighed with a roll of her eyes. Looking up at her wrists again, she tried to yank them free. "I bet you would need to have that damn book in the same room so you could see how to do things the right way. After all, it wasn't in your training. Oh, wait!"

she smiled sweetly at him. "You didn't have any training. You don't know how to give pleasure or get it."

Kane felt the tick in his cheek quicken. Never had one person gotten under his skin the way Jada was managing to do right now. He wanted to beat her and fuck her so hard his cock was straining against his zipper painfully. Something he was starting to hope she *would* notice. He pushed off the wall and walked around her again.

Kane was beginning to think that if she did notice the affects he was starting to have being in the same room with her then maybe she would curb that tongue of hers. Ah, her tongue, he thought. What would it feel like licking the head of his cock as he pushed the thick length into her heated mouth? A mouth on his cock was something Kane knew he wanted to experience, ever since he saw it in the book.

He tried to suppress the groan that reached his lips before she heard, but failed. Jada looked at him with an amused expression on her face.

"Ah, what's wrong, Kane?" she cooed at him. "Am I starting to get to you?"

Kane suddenly felt as if he'd had enough. "The only thing I'm starting to notice, or what's getting to me, as you put it, is that scent." He stopped walking and stood behind her. Even with her standing on the chair, she was still short. Kane grinned at the fact that she barely reached his chin. He enjoyed that he still had to look down at her.

"And what scent is that, you freak?" she asked him in an annoying voice. "That's all you talk about."

He strongly gripped her hips, and though she attempted to kick out at him, he firmly held her in place. He bent slightly so his breath touched her ear as his lips moved close, keeping his mouth inches from touching her. He answered her with a purr to his voice, "Your scent. A scent that is so pure it calls to my blood." Both hands moved around her hips to the front of her jeans. Kane smiled at the sudden increase in her breathing and at the smell of her fear mixed with the first stages of arousal. He knew deep down in his soul that this would happen if he touched her. That if he let the control he kept so tightly closed loose then he would have this one woman under him for hours, maybe days. "I can smell it," he told her in a husky voice that seemed to only deepen. "I can smell the sudden dampness that I have caused by just standing this close and touching you the way I am now."

"This isn't funny, Kane," Jada breathed out, yanking on her arms. "Let me go right this second."

"Why?" His fingers found the snap and zipper of her jeans as he pressed his body closer to her backside. He pulled while he nudged her back to feel the hardness that was between his legs. In a slow, agonizing motion, he pulled the zipper all the way, opening her jeans as wide as they would go.

"Kane!" she cried out. "What the hell are you doing?"

"What does it look like I'm doing?" His hands slid inside her jeans to her hips where he pushed them down over her legs. He smiled at the French cut pink lace panties hugging her slim hips. With forced determination he removed her socks and shoes as well and gave her jeans a hard yank until he had them off, tossing them to the side, chuckling the entire time. He actually found humor in her ineffective attempts to kick out at him.

"You son-of-a-bitch!" she gritted with fire in her eyes. "How could you do that?"

"Why, Jada…" He grinned as he walked around to her front. "I would never have thought *you* were the kind of girl to wear such sexy panties. I think I like the white ones better."

"Goddamn you, Kane!" she groaned.

"Is that the best come back you can give me now?" He shook his head as his hands went to his hips along with making a tsking sound. "Guess it's true about stripping away the defenses."

"Very fucking funny," she snarled back.

"Hum, still lippy I see." He walked back around her, hands on her waist and flat against her belly. "Guess I'm going to have to take something else away."

"Don't you dare!"

Kane grabbed the back of her shirt and gave it one hard yank. The thin material ripped down her back and Jada screamed from the force he used to pull it away. She shook when he whistled behind her.

"A matching bra? Now I really am impressed."

He walked back around to stand in front of her, licking his lips as he went. He felt the sudden change within him, as he looked his fill of the woman who stood before him in nothing but her undies. Even the deep blush on her face seemed to trigger more pain to his crotch.

Before he could talk himself out of anything, he was pulling his shirt from his body. Jada watched with bulging eyes as each rippling muscle slowly came into view, along with scars from all his beatings. Normally he didn't want others to see the scars, but this time, in this moment it didn't seem to bother him too much.

The moment he turned his back on her to toss his shirt aside, he knew he was giving her a great view of his back and the proof of the life he had lived in the lab. Deep scars lined his back in a criss-cross manner showing the beatings he'd endured. Some even went around his shoulders to touch his chest.

But Kane had a good idea that that wasn't what had Jada gulping for air. He could smell the change in her scent as well as the thick sweetness of her desire. If he had to bet on it, he would say that her panties just became very wet just from the intense look in his eyes.

"Your eyes are red," she whispered.

He knew what she was talking about. Drake explained to him that his eyes would change color when his sexual need came. That they would change to red when he was in heat. But he wasn't in heat now so he didn't care why they changed.

"Kane." She swallowed hard as he circled her as a predator would his prey. "I think it is time for you stop this game. It's starting to get out of control."

He walked around Jada a couple of times more before he stopped behind her again. "What game are we playing?" he asked softly in her ear, causing her to jump.

"Kane, this isn't funny," she whined. "You need to let me go. Now!"

Kane reached up to her wrists but it wasn't to set her free. His hands wrapped around her wrists under the leather as his body pressed as close to hers as it could. "I'm in complete control, Jada, but it's slipping fast."

* * * *

Scorching heat wrapped around Jada as his hands slowly skimmed down her arms, turning at the last second to run his knuckles down her sides. Chills mixed with his body heat hit her and Jada found it was all she could do to steady her breathing.

All the way down her legs and back up to her hips his hands moved. His chest rubbed against her back while his face buried itself in her hair, moving her head to one side. Lips grazed her shoulder, neck, and up to her ear while his hands continued to roam her body but not once did he touch certain spots on her that were slowly waking up, wanting to be touched.

"You are so soft," he told her in her ear with his rough voice. "And you smell so damn good." His hands went from her belly up to the undersides of her breasts. "I don't think I've ever had the pleasure of touching someone for myself," he said against her neck. He let out a sharp intake of breath as his thumb hooked into the tiny clasp in front of her bra, popping it open. "You smell sweet and hot." He licked her shoulder. "Good enough to eat, maybe."

Jada's head went back on his chest as two hot hands closed over her breasts, squeezing her flesh. Her nipples suddenly became so hard they throbbed in his hands, begging for attention.

"Kane, this is not a good idea," she managed to breathe out.

He brushed her hard nipples with his thumbs, sending tantalizing chills racing down her body to pool between her legs while his lips skimmed up to her ear, licking the lobe. "I think this is the best idea ever."

* * * *

The moment his hands left her breasts, Jada wanted to whimper from the loss. Her mind screamed a sigh of relief, yet her body begged for him to come back. It wasn't until she saw his jeans being tossed in front of her that she realized things would never be the same between them again. She knew that the moment they left this cabin—the safe zone she put between herself and Kane—would forever be gone and could never come back. It both terrified and excited the hell out of her.

The last of her struggles stopped as his hot lips touched her back and Jada almost screamed from the pleasure of his heated caresses. Nothing in her whole life felt this good or had her craving for more. And that was what she was doing—craving for more of his touch.

"Kane," she rushed out as his body, and mouth began a trail around to her front, "You really should stop." Jada tried again. "This isn't right." Yet, deep down inside her, though having him near her scared her, she was also excited by his touch. She felt this was right on some level. She just didn't want to admit that to him…or herself.

Kane left a scorching trail of heat all the way around to her belly with his mouth. Jada's breathing went into overdrive as she watched him sit down in front of her, in the other chair, naked. She closed her eyes, taking several deep breaths, trying to get some control and think of the best way to get him to stop and let her go. Nothing came to mind.

"God, this isn't happening," she groaned, struggling with her warring senses.

"Oh this is definitely happening." He looked up at her and the heated expression she saw had her mouth going dry. "Very much so."

His hand moved up her back, grabbed her bra, and ripped it off. "And I'm going to enjoy every minute," he finished with a rip to her panties then placed one of her legs over his shoulders.

* * * *

Kane parted the swollen lips of her pussy with his thumbs and licked her from ass to clit. The moment he reached her clit, he sucked the bud into his mouth, Jada cried out. Kane moaned back his pleasure against her. Nothing in the labs and nothing from the books could have prepared him for this kind of pleasure, and he found that he wanted nothing else but to get lost in it, in her.

He licked at her hard a few more times before he took one of his thick fingers and pushed into her. She was so tight, so hot, and wet that he had to close his eyes and fight back the sudden orgasm that threatened to erupt from his own body while he sat there. Jada was scorching heat that he wanted to dive into. He wanted his dick where his finger was. Wanted her hard nipples in his mouth as he pumped his hardness into her over and over again. To fill her so completely that they both knew they would never find this kind of completeness ever again.

Kane sucked hard on her clit as another finger joined with the first and he used one more to tease the rim of her ass. With a quickness that matched the raging need within him, he moved his hand and pushed his finger into her ass. He sucked her hard and finger fucked her in both ends fast. He wanted to hear her scream his name as she came and she did scream when he moved his fingers. He couldn't wait to take all of her sweet cream as the pleasure washed over her into his mouth, just like he could barely wait to have his cock replacing his fingers, all three of them.

"Kane!" Jada screamed his name and came, tightening around his fingers.

The leg that was over his shoulder seemed to wrap around his head as he drank her pleasure, and kept up the pace of his hand. He had to close his eyes and hope for control. Willing his orgasm back wasn't easy, he tried telling himself that now was not the time. Yet, the more he tried to fight with what was right in front of him, the quicker he found he was losing the battle.

Keeping his hand pumping inside of her, he stood up. He was rock hard and so ready to experience what true sexual pleasure was all about—to know what having a woman for one's own pleasure was and not to fuck because of being drugged, or forced into it.

His lips kissed a fiery trail up her body stopping for only a split second to suck on a hard nipple. He could tell she was still in a daze from her orgasm and decided to use that to his own advantage.

Everything within him screamed that this was right. That this was what he needed and should take. To embrace what nature was giving him. But a small voice whispered that this might be wrong also. That maybe he shouldn't take something that didn't belong to him. He snarled at that thought. This was his woman. His! He had every right to take what was rightfully his, and shouldn't feel guilt at how or when he took her.

"Mine," he growled softly against her skin, pushing the guilt back.

Quickly he removed his fingers from her snug heat and replaced it with the thick mushroom head of his cock. Wet heat poured over the head making him want to hiss at the sweet torment. With determination Kane managed to push only the head of his cock into the tightest woman he ever had in his life. He had to stop to catch his breath and fight for some kind of control.

Then he took hold of her legs, wrapping them around his hips and held onto her ass. He looked down at his thick shaft; watched it as he slowly worked it in, then Kane growled at the tight blazing heat that greeted him.

* * * *

Jada thought she was dreaming. She was still feeling the aftershocks of star blinding pleasure—still coming down from that high when she felt Kane move and wrap her legs around his hips. His big height, even with her standing in a chair, still made him taller than her. But his hips were evenly proportioned against hers.

She'd only read or imagined what darker sex could be like. It both thrilled and scared her at the same time. She both did and didn't want him, but desperately needed his hot touch. When she opened her eyes, and felt his heated body mingling against her, she knew that everything she had was lost to him.

She bit her lower lip to hold back the whimper while he pushed his way inside her body. He was so big, so thick, that he stretched her to a point where she felt he was ripping her in two. He was blistering steel forcing his way into a place that seemed much too small for him; blistering steel that burned with each thick inch that parted her unused muscles to accommodate him.

"Wait," she rushed out, and strained slightly to reach onto the exercise bar above, with all her might. Jada even tried to pull herself up and away from Kane, but he was stronger and brought her down to impale her on him. "It's not working." Jada tried to move her hips away, only to be rewarded with his fingers biting into the tender flesh of her ass. She would likely be bruised by tomorrow; yet, this mating was thrilling, and somehow, she had a feeling her life would never be the same again.

"Yes, it is," he told her in a tight voice, his head down, watching as they joined.

"Kane, please!" she cried out." I...I..."

He stopped moving and she thought there was a chance that he would stop after all. Kane moved his hand between their bodies, and touched her hard clit, rolling it with his finger. She moaned and again tried to get away from his probing fingers invading her flesh.

"It's mine, Jada." His voice was so thick and deep it gave her the chills.

"What are you talking about?" she whispered, her breathing hard and desperate.

He looked up at her and she gasped. His eyes were an even deeper shade of red and the veins in his neck were straining, as if he was holding something heavy or holding something back.

"You've been keeping secrets." She shook her head no and bit her lip to still the whimper. "Yes, you have." He moved just enough to force the whimper out. "I can feel it."

"You're out of you mind," she breathed out. "And you don't know what you're talking about."

"I might be, but not about this."

* * * *

Kane closed his eyes when he touched her virginity again. Slowly he pulled what little amount he managed to get in, out and slid slowly back in. Two more times he did this, groaning at how her muscles seemed to relax so much better than that first time but were still tight as ever.

He played with her clit, touching it and learning all there was to learn about the little nub that seemed to give her so much pleasure. It was fascinating to watch her face when he rolled it, and it excited him to hear her moans when he gave it pressure. Each thing he did to her was exciting and had him wanting to learn more and do more; not only to her, but also for them both.

Her legs tightened around his hips and another orgasm hit. Kane used that distraction and surged into her. He tore past her innocence bringing a cry not only to his lips but also to her own.

Jada screamed, and he held her tight. Tears came to her eyes from the force of his invasion and it took his last remnant of control to stand perfectly still. She was working on her breathing and Kane freed her wrists, picked her up from the chair, and held her against his body as he walked to the back of the cabin, pinning her up against the wall next to his bed.

He was on fire. His body burned in not only places but in spots. He felt as if he needed to get closer to her. As he pushed her up against the wall, his hands dug into her hair, pulling her head back. Lips nipped and sucked on the tender skin of her throat and shoulder, and he moved his hips.

The controlled man that he had been was gone. Out came the beast, pumping into her hard and fast. All tenderness was gone, and quickly replaced with the burning need to consume and to brand this one woman his!

He plunged into her sharp and short. At most, half of his hardness left the tight hold, only to piston back inside the sweet tightness that awaited him. Everything was alive on him. He felt each ripple of muscle within her and each sensitive spot that he had but never knew.

It was both heaven and hell. He couldn't take much more of this torture, yet was helpless to stop. Then he felt her arms pressing against his chest one moment, then relax and go around him in the next. Satisfaction tore through his body for he knew she wanted him, yet her pride resisted him at the same time. He knew he could make her his, for all time, and she could fight it all she wanted, it wouldn't work. She was his.

Faster and harder he moved, slamming her into the wall with his movements. Closing his eyes tightly, Kane felt the tiny chills race down his spine to swell up in his balls. His head moved back and forth, as he worked hard to fight off the orgasm that was gripping him. He whimpered at the fight he was losing. Yet, when he heard her cry out his name, and her nails dug into his back, Kane knew then that he didn't have to fight any longer.

With his eyes shut tightly, his cock erupted. Deep within his soul, his seed left his body in a rush and entered hers. He stood as still as a statue with Jada wrapped around his body limp as a baby, breathing hard. But he wasn't finished or completely satisfied. He was still hard within her and wanted much more. He felt as if there was something not complete yet.

"Oh, fuck," he moaned, resting his head on the wall, closing his eyes. "More!"

He pushed them off the wall, and dropped down to the bed with her under him. He kissed her deep, preventing anything she might to say to kill this moment. His cock still throbbed and he was powerless to stop his hips from moving, stroking inside her again. This time was somewhat gentler, but not much.

Kane rocked within her, the hunger inside him only got worse instead of dulling. He thrust his tongue into her mouth to match the thrust of his cock.

Bracing his weight on one arm, he moved a hand down between their bodies, touched her clit, then not missing a beat of his movements he took juices that came out and pushed it back to her ass. He wanted all of her, and he would have her.

Two fingers he used for her rear. Kane pressed them inside her with a bit of difficulty and fucked her with fingers and his dick. Jada arched and broke the kiss. She tried to push against his shoulders and he moved his mouth to her throat.

"You feel so good," he whispered against her skin.

One, two, three, four, and it was coming again. Kane bit the cover, and shook from his orgasm and fought to catch his breath.

"Not enough," he shook his head, not understanding what was going on. "Not nearly enough. I need more."

Chapter Five

She was exhausted and didn't put up a fight when he flipped her over to her stomach and parted her legs wide. He slid two fingers inside her and brushed her arousal mixed with his cum back to her rear. She froze, and then whimpered, knowing where this was going. He couldn't mean to take her that way…he couldn't! When he worked the moisture over her crevice again, and again, she gasped, knowing he meant to take her in the one place she knew without a doubt wouldn't fit. "No, Kane! Enough." Jada started to get up on her knees to crawl away when he stopped her.

He grabbed her hips and dragged her back to the center of the bed. "It's not enough yet. I can't stop."

She shook her head. "Damn you!" she yelled when he pushed one finger into her.

"You'll feel some discomfort at first…at least that's what the book said. Then, afterwards, it'll feel so good. Trust me."

A tear slipped from Jada's eye and she shook her head. "No. I don't trust you. Give me one damned reason why I should after what you just did to me."

"You're mine, that's why. You might not think so right now, but you are. I *feel* it. Mine," he growled.

"No, I'm…"

"Don't lie. No more lies."

"I need to think. I—"

"You need to feel, princess. We both just need to feel."

Jada heard the pleading in his voice and knew she couldn't deny him. She wanted him, too, but she'd be damned if she made that confession yet. He was using her, and she was powerless to tell him no. She'd allow him to take her into this unexplored world of sensuality. She'd only slightly envisioned exploring before, now it was here. She thought how she'd taken his heated touches and his bruising body—the thought made her shiver with delight. But she didn't dare show him all her true feelings, not until she could trust him. Bitter disappointment swept through her then as she felt his big hands tighten bruisingly on her hips, as she thought about how so many people had disappointed her, hadn't been there for her in her life.

With some resistance, he eased the head into her ass and she froze, and then gasped with the pop she felt from that penetration. She stayed as still as she could, trying to get used to the full feeling of him deep inside her.

She couldn't breathe, couldn't bring any air into her lungs while he kept pushing into her, filling and stretching her ass to a scorching burn. Nothing could have prepared her for this. Yet, she hung on, guessing the pain would subside after awhile, remembering his words—his promise.

"Argh!" Kane yelled behind her and lunged forward. He buried himself, and the forward motion caused her to drop the top half of her body down to the bed.

She couldn't do anything but lay there and let him have his way with her. He moved a hand between her legs, teasing her clit, mixing the pain with pleasure, all the while fucking her ass hard and steady. She fisted her hands into the blankets and fought within herself, with the orgasm that she felt slowly surfacing. Jada hated to admit it, and refused to say it aloud, but it was starting to feel good. Real good.

"You feel so good," he moaned behind her, his hips making a steady penetration into her. "So fucking good! I don't want this to end."

Jada shook her head and moaned, concentrating on her building climax that managed to stay just out of reach. "I can't...I can't..."

"Yes, you can." the hand between her legs rubbed and rolled her clit quickly. "Come for me again, Jada. Finish us both off together."

He drove those two fingers into her pussy, with his thumb rubbing her clit. Those fingers of his matched the thrusts in her ass and it wasn't too long before new and powerful sensations hit her.

Jada gasped and struggled to breathe and before she could stop herself, she was bearing down and pushing back against him. Sweat covered her face and mixed with a few tears. Slapping of flesh against flesh could be heard as well as the heavy breathing and panting from Kane behind her.

She felt him swell inside her. His fingers fucked her pussy quicker and stars exploded behind her eyes. Jada screamed and reared back and Kane bellowed.

* * * *

Kane shoved forward one last time, giving everything he had—taking everything she had. She screamed, clamped down around his cock, and Kane was in heaven. One orgasm turned into another until the third came, pushing that last strand of control out the window.

His climax came and he reared back, yelling his release. The ecstasy that hit was unlike anything he ever *thought* to experience in his life. He couldn't decide if this one was better than the first, but knew that it was all heaven and he was for sure going to do it again. Kane's teeth sank into her shoulder while his cock still pumped in and out of her body, releasing every drop of seed he had in her ass. He wanted to draw it all out for as long as he could, but knew that all great things ended.

He collapsed on top of her, crushing her into the bed, gulping air in. It took a few more moments before he was able to pull out of her and move to the side.

"Don't move," he ordered, then wobbled to his feet and went into the bathroom. He quickly cleaned himself up then went back to Jada and tenderly cleaned her as well. First her backside. Then he turned her over gently so she faced him and that's when he heard her sobs. Guilt hit him hard. With ease, he slid back into the bed, wrapping her into his arms. She struggled some, but the fight wasn't normal. No, as Kane rested his head on the pillow and held her tight against his chest, spoon position, the first thing that came to mind was that he might have broken her, and that was the last thing he wanted to do.

"I'm sorry, Jada," he whispered against her hair, resting his chin on top of her head. "Shit, I'm so sorry. That wasn't planned. I—I didn't want to hurt..." He couldn't finish, couldn't come up with the right words to say.

What was worse was that she didn't say anything to him. Kane moved slightly and looked down at her. She'd fallen into a deep slumber, which added more weight to the guilt. He never felt guilty about things, but this time when it came to her and what he did, he had a hell of a lot of it.

His eyes moved from her face to her shoulder, and he frowned. A strange crescent-moon bite mark was on her shoulder, and that could only mean one thing according to what he was told.

Jada had his mark. A mark like that meant that he mated her to him for life.

He sighed, rubbing his eyes. What was he going to do now? *You made one hell of a mess.* He wanted to yell out his frustration, but instead hugged Jada tighter. She stirred in his arms and mumbled something in her sleep.

"What am I going to do now?" he whispered.

He lay with her for hours, awake thinking about the situation. He couldn't come up with an answer to his question, which meant that he was going to have to go to Drake for help. It was the only thing left.

Carefully he slipped from the bed and found one of his shirts for Jada, placing it on the bed next to her. He knelt down next to the bed and watched her sleep, enjoyed the simple act of watching her. He reached out and touched her hair, face, and shoulder before she rolled over to her stomach, giving him her back. He smiled.

His smile faltered when his eyes landed on her shoulder again. The mark. It was now turning color, bruising, and he hated that he caused her pain. Okay, so he brought her to the cabin with the intentions of teaching her a lesson, or that was at least what he thought he was going to do.

He wanted to humiliate her some by stripping her, but things got completely out of control. Sex with Jada was *not* his plan even though he couldn't stop thinking about it.

A new guilt hit him. First times were supposed to be special, at least for the girl, according to what he was taught about sex, and he had fucked that up for her. He took what he shouldn't have taken and did it brutally. Then he thought about Jada; she had said 'no', but she'd shown she'd wanted him, hadn't she? Yes and no. She'd been hesitant, probably scared shitless, but she'd wanted him—he knew she had. Had felt her sensual emotions reaching out to him. He hoped she still did want him.

When his legs started to go numb, he stood up. Kane tore his eyes from her sleeping body to pick up her jeans on the floor. It was the only thing she had that wasn't ripped. He folded them and placed them on the table for her to find when she woke up along with her socks and shoes.

He picked up his own jeans, got back into them before he went back to the bed and knelt next to her one more time. Kane gently brushed some hair back from her face and touched her bruising shoulder with that had his mark. He just couldn't get over how rough he was with her, and the proof was on her shoulder. He was pretty sure that she was going to be sore when she woke up, and pissed to a point of wanting to kill him. He smiled at that thought, just because of her size. Jada wasn't scared to stand up to him and he enjoyed that.

"Forgive me," he whispered to her. With tenderness that he normally never had, Kane kissed her once on the forehead, then the cheek. "I shouldn't have been so rough with you. I promise it will be even better next time."

It was four in the morning when he slipped out of the cabin. Hands in pockets, head down with his guilt, Kane headed back to Drake's. He kept thinking about how pissed Jada was going to be when she woke up. And the sick part of him was looking forward to it. But that wasn't what had him worried. He needed to talk to Drake and get some answers. He knew what he had done, sort of understood it, but thought it might be best if he talked to Drake before Jada came storming home.

As usual, the house was quiet when he opened the front door. Before he went to Drake's room, he turned for Sasha's. Kane was a bit shocked to find Drake already up, dressed, and tucking his sister into bed.

Drake moved his finger up to his lips, indicating to Kane to be quiet, and then he motioned for Kane to follow him out. Kane ended up going back downstairs and into the kitchen.

"I'm going to suspect that you're here early to let me know that you caught Jada trying to run," Drake said.

Kane rubbed his face. "Not exactly." He couldn't look at him. It was the sign that something was up because he always met Drake in the eye.

"Kane, what's going on?" Drake asked.

"I caught her climbing out the window. And, and," Kane stuttered, still not looking at Drake. "She's sleeping at my place."

"Why?" Drake trailed the word out and this time Kane looked up at him. "What did you do?"

"I don't think you really want to know."

"Oh, I think I want to." Drake crossed his arms over his chest and his eyes narrowed on Kane. Kane felt like he was a little boy and his father was looking down at him after he pulled a bad prank. In a strange way, Drake was looking down at him and he was Kane's father. "Give."

Kane swallowed hard and took a deep breath, letting it out loudly, "I've done something that I really shouldn't have done."

Drake frowned. "I'm listening."

Kane started pacing the kitchen and rubbed the back of his neck. How the hell could he tell Drake what he'd done? "Well I um, I caught Jada trying to run away again and I stopped her like you asked me to do."

"Okay." Drake put his hands on his hips. Kane got a very uncomfortable feeling when he took a quick glance at him. "And?"

"And I took her to my cabin."

"Kane—"

Kane shook his head. He started to think about why he took her there and the words began to flow. "And she just started her mouth again, said one too many insults, and then I wanted to teach her a lesson. You know. Let her know that her mouth would only get her into trouble. But it all went wrong. Everything went wrong," he finished with a groan.

"You're not making any sense." Drake sighed. "What're you talking about?"

Kane stopped his pacing again and looked at Drake with a hard expression on his face. "I had sex with her."

Drake stared at him without saying anything. His mouth opened, he blinked fast many times before his hands came up, one rubbing his face the other shaking a finger at him. "I know I didn't hear you right. What did you say?"

Kane swallowed hard again before he spoke again. "I had sex with her," he repeated.

Drake scratched the side of his face and turned his head to the side, eyes still on Kane but he clearly was confused about what Kane just said. "And um why...why would you do that?"

"Be...because." Kane started to stutter out. He cringed and pressed his fingers to the bridge of his nose. "I don't know. Because I wanted to."

"Why do I get this feeling that there's more you're not telling me." He didn't answer Drake. "Kane...what else happened with you and Jada out in that cabin?"

When he met Drake in the eye Drake shook his head, turned and left the kitchen. Kane followed him. "Son-of-a-bitch!" Drake yelled. "Did you mark her?"

Kane took a deep breath and only met Drake in eye, keeping his mouth shut.

"Motherfucker!" Drake yelled again.

"Tell me that this mark doesn't mean what I think it means?" Kane asked him. "Please, tell me everything is going to be okay."

"Oh, it means *exactly* what you think it means." Drake chuckled without humor. "And no. Everything *isn't* going to be okay."

"So what do I do about it?" Kane asked.

Drake choked in mocking laugher. "This isn't something that goes away or can be fixed. This is for life! You have marked Jada as your mate. There is no going back."

Kane rubbed his face and sighed deeply. Guilt washed over him hard and heavy. "She is going to be so pissed. I wasn't exactly easy and gentle."

Drake laughed, "Pissed? She is going to be out for blood and your nuts." Kane gave him another quick glance before turning and going back into the kitchen. "What else happened, because you're acting like more shit happened."

"Oh, more shit happened." Kane went right to the fridge and pulled out a beer. He twisted the top and downed half of it in one big gulp. "And I think it's best if I kept it to myself," he said with a tight voice, thanks to the gulp he took.

Time stood still and Kane finished his beer before Drake spoke again. "Did you take her like a male on moon night?"

"I don't know what you mean." He kept his eyes down and thought about how he did take her.

Kane feasted on her flesh and hungered for so much more. He would swear right now that he could live off her taste and hunger for no other. Even now, he couldn't stop thinking about her taste and how much he wanted it. Standing in the kitchen his damn dick throbbed to match that want.

"The hell you don't!" Drake's voice was short and had the effect of making Kane cringe. "I told you everything there is to know about the heat cycle. You know how we take our mates on moon night, how rough, and dominating we become. Did you fuck her like that?"

Kane met him in the eye and stood up straight. "Yes."

"Son-of-a-bitch," Drake groaned.

"What should I do now?" Kane couldn't keep the desperation from his voice. "I need advice here, so what the hell do I do?"

Drake rubbed his face quickly and shook his head. "Protect your nuts and go on the offensive," he shrugged, "Because she is going to want to kill you once she wakes up."

* * * *

Jada jolted up and awake from a deep sleep with a gnawing, raw pain between her legs, not to mention in her ass. The memory of what Kane had done to her hit like ice water over the head. She lowered her head to her hands and took several deep breaths, pushing the tears that threatened to fall. She wasn't going to cry. Not here, not now, not again.

"You bastard." One tear slipped free and she grabbed the shirt he'd left on the bed for her. Jada didn't know what time it was, but she did know that she was going to kill Kane.

Wincing as she dressed, Jada felt her anger boil over. How in the blazes of hell could this have happened? How could one moment she be having words with Kane then the next she was tied to a beam with him touching her? Of all things to happen, having sex with him was one of the things she didn't want to happen—hadn't planned on it happening.

Sex was something she was always afraid of, mostly because of her grandfather. He pounded into her that to lie down before being married was one of the dirtiest sins out there. That her sin would fall on that of a child, if she had one. Just like her. And it wasn't pleasurable but painful. *Well part of that is the truth. She was sore. But, man, if she didn't have one hell of an orgasm!*

Damn! He'd made her want him—want to have sex with him—made her forget all about her grandfather's warnings. "When I get my hands on you," she mumbled to herself as she worked to get her shoes on. "I am going to skin you alive."

Dressed with his shirt and his scent around her, Jada stormed out of the cabin. She stopped and picked up a thick piece of wood before heading towards the house. She was hurt and angry and if she was going to have to face Kane, because she was damn sure he was at the house, then she was going to cause him pain. It was only fair.

Jada ran all the way to the house and went around to the back. She stormed inside and swung wide at Kane the moment she saw him. "You bastard!" she yelled.

"Oh, shit!" was the only thing Drake managed to get out before Jada came swinging at Kane. Both men ducked in the nick of time.

"You no good rotten piece of shit!" she screamed, swinging again with her wooden weapon.

Kane managed to jump back out of the way so she swung at air only. "I knew she was going to be upset but this is beyond anything I could have expected," Kane said.

"Shut up, Kane," Drake growled. "Jada! Will you get a hold of yourself!" Drake yelled at her.

"You don't know what this rotten mutt has done to me!" she screamed, taking a swing at Kane again and huffing from the effort.

Kane gave her a cheap grin as he again jumped back from her

swing. From the look on his face, she knew that Kane was playing with her, and that pissed her off even more.

"Name calling will only get you into trouble again, Jada," Kane warned with his grin still in place. "It's what started this in the first place."

"When I get my hands on you I am going to slice your balls off and feed them to you in a fucking stew!" she screamed at him.

"Why do I get the feeling that there is more to this story? Want to share the rest?" Drake asked Kane.

"Nothing more to tell, Drake," Kane said in his emotionless, calm voice that Jada was beginning to hate. "Just a temper tantrum that I need to get under control."

"Think that might be a good idea." Drake sighed, and added, "Before she trashes my house!"

Jada took another swing at Kane and this time Kane caught the wood. He yanked it from her hands, slamming it on the counter behind him.

"Now that we have that out of the way," he told her, crossing his arms over his chest, leaning on the counter in a lazy manner. "Want to talk?"

"Talk!" she gasped. "Now you want to fucking talk?" Kane frowned when she turned her back to him and began to rummage through a drawer. "I'm not going to fucking talk to you. I'm going to kill you!"

* * * *

Kane rolled his eyes and sighed when he saw her bring out a large butcher's knife from the drawer. Before she had a chance to turn the thing on him, Kane was on her. He wrapped his arms around her tiny form, one hand over hers, putting enough pressure on her wrist to force her into dropping the knife.

"Ow!" she cried out. "You're hurting me."

Kane plucked her off her feet and walked them both out of the kitchen, heading for the stairs to her room. "I'm not hurting you, only holding you so you won't hurt yourself."

"Bullshit! And this is not holding me, this is pinning me down." she cried as she tried to twist her body out of his arms. "And all you have done is hurt me since we have come face to face."

Kane grunted when the heel of her foot made good contact with his leg. He worked at holding her tightly with one arm while he opened and closed her bedroom door, locking it behind him.

Kane walked over to the bed and dropped Jada on it with a little extra force. He grinned again when he heard her scream in the pillow as he took a desk chair and dragged it over to the bed. He straddled the chair watching her as she hit and kicked on her bed, screaming out her frustrations.

"Finished yet?" he asked her calmly, knowing by the way she acted that it only added to her aggravation.

Jada turned on her side and tried to lunge at him. Kane caught her and like a child, he tossed her back on the bed. This time Jada's screams of frustration suddenly turned into sobs. All of a sudden, she started to cry face down on her bed. Kane was speechless. He didn't know what to say or how to comfort her. Hell, he didn't know what to do in general. If she was screaming and fighting him, then he would know what to do. This crying he didn't know shit about.

"How could you?" she sobbed, keeping her face hidden. "How could you do that?"

Kane sighed. "I'm sorry about your shoulder."

Jada turned around quickly, looking at Kane as if he lost his mind. "I'm not talking about my fucking shoulder, you moron." She sniffed back her tears, wiping at her face quickly. "You know damn well what I'm talking about. How could you do all that to me?" she cried.

Kane took a moment to think over his words carefully. Deep down he knew that no matter what he said to her now, Jada wouldn't be happy. "I'm not going to apologize for taking you. I've been struggling since you came here not to touch you. I took what I felt was mine."

"What was yours?" She laughed in disbelief as she cried. "What was yours? How in the hell do you figure that you had any right to do that to me? You took the one thing that was mine—the one thing that I will never be able to get back or give *freely*."

"That one thing belonged to me!" he informed her harshly. Softening his face, he went on, "I never meant to hurt you or do all the things I did." Kane spoke as soft and as gently as he could, but inside he wanted to shake some sense into her. "I'm sorry. I should have known this would happen. I saw the signs and ignored them."

Jada shook her head at him. "You should have stayed *away* from me if you knew this was going to happen."

Kane looked her dead in the eyes. "Then you have as much to learn about all of this as I do. Once I picked up your scent, no other woman would do. Drake taught me that." Kane made sure that he had her full attention before he went on. "I picked up your scent the night you were taking photos of me and that woman. I picked it up again the first day you showed up here. To stay away from you made it this bad. What do you think it would have been like if I fought it longer? It would have been worse."

"Worse!" Jada frowned at him and scooted off the bed as far away from him as she could get. "You did wrong here, Kane. So wrong." When he reached out to touch her, Jada jumped back. "Don't." Her hand went up and her finger pointed at him. "Don't touch me. Ever again."

Kane cocked his head at the challenge. "I plan on touching a lot more of you, Princess." He stood back up, hands going to the snap and zipper of his jeans.

"What the fuck do you think you're doing?" She backed away from him, but lucky for him there weren't too many places for her to go.

Kane stripped to his bare skin before her. He stood in all his naked glory, letting Jada get her first good look at his body; including the large cock standing at attention. Something he didn't do back in his cabin. "Just what I said I was. I'm going to touch you."

"You're crazy!" she said in disbelief. "You are really out of your mind if you think I'm going to let you fuck me again."

Kane walked up to her, or more like backed her up against the wall, standing mere inches from her. He grinned, sniffing the air around him. "I must be crazy because I want you again desperately." He leaned into her and braced his hands on the wall above her head. "You want me just as much as I want you. I can smell it."

Jada swallowed hard. "No, I don't."

Kane smiled. "I can smell that lie as well as I can smell you." He touched her jaw, running his hand down her neck over her breasts to her jeans once again. With a jerk, he had the snap undone and the zipper down.

"Stop that," she whispered.

Kane rested his forehead against hers. Both hands went to her waist. Fingers slipped into the waistband of her jeans and he groaned loudly. She didn't have any panties on which reminded him that he ripped them off her.

"You look good in my shirt," he purred, going down to his knees. His shirt almost reached her knees due to her petite frame.

He helped her once again out of her shoes so the jeans would come off, but he didn't take them off. Instead, he rubbed her legs and tried to get her to calm down. To still her temper. "But you look better out of it." Kane stood up with the bottom of the shirt in his hands. He moved it up to her stomach before she stopped him from taking it off her.

"I can't and won't do this," she whispered, tugging his hands free of the shirt and pushing away from him again. When he turned around, she tossed his jeans at him, which landed in his face. "Put them back on."

"Nothing is going to change what happened," he told her while he got back into his jeans. "We crossed a line and there isn't any going back."

"You're right." She hugged herself, more tears falling from her eyes. "You did cross a line. And I can make damn sure it never gets crossed again."

"You're my mate, Jada."

She held up her hand and shook her head. "No, I'm not." Her voice shook, making him want to go and wrap her in his arms. He hated how broken she sounded. "I'm just a girl you used."

She rushed to the door, unlocked it, and was out before it dawned on him that she was running away from him again. Kane quickly zipped and snapped his jeans closed and went after her. He made it down the stairs and was about to go out the front door but stopped with Drake's yell.

"Kane!" He turned and frowned. "Let her go."

"Drake…" Kane couldn't keep the growl from his voice. He didn't get to finish what he was about to say.

Drake held up his hand, "Give her some space man. She's a human who's just been claimed. No human takes the news well."

"I can't let her go," he said through his teeth.

"She's not going anywhere. Cole is heading this way to get her so he'll meet up with her."

"I don't need Cole fighting my battles!" He could feel it. The need, the domination, the challenge that his mate was giving him. Everything that Drake told him he would feel after he claimed someone.

"No one is going to keep you away from your mate, but you need to understand that she needs time to digest all of this." Drake rubbed his face and sighed. "Put your sister in her shoes. Wouldn't you want space between Sasha and her mate if she was claimed like that?"

"Don't bring Sasha into this." Kane didn't bother with keeping the threat out of his voice. "She'll not be a part of this shit."

"And you don't get to make that decision."

Kane lost it and grabbed Drake by the front of his shirt. He pushed him back, slamming him up against the wall. He snarled in his face. "No one will touch my sister, ever!"

Drake hit him in the side of his face with the side of his arm, knocking him down to his knees. Before he could right himself, a solid punch landed in his stomach.

"Hey!" Carrick came running down the stairs. She went up to Drake, pushing him away from Kane. "What the hell is going on?"

"Nothing." Drake shook his hand and rubbed it, but his eyes were still locked with Kane's. "Just having a disagreement."

"With your fist?" Carrick's voice pitched. "You know that shit doesn't solve anything."

"No, but it makes me feel good." Drake shrugged off Carrick's hands and backed away. "You want to be a man, Kane. Get some fucking control over that temper. Your sister has the chance of being claimed just like Jada and there isn't a damn thing you can do about it. And you come at me like that again I'll knock the piss out of you."

Kane kept his mouth shut and rubbed his jaw. He tasted blood, felt inside his lip and swore under his breath. Busted lip.

"You okay?" Carrick came over to him, but he backed up before she could touch him.

"I'm fine."

"Yeah, everyone is fine," she sighed. "My ass! You all start acting like a bunch of pricks a few days before the full moon."

"Full moon?" Kane couldn't stop the frown. Since Jada came, he hadn't thought about it or for that matter knew when it was coming. "How long?"

"What?"

"How long before the full moon comes?"

"Couple of days."

He sighed and rubbed his face. Time. What he needed was more time and Jada wasn't going to give it to him. Stefan told him two years ago that once he had his mate his heat would be different. He wouldn't be kept from her and if he were then he would hunt her down. There was a possibility of hurting anyone that might try to stand in his way.

"Shit," he breathed out heavily. "I don't need that to come up right now."

"Kane, what's going on?"

He met her eyes and rubbed his jaw again. "I fucked up, Carrick. I became the animal that Stan has been trying to get me to be for years." He stood up. "I took what wasn't mine to take."

"Well then I say give her some space." She touched his cheek gently and smiled. "And make up with Drake." She gave him a small slap. "Not healthy for you to fight with your father, even if he is old enough to be your brother."

Kane couldn't help it and smiled at her. "Yes, mother."

Carrick shivered and turned away from him. "Hate it when you call me that."

Chapter Six

Jada spent the night locked up in her room away from Kane and everyone else. After some arguments, and lots of screaming, she ended up locking herself away since she couldn't get them to let her leave or go stay at Cole's place.

What really surprised her most was how much she was crying over all of this. She wasn't crying over Kane, but more over how fate fucked her over again. She landed in the protection of animals without manners. In her eyes, it wasn't any better if she was out on the streets looking over her shoulder like before. At least that way she would know who was attacking her and what they were after. With Kane, she didn't have a clue as to what was about to hit her until it was too late.

Twenty-four hours since the encounter and her body felt like it had been through some battle, reminding her every time she moved that Kane took something that didn't belong to him. Jada spent most of the night pacing the room, trying to think about what she was going to do in order to get out of this mess, but all she ended up doing was crying.

When she stopped at the window to stare at the night she saw Kane standing outside the watching the window. He was still keeping an eye on her, waiting for her to try to run again so he could get his hands on her. She could feel his eyes on her, just as if she could still feel his hands on her body and his cock inside her tender pussy.

With frustration, she closed the blinds after midnight, blocking everything from his eyes and went back to her pacing. Two more times she tried to get some sleep but failed. On the fourth try, she gave up with a groan, flipping the covers from the bed only to start the pacing again. It was now three in the morning.

"Can't sleep, Princess?" Jada spun around and there he was. Kane. "Neither can I it seems." He stood in the doorframe, or more like leaning against it, arms crossed over his chest. His face showed no emotion, which only added to her bad mood.

"What are you doing here?" she demanded, hugging herself.

"What's it look like?" he answered. He showed her a plate filled with food. "You didn't come down for dinner, so I thought I'd bring you something and we can talk while you eat. And I come to check on

Sasha each night."

"I'm not hungry," she stated, glaring at him. "And I've said all there was to say to you."

Kane walked into her room, kicking the door closed. He went over to the nightstand, putting the plate of food down. "Jada…"

"No, Kane. It was agreed that you would stay…"

"No!" he growled. She heard the anger in his voice then. "*You* demand that I stay away and Drake agreed with you for now. *I* never agreed to stay away from you." Both hands went on his hips. "You have my mark."

"Only because you forced it on me!" Her chin trembled with a fresh set of tears. "Just like you forced yourself on me. The mark means nothing."

"The hell it doesn't!" he yelled. "That mark means one thing…" He pointed his finger at her. "You're mine, dammit."

"Yours?" she breathed out in disbelief. "Listen to yourself. I'm not your damn possession. I don't belong to anyone."

"That mark on your shoulder means a hell of a lot more than either one of us completely understands," he informed her with gritted teeth. "You are bound to me as I am to you."

"I'm not bound to you!" she screamed. "I'm not bound to anyone, you freak." She motioned at the door, anger boiling over. "Get out." Her legs gave out, causing her to drop to the floor. Not eating much for a couple of days and no sleep was starting to take effect on her body.

"I'm not going anywhere." He grabbed her arms, forcing her back to her feet. "I can't walk out of here alone. Don't you understand that? Don't you comprehend what all of this means?" He shook her. "I've had a taste of you. You are in my system for life. Nothing else will do but you."

"The only thing that I understand is that you hurt me," she told him through her teeth, thrusting her chin up at him. "And no matter what you say or try to do it will never go away. You took something from me that you had no right to do. You were told to keep an eye on me, not rape me!" she yelled in his face.

Kane's face paled. He released her slowly, but his eyes never left hers. "I didn't rape you." His voice shook when he spoke and she saw a flash of pain in his blue eyes causing her to flinch. He reached out to touch her face and Jada couldn't stop herself from flinching away once more, as if he was going to hurt her again. "I would rather die, than hurt you. If I could do this all over again I would." She stayed still as a statue when he bent over and kissed her forehead. It was something tender that she didn't expect from him. "I'm sorry, I really am, but I'm not going to keep fighting a losing battle within myself."

He turned and walked out of the room, closing the door softly. Jada exhaled the breath she didn't know she was holding and slumped back down to the floor. Her whole body started to shake uncontrollably.

"What the hell just happened?" Drake slammed the door open, making her jump up quickly from the floor to stumble back against the bed. She didn't look at him, but lowered her face to her hands, elbows resting on the knees. "What the fuck did you do to him?"

"What did I do?" Jada looked up at him in disbelief. "What about what the hell he did to me?"

"I thought you knew something about what we're like." Drake put his hands on his hips, glaring down at her. "We have no control, Jada, when our mate is around. You can't blame him because of what his nature forced him to do. I was under the impression that Chase explained things to you."

"Oh, that's just perfect," she spat as she rose to her feet, slapping her legs, fresh tears falling down her face. "Let's pity Kane, because he just did what nature told him to do. Fuck you, Drake!" she yelled. "He hurt me beyond anything I've ever been hurt before in my life. So don't you stand there acting like I did something major to him."

"You did do something major," Drake told her through his teeth. "It was written all over his face when he walked out of this house. What the hell do you think is going to happen now in a couple of days?" He cocked his head to the side at her, but she didn't understand the question.

"What are you talking about?" she sighed.

"Full moon, Jada," Drake raised his arms up in the air, bringing his hands down to slap on the sides of his legs. "I know you have some idea what happens then."

"It has nothing to do with me." She turned her back on him, but Drake wasn't going to let her do that.

He grabbed her arm, forcing her around to face him. "It has a lot to do with you now. You're mated to him. He will go into heat and hunt for you to claim you completely. Just so you understand what I'm talking about, I'm going to be very blunt here. He is going to take you until the need he feels for you has calmed down in his veins."

"News flash, Drake." She jerked her arm free, glaring up at him. "He already has."

"I'm not talking about that, damn it," he sighed, rubbing his face. "Full moon night is going to be worse."

"Well, he can just do like he has in the past."

Drake groaned. "You're not getting it."

"Oh, I understand perfectly." Jada was gritting her teeth so tightly her jaw started to ache. She turned around, eyes narrowing. "You want me to lie down and be his whore."

Drake narrowed his eyes on her, "Are you *really* that stubborn? You really think that's all it is? That it's just about the sex?"

"Isn't it?" she gasped.

Drake opened his mouth to answer but stopped when they heard a loud yell like growl. Jada went over to the window, but didn't see anything. It didn't take a genius to figure out that it was Kane out there yelling like an animal.

"That's why," Drake said. "He's a mated man. Nothing will keep him away from you and I mean nothing now. You might have gotten away with him walking out of this room alone, but don't hold your breath that it's going to stay like that. Full moon is a couple days off so brace yourself. Kane *will* be back—for you."

* * * *

Kane howled at the top of his lungs because of the grief he felt deep inside. *You were told to keep an eye on me, not rape me!* He kept hearing those words in his head, words that were true but he didn't want to face them.

He was supposed to watch her, not touch her, not tie her up, and have his way with her. He sure as hell wasn't supposed to hurt her as he had. Now Kane was in a bind, because he didn't know what the hell he had to do to make it right. Then to add more trouble he had to look forward to the full moon in a couple of days and had no clue on what he was going to do.

"You didn't rape her." Kane stopped his walking when he heard Sasha's soft voice. He turned around and there she stood, hugging herself with her thick coat on. "You didn't."

"What are you doing out here?" he asked.

"You didn't rape her," she said again.

"I hurt her," Kane breathed out. "So it might as well be called rape."

Sasha smiled, rushed up, and hugged him around the waist. Her touch brought him down to his knees and Kane didn't hold back his pain. With his sister holding him, he cried.

He didn't know how long he stayed on the ground, holding onto her, but he stayed like that until there were no more tears left to fall. Once finished, Kane stood up and with Sasha by his side headed for his little cabin.

The temperature was dropping, the smell of snow was in the air, but the guilt on his shoulders blocked it all out. Once inside the cabin, Kane sat down on the large sofa, staring at the cold fireplace. Sasha had a fire built quickly and was fixing some hot cocoa for them both. When she handed him a mug, she sat down next to him with her legs tucked underneath her saying nothing.

Carrick explained to him once that every girl remembers her first time, so if he was lucky enough to have a mate that was still innocent he should take it slow and easy with her. Guess he fucked that one up.

"You're being too hard on yourself," she said. "I'm sure once she's calmed down she will forgive you." Kane turned his head toward Sasha who giggled, "Eventually."

Kane sighed. "You've been in my head again."

She shrugged. "Can't help it. Old habits die hard you know."

"So you know what I've done then?" She nodded. "Shit," Kane groaned, tossing his head back on the sofa.

"Kane, you didn't rape her, even though she said you did. I looked it up." Sasha had a proud excited look on her face when he glanced at her again. "Nothing pleasurable comes out of rape, and from what I saw, she was enjoying the things you were doing."

"Sasha, I don't want to have this conversation with you." He sat his cup down on the floor and stood up. Kane walked into the bedroom and his eyes went right to the bed and the bloodstain in the middle. Quickly he went to work at stripping the bed before Sasha saw it.

"Okay, but if you change your mind you know how to find me." Sasha took her cup over to the small table slipped back into her coat and smiled at him. Kane stopped what he was doing when she came into the room, pulled him down to her level, and kissed him on the cheek. "And stop beating yourself up. Everything will work out. Trust me." She'd shocked him again.

Staying in the cabin alone didn't seem to sit well with him like it once had. Night came with an overcast sky, some snowflakes, and the reminder of a full moon that was too close for his comfort.

Nevertheless, he did stay put, watching the snow come down, feeling the burn start in his veins, and plunged into his guilt.

The entire next day, Kane thought about what he had done, what he wanted to do, and what needed to be done. Okay, so bringing her to the cabin, tying her up, and stripping her was a mistake. He'd admit that one. As for the sex part, well that was something different. He didn't feel ashamed of it, only bad for how rough he was since it was her first time. He should have stayed away from her after he kissed her, but he just couldn't do it. After what he felt once he saw her swimming, that definitely should have been a big sign to stay away from her. But did he listen? Fuck no!

It was just like now. Kane couldn't calm his body down, release the tension that was present in his body, or stop it from traveling down to one hell of a raging cock, which seemed to get worse the more he thought about it. It was only twenty-four hours until the full moon, and the plan was to stay away from Jada, to give her time to calm down, but it didn't feel like it was going to happen like that.

Nope, not at all.

He was hard, tension quickly rising in his body, fire burning inside. Kane paced his tiny home, his one and only thought was to touch her, go to her, claim her and still this blaze inside of him. He wanted nothing more than to feel the heat of her body and the silkiness of her skin against his own. The more he thought about it the more he didn't give a damn if she was pissed. He just needed to satisfy this ache for her that he had.

One taste of that body and Kane was lost the second it happened, he just didn't know it then. He smiled at that thought though. She was his natural drug and boy did he hunger for a fix. She stood her ground with him, not knowing that the simple act itself was enough to have his animal side raging with the need to take, claim, possess, and dominate. Kane explained that to her several times but she seemed to ignore it, and it was fine with him. He never thought he could or would enjoy someone challenging him the way his little Jada did.

"Fuck it." Kane growled, having enough of this alone shit. "I'm taking what belongs to me."

He rushed out the front door, jerking his coat onto his thick shoulders. He thought for a second that he might be making a mistake by going up to the house in the condition he was in, but there was no damn way he could stay in his cabin for one moment longer alone. Jada might be pissed at him, even hate him for how he fucked her against the wall her first time, but she also needed to understand that he couldn't be alone. Not with his heat right around the corner.

Snow was falling thick now and the wind was blistering cold when he stepped outside to go over to Drake's. Kane could barely see where he was going and it was only four in the afternoon, which meant that the storm was going to be even worse than what any of them had thought. He knew that they were going to be in for a big snowstorm by tonight, because this stuff was coming in thick and acting crazy.

The walk took him longer than it would normally. When Kane walked into the house, he was surprised that it was quiet when he stepped inside. He rather expected everyone to be in the front room sitting in front of the fire that burned, giving off a low glow of light in the dark room. The smells and noise that was coming from the kitchen told him that baking was going on.

"I was starting to wonder how much longer you were going to hold out." Cole came out from the kitchen alone, smiling at Kane, with a cookie in his hand. "I told Drake that you would be here before night and here you are."

Kane shrugged out of his coat, hanging it up before he went to the fire to warm his hands. He decided to play it cool and not let on why he was here. "Thought I would come and check on Sasha."

"Bullshit," Cole snorted. "You came to irritate Jada again."

"I don't irritate." Kane frowned, keeping his eyes on the fire. He worked extra hard at keeping all emotions from showing. Kane didn't need Cole giving him shit, not now when he felt like he was about to explode any second. "I thought you were leaving for the weekend?"

"I was, but we're in for a bad snow storm, so I have to endure the heat alone this month. She's upstairs, taking a shower." Cole indicated with a nod. He walked up to Kane, standing next to him, rubbing his own hands for warmth. "Carrick got her to come down for dinner, but she went right back up when Drake started in on her about the full moon. She's pretty close minded right now."

Kane fought with his legs to stay put. He didn't want to appear too eager to go up and see her. When he felt Cole's eyes on him Kane turned, looking him right in the eye. "Say it."

Cole turned also, looking Kane head on. "We all know she's yours, and that she needs the time to come to terms with it. Go upstairs and talk, because the two of you really do need to talk before tomorrow night. You get one true mate, Kane, don't fuck it up."

Kane watched him turn away and start to walk back into the kitchen. "Cole." He stopped walking, turning back around. "How did you know?"

Kane watched Cole closely. This whole mating thing was so hard to understand. He didn't know if he could be a man and not the animal Jason almost turned him into. Now that a mate had been tossed into his life, Kane still didn't know what was wrong or right. What he felt at the time was right when he took her to the cabin. Being inside her felt right. What had him thinking it wrong was what if it was Sasha and not Jada? What would he do if someone treated his sister as he treated Jada?

"Sometimes we just know." Cole sighed deeply.

Kane opened his mouth to ask more, but Cole stopped him with his hand held up. "Go up there and do what it is you have to do. Make it right with Jada. Lord knows she'll be a pain to live with if you don't."

Kane placed his hands on his hips, watching Cole disappear into the kitchen. He thought maybe he should go in there and say hi to Sasha, but he couldn't move. His hearing picked up the faint sound of water running. Jada was taking a shower. That image alone gave new life to his cock, causing the unwilling member to thicken, harden, and press tightly against the zipper of his jeans. Out in the cold snow he was able to cool off, but now, with the image of her wet body, he was once again on fire.

God, he wanted her! Kane couldn't suppress the need that raced in his system like hot lava. That time in his cabin started something he couldn't fight, and when she came, charging after him pissed and ready to kill, it only caused Kane to want more. He felt as if he needed to feel her sweet cunt fist over his cock like he needed to breathe. Had to have it stretched around him in an almost brutal, painful pleasure while he pumped hard inside her.

"Shit, I'm fucked," he whispered to himself, looking into the fire one more time, debating what he should and shouldn't do.

Rubbing his face, Kane made up his mind. He was going upstairs to see Jada. What he was going to do once he got there, he had no idea. He just knew that he couldn't stand not being around her.

Kane took the steps two at a time. His heart pounded in his chest with each step he took, reminding him once again of the need that raced in him. Hell, his hands were shaking with the desire to touch her. For Kane, this was not normal, not by a long shot. He never, *ever* was this way when a woman was involved, but then again he hadn't been around one who turned out to be his mate.

He stopped at the door to the bathroom. Steam came from the top and bottom of the door as well as the sweet scent of Jada. He closed his eyes, inhaling the sweet scent, hungering for more, welcoming the burn of the upcoming heat.

He had to force himself to move again. Kane wanted to stand there, taking her scent in, letting it wash over him for the longest time but that wouldn't fix the problem or ease his pain. He was tired of standing in the shadows. Tired of getting bits and pieces of a scent without touching the owner. He had to touch her, had to ease what was burning within him, even if that meant she was going to hate him for the rest of his life.

Kane forced himself to walk away from the bathroom and go to her room. It was dark inside with a slight chill in the air. He looked around. The bed was a mess, which meant that she was still not sleeping. The dresser was open with clothes hanging off the side, and a few on the floor.

He touched nothing, didn't even turn the light on. Kane closed the door silently before walking to the far corner to the right where it was the darkest. Bending over, he unlaced his boots, slipping his feet out of them and then his socks. Tension gripped him as he worked at stripping his clothing. He didn't plan on what he was doing, but from the look of the bed, Jada needed some rest just as he did. A full night without sleep was unbearable and he didn't want to do another night without it. Therefore, his plan was to climb in that bed, wrap her into his arms, and get the needed sleep they both required. He also knew that she would fight him on it every step of the way, which would more than likely take things to the one place that would surely get him into trouble all over again.

Once he was down to his tight boxer briefs Kane waited. He stood as still as a statue listening for her steps. Each and every one of his nerves were on high alert as well as his cock straining against the thin cotton, demanding to be set free. Not even the chill in the room could calm the raging need his cock now carried.

The air shifted and Kane tensed more. Jada was coming down the hall towards her room; he could smell the difference in the air. He fisted his hands waiting, preparing himself for that fight that was sure to come. One way or another Kane was going to make her understand that she belonged to him!

The door opened and Kane pressed farther into the dark shadows. He was surprised that she didn't turn the light on or sense that he was in her room, but glad all the same. It gave him the better opportunity to watch her as she moved.

She was wrapped up in a towel with another on her head. Kane forced himself to keep his control and not go to her. He fought with his beast to stay put and let her do what she needed to do. The time would come soon enough when he was able to touch her, sooner than either of them knew.

She rubbed her hair viciously before dropping the towel into a small pile of clothes on the floor. Her back stayed to him, even when she went to the dresser and began to brush her hair. Kane noticed how she looked out the window while she brushed her hair and he started to wonder if she was watching for him.

Once she was finished the next thing she did almost caused Kane to let a sound slip from his lips. In fact, Kane had to bite his lower lip to stop a sound from escaping when the towel around her body slid to the floor, letting him get a full view of her naked backside.

She was gorgeous. Plain and simple.

Kane's whole body shook with need and it took the last amount of his restraint to not rush over and fuck her hard and deep. Standing there watching her pull out a loose set of boxer shorts, slipping them up her legs to cover the round rump he couldn't get out of his mind was driving him crazy. He was starting to think that coming up here was a very bad idea and not having sex with her out of the question.

Kane had to close his eyes as she finished. He couldn't watch her slip the tight tank top over her breasts, knowing how bad he wanted to taste them. Couldn't watch her hide the body he'd dreamed of since the first time he touched it. Only when he heard the sheets move and a deep sigh come from her did he open his eyes. Jada was in the bed, on her left side on the far side of the bed. For Kane, she was in the best position for him to creep in behind her.

He waited.

He wanted some time to pass before he moved, wanted Jada to be relaxed and somewhat sleepy before he slipped in behind her. Once he sensed she was relaxed enough Kane moved from his hiding spot to the bed. Carefully he picked up the blankets and slipped in behind her. With delicate movements, he scooted as close as he could get to her, slipping one arm under her neck and the other around her waist. As soon as his body heat reached out to her, her body tensed.

"What—what?" she mumbled sleepily.

"Shhh," Kane whispered in her ear.

"Kane! What the hell are you doing back here?" She tried to twist in his arms, but Kane tightened his hold on her.

"Neither one of us has slept since that night." Kane rubbed his face into her still wet hair, closing his eyes at the scent that wrapped around him. "I can't fight this." His voice lowered, thickened." It's killing me being away from you."

"Get out!"

Kane took a deep breath, letting it out slowly. His arms tightened, pulling her back closer, bending his knee, which slipped between her legs. "I can't."

"Kane, I'm warning you." She fought to twist in his arms, which only forced Kane to hold her even tighter.

"Warning me of what?" he purred the words, letting a small hint of danger thicken with them. "Remember the last time you warned me? You ended up…"

"I know what fucking happened!" Jada snapped. "You don't have to remind me that you're a damn animal with no goddamn control. Now get your fucking hands off of me!"

Kane smiled, even though she couldn't see it. The anger that radiated in her, mixed with the lingering lust that he could smell. "Must I remind you once again about that animal statement?"

Deep down Kane loved it, though. He didn't want to tell Jada that when she made her snide remarks about him being all animal, it fueled him. Her smart-ass temper was all it took for Kane's animal to come out, waiting to be stroked by her.

"I can smell it," he stated, moving his head to her shoulder and licking the mark he left there. Jada trembled in his arms. The arm he had over her waist moved to her belly, feeling the soft skin quiver under his hand. "Just like I can feel it in your body. The attraction is there, rising to match the heat that is building inside of me."

"Kane, please," she begged softly, moving her head to his shoulder. "Don't do this to me."

"I want you, Jada." He licked at the mark again before he let his teeth scrap it. "I feel as if I can't breathe unless I can touch you." He moved his fingers with skill, slipping them inside the waistband of the boxers she wore to slip down to the slick junction between her legs. "Can't think beyond what you taste like, feel like." Kane cupped her with his whole hand, hissing in her ear, "God you burn."

Both of her hands closed around his wrist between her legs. "Kane!" she hissed the words out in a rush, and strangely she made no move to try to move his hand away.

"I need you." Kane couldn't hide the rough edge to his voice. He moved his fingers slowly, spreading the outer lips of her pussy before moving his middle finger in a teasing manner up and down. "I can't stop thinking about how you felt when I pushed my cock deep inside you. You're so tight it feels like a hot, tight fist is closing around me and I want more." He pushed two fingers deep into her pussy, growling lightly when she arched back against him, her ass grinding into his hardness. "I need more, Jada. I feel like I'm that animal you accuse me of all the time and only you have the power to make me the man I know I can be. And I promise you no pain. I won't hurt you again."

"We can't do this." She tried to sound serious but failed with a moan, arching her back. "*You* can't do this to me again. It isn't right."

"I can't think of anything more right. Don't fight what it is," Kane spoke soft, his fingers fucking her tight pussy in slow in and out strokes. "We belong to each other and I can't stay away from you. I *refuse* to stay away."

Jada shook her head. "Damn you," she moaned, her hips thrusting to meet his fingers' movements. "Oh shit," she breathed out, bending forward, as much as his arms would allow.

"You're close." Kane licked and suck at the mark again, increasing not only the pressure at her shoulder but the spread of his fingers. "I can smell it."

"Kane, please," Jada begged, arching in his arms once again, her grip tightening on his wrist.

"I love when you come." He used his free arm, the one tucked under her neck to pull her tank top up, never missing a beat with his fingers fucking her tight cunt. "And I want to feel it again. Need to feel you lose that tight fucking control you keep." He finished with a deep growl, almost ripping her top from her body.

"Fuck you!" she moaned.

"I plan to."

Kane shoved another finger deep inside her hard and shattered her control. Jada screamed out, her whole body convulsing around him, her ass bumping into his ever-painful cock.

He quickly moved. Turned her to her back with a little extra force, gripping the boxer shorts and yanking them from her body.

Before Jada even had a slight chance to protest what he was doing, he had pulled his own boxers from his body. He pressed the heat of his flesh to hers, glorying in the silky feel of her skin against the hard contours of his own.

His hips wedged between her thighs, his needy cock resting on her belly while he waited for her to not only come down from the high of her orgasm but for her to start fighting. Kane figured out one thing for sure about Jada, she never ever gave in easy, not even when her body was on fire begging for the fulfillment.

Kane took hold of his throbbing cock, rubbing the sensitive mushroom head up and down the wet slit of his heaven. "Still want to deny this?"

Her hands went up to his chest, nails raking the skin to bring forth a hiss from him. In fact, Kane had to close his eyes as she moved her legs, bending her knees and raising them up his side, opening herself wider for him. "You're an asshole, Kane."

Kane smiled, showing her each and every one of his pearly white teeth. "And you can be a real bitch, Princess."

He shoved hard, impaling every thick inch of his cock as deep as he could get it inside her tight pussy, bringing forth a gasp from her. He growled at the exquisite glove-like grip she had on him. He slightly raised his body up on his arms, just enough to keep most of his weight from crushing her.

With her legs almost tucked under his arms, nails digging into his side, he moved. He pulled his throbbing cock almost completely out, driving back in as hard as he dared. Slowly he moved, building it up. Kane wanted her screaming, begging him to fuck her, to take, claim, and brand. To let loose the animal inside for only her to tame.

"Mine," he growled, withdrawing slowly before plunging back in. Each movement brought a gasp from her lips. "Admit it."

Jada shook her head no, bringing a warning growl from him.

Kane picked up his pace, ramming into her slightly harder, but with the same slowness. "Mine!"

Her nails dug harder into his back and Kane hissed in the pain, loving it. "Never." She moaned, her hands moving lower down his back to his ass. "I'm not yours. Never will be."

Kane lowered his chest to hers, grabbed a fist full of her hair and yanked her head to the side, exposing his mark. "By the time I 'm done with you tonight, and after the full moon you will be screaming it." he snarled the words before his teeth clamped down on the mark and bit her hard.

Jada cried out and bucked under him and Kane let go of his inner animal. He pounded into her with brutal thrusts, forcing her tender pussy to stretch and take all he had to give. He fucked her hard, taking and taking, only letting her have a very few seconds to catch her breath.

When she was close, when her pussy started to tighten on his cock and the nails dug even harder into his ass, letting Kane know her orgasm was very close he stopped. He also let go of the mark, grinning slightly at the bruised color of it.

"You can't have it," he whispered in her ear, his voice thick with need as his cock throbbed within her. "You want to come, then you say that one word. Tell me what I want to hear."

Jada shook her head. "Damn you," she cried. Her hands went up to his chest, pushing at him in a very feeble attempt and hitting him. "You fucking dick! Get off."

"I will, Princess," he purred, licking at her earlobe. "But the question is will you?" He moved again, slowly stroking inside her. "If I have to, Jada, I will fuck you all night long until you pass out. Then in the morning start it all over again. I'll stay inside you until you admit that you belong to me. In case you think that I can't hold back my orgasm, then just think back to when you watched me in the lab. I fucked that one girl without coming once."

"Don't do this, Kane." She panted, begged, "Please!" Once again, he pounded into her hard, stopping when he felt her body about to come. "You bastard!" she yelled, a tear falling from her eye. "You're nothing but a fucking animal on a goddamn, mother-fucking power trip." She shook her head, "I'll never give you what you want. I belong to no one!"

Kane shoved hard, rotating his hips, grinding against her swollen clit. "Then by all means, let me show you my power and who you fucking belong to." He snarled at her when she moved her hand between their bodies to pleasure the clit that was straining for attention. Attention that Kane knew would give her the orgasm she was seeking, if only she would submit to him. He *knew* she wanted him. Why did she lie about it? His grip wasn't nice or gentle when he stopped again and took hold of both her wrists, pinning them over her head. "Don't think so, Princess. The only pleasure you're going to get it is from *me* tonight!"

"Stop it, stop it," she begged, tossing her head back and forth as she tried to move her hips and grind up against him. Sweat beaded on her forehead, slipping down her neck. "Kane, stop!"

"Mine!" he growled again, shoving his cock hard into her tight sheath, fighting the change that was starting to threaten to erupt from not only his body but his soul. The beginning of his heat was growing with each second he tormented her, reminding him of a demand that he was soon to get satisfied. "My pussy." He withdrew. "My woman." He shoved back in hard. "My fucking mate!" he yelled, giving in and letting his beast out.

Hair started to sprout over his body and his cock thickened more. Kane withdrew slowly, only to mercilessly thrust back in, bumping her hard clit with his pelvis. Jada was twisting, grinding, and begging him for her release.

"Fine, damn you!" Jada screamed, her eyes still closed. "Yours." She started to sob, tightening her legs around his hips. "I'm all fucking yours!"

Kane growled a primal, dominating growl of pure victory. He drove inside her with such power that it took his breath away. Over and over again he pounded into her, enjoying her screams and her nails. He braced his hands over her head, letting her delicate hands roam freely over his body.

The pleasure at having not only her hands on him but also the admission that she belonged to him was exquisite. She whimpered under him, clawed at his skin and still Kane pounded into her. He couldn't get closer, couldn't get enough of the tight friction or feel the branding of her pussy on his cock. He wanted it all and with his body, he demanded it. However, he lost his control when out of the blue she bit him hard on his chest next to his right nipple.

Kane yelled a primal yell that was all animal, nothing human. He tossed his head back, ramming into her with all his strength, which had her crying out in release. His cock exploded. Thick, rich seed shot out of his cock in pulsing tidal waves leaving his body shaking.

Both breathed hard but Kane could not find the strength to move from her. He wanted to stay this way, his cock buried to the hilt inside Jada until he died, for nothing in his whole life ever gave him this kind of pleasure. Not even his moments with Sasha as she grew up gave him the peace. Somehow, Jada was the one to calm him like no other would and that thought alone scared the hell out of Kane.

"Mine," Kane breathed the words out, resting his head on the pillow next to her head, "My mate." He licked at his mark, feeling her shutter under him.

"I hate you," Jada whispered the words softly. Kane smiled, but kept his mouth shut, knowing she was just angry that he'd made her give into his demands.

He moved so he could look at her face. Jada was out cold in one of the deepest sleeps he had ever seen. He kissed her cheek, wincing when he slipped from her body, ignoring how his body still ached. Kane wanted to fuck her again, to assure her once more that she belonged to him but he didn't. He knew she needed some rest, just like him. After all, tomorrow night was the full moon, a new experience awaited them both.

Adjusting his body so it looked and would feel like he was still on top of her, but his body weight was really to her side, Kane wound his arms around her. He let his body cool while his warmth reached out to her. Using his legs, he brought up the blankets, tucking them in before resting his face behind her head, taking in her scent. Letting out a deep, sleepy sigh he closed his own eyes and let the long awaited rest over take him. Finally, he was able to sleep like he needed with his woman, his mate tucked in his arms.

Chapter Seven

From her window, Sasha watched the snow falling. She loved the snow, even though it was bitterly cold for her. Loved the pure white look on the ground and how fresh the air smelled. But her enjoyment slipped away when she saw a figure running away from the house towards the woods. At this time of the morning, and with the temperature dropping as fast as it was, no one should be outside. Straining to make out who it was, Sasha gasped and covered her mouth with her hand.

Jada!

She couldn't believe what she was seeing. A major storm was coming and Jada was out in it. With the temperature dropping so fast, and the snow thickening to a point that one couldn't see a hand in front of their face, Sasha didn't understand why Jada would try to go out in it.

"Oh, God!" she gasped.

She pushed away from the window and ran from the room. Sasha knew that Kane spent the night with Jada. But she didn't hear anything, so she wasn't completely sure if they had fought again or not.

She barged into the room, making so much nose that Kane jumped up. When he saw her he quickly covered himself up and looked around the room.

"She's outside," Sasha rushed to say. When Kane frowned she quickly went on, "Jada. I just saw her outside and the snow storm has hit."

"Shit!" Kane stood up with the blanket wrapped around his waist. "Turn around."

Sasha did and bit her lower lip. "The snow is bad, Kane. It was getting real bad while you two were sleeping. Cole called Drake and told him that it was going to be real bad this time." She turned back around when she heard him zip his jeans up. "She can't be out there. She'll die! And why would she leave when the full moon is tonight. Isn't she going to help you with it?"

Kane grabbed hold of her arms, stopping her from panicking. "Calm down. I'll find her."

Sasha nodded and took a few deep breaths.

"Now, which way did she head?"

She licked her lips. "She headed for the woods."

"Okay. Go wake Drake up and tell him. Also let him know that I'm going to take her back to my place since she is already in the woods, and like you said the moon is tonight. Tell him I'll call him with the phone he gave me once I get there." She nodded again and he kissed her on the top of her head. "Don't worry. I'll find her before anything happens."

* * * *

Like Sasha said, the storm was coming in hard, fast and thick with the wind blowing the white shit in his face. Seeing anything in front of him was almost impossible and by the time he reached the edge of the woods he was shaking from the cold temperatures. But the cold did little to ease his anger at her trying to leave again, or the burn from his upcoming heat.

"Jada!" Kane yelled against the wind and the thick snow. Twice he slipped and fell down over lumps and dips in the ground that he couldn't see. "Jada!"

Why did she leave? He didn't understand why she would come out in this shit and leave. He thought they'd come to some kind of understanding, but apparently not. She was still pissed at him and he knew that, but that damn anger of hers was going to get her killed. That is, if he didn't do it first.

He wasn't moving fast or making up much ground. The wind seemed to be pushing him back and draining him of energy like the cold took away his body heat but not the heat of his sexual need thanks to the full moon that was coming. He fell to the ground again, his strength slipping with each second he braved the storm. Kane was starting to think that this wasn't a normal snow storm but a blizzard. He saw footprints, but they were quickly being covered over by fresh snow. That gave Kane the extra oomph he needed to push himself up and go forward. He had to get Jada out of the storm. If he was fading this fast out here, he could only imagine how she was doing. Then once she was safe, he was going to beat her. Put her over his knees and beat her for her stubbornness, and not stop until she begged him to fuck her.

Kane had to stop again and lean against a tree to catch his breath. His feet were going numb and his legs were starting to feel like they weighed a ton. He reached his hand out, trying to block snow from his eyes as he looked around for any signs that Jada had come this way.

He saw none. And with the wind so strong, her scent was almost impossible to detect.

"Can she get any more hard headed?" Kane asked himself as he pushed off from the tree. "I swear!" then he yelled her name again.

Kane managed to walk only a few more feet before he had to stop again to rest. His fear was starting to get the best of him. He couldn't last out here much longer, but he couldn't go back without her. He also didn't want to think that she might be hurt out here, but he couldn't push that thought away.

"Jada!" again Kane tried to call out to her, only to be slapped with his own voice.

Kane waited a few moments to draw up some extra strength. He didn't know how much longer he was going to be able to stay out in this and look for Jada on his own. He might have to go back to get Drake to help him.

After the fourth stop to catch his breath, Kane pushed off from another tree and started to turn back towards his cabin to call for help. He opened his mouth to yell for her again when he tripped over something on the ground. He went down hard face first. With the wind knocked out of him, it took a few seconds before he could breathe again. Shaking his head, he looked over his shoulder at what it was that had tripped him and his heart sank. Jada was on the ground passed out with snow quickly piling on top of her. Next to her head, the snow was the color red.

"Jada!" Kane yelled, crawling towards her. He reached out, grabbing her under the arms and dragging her back to his lap. Brushing snow from her face, Kane leaned down to see if she was still breathing. On a sigh of relief, he closed his eyes and said a silent thank you. But that was short lived when his hand came away from her head with blood on it.

Jada never opened her eyes or showed any sign that she heard him. He turned her head to get a better look at where the wound was and how bad, but with the snow coming down he could barely see a thing. Kane looked around to get his bearings to figure out how far away from his cabin he might be.

"You still need a spanking for scaring me to death." He scooped Jada into his arms and struggled to get up on his feet. "But for now we need to get to the cabin and I need to get you warm and fast."

The normal walk that would have taken Kane moments to make ended up taking him forever. With Jada out cold in his arms and fighting the wind with each step he took, he thought he was never going to reach it. The moment he saw his cabin, Kane felt a small sense of relief and gathered extra energy and strength.

Shifting Jada's weight, Kane took a deep breath and pushed his way through the storm. After what seemed like the longest walk in his whole life, he reached the door to his tiny haven. Only when his hand touched the cold knob did he let out a much-needed sigh of relief. Balancing Jada's weight he managed to open the door and step inside.

Inside was dark and cold, but it still looked like paradise to him. Kane placed Jada on the sofa, went back to lock the door, and then went to the fireplace to get a nice size fire going. It took him several tries because his hands were shaking before he was able to light it. Once finished he went over to Jada and checked her head.

She had a cut on the side, under her hair at the back of her left ear. It didn't look bad enough for stitches, but it still needed to be bandaged up. Her lips were blue, face pale, and body shaking when he left her side. He went to the bathroom to get his first aid kit. In the bathroom, he quickly stripped off his wet cold clothes, grabbed some towels, and then grabbed blankets from the bed.

Naked and cold, he dropped the blankets and the first aid kit on the sofa. Dropping to his knees, Kane went to work on stripping Jada as well. The only way to get her body heat up was to hold her and share his body heat.

She was freezing. He wrapped one blanket around her before he cleaned her wound and put a large bandage over the cut. Once that was done, he put wood on the fire, picked her up, and slid onto the sofa with her facing the fire. He wrapped his arms around her, as well as the blankets that were on top of both of them, and then started to rub her arms and legs.

She was shivering and he held her tighter, doing everything he could to get her warm. The fire crackled, the wind whistled outside, his heat building. In his arms was his very stubborn mate.

The cell phone that he kept on the table buzzed. Kane reared back, looking at it, then rolled his eyes and moved away from Jada. She whimpered when he left and tried to snuggle into the spot that he'd vacated. He grabbed the phone and went back to the sofa, moving her just enough so he could get back in the spot and hold her close. Jada tried to bury herself into his chest and almost got on top of him, but stopped with her head on his chest and one leg over his waist. He readjusted the blankets then answered the phone.

"Yeah."

"Did you find her?" Drake asked.

"I found her." He glanced down at her and hugged her. "She's out cold. Hit her head and freezing."

"Do you have enough food to stay put? This storm just turned into a blizzard and everyone is stuck in the house."

"I have plenty, and enough wood on the porch and inside to keep the fire going which should keep us warm since the place is small. I don't want you to go out in this shit. It's too dangerous out there. I almost didn't find her."

"Have any idea why she ran?"

"None. I thought we had come to some kind of understanding last night." He sighed and rubbed his face. He was tired, not just because he hadn't been sleeping since their first time, but because of his upcoming heat and having to fight that shit outside drained him of energy. "How long is this shit supposed to last?"

"You're not going to like this, but a report just came through and it looks like we're all stuck indoors for at least two days. So we'll all be confined during the heat."

Kane couldn't keep the growl from his throat, "What about Sasha?"

"Don't worry. I've got a plan and she'll be safe. I promise."

He didn't like it, but there wasn't anything he could do about it. "Okay, make sure she knows I'm fine and once this storm is over tell Sasha I'm expecting some cookies. That'll keep her busy while this storm passes over us."

"Stay inside, and I'll call you later."

He hung the phone up and wrapped his free arm around Jada.

"Why are you holding me so tight?" Jada's raspy voice startled him.

Kane took a deep breath and looked up at the ceiling. "Because I found your sorry ass out in the damn snow passed out." She pulled away from him, and he let her go. "Care to explain to me why the fuck you would go out in this shit?"

She shook her head, eyes narrowed on him. "No I wouldn't." Jada pulled away from him, pulling one of the thick blankets tightly around her. "Who the hell asked you to come for me in the first place?" she snapped.

"Who asked me?" he also sat up, but didn't cover his nakedness. "You would have frozen to death out there if it wasn't for me,

Princess."

Jada bent over to one of her boots picked it up and threw it at his head. Kane ducked just in time before it hit him. "Go to hell! I never asked you to come after me. I never asked for this shit!" she yelled.

"And you think I did?" he yelled back. "We both are in this together. We both are wanted by that fucker Stan, and we both are mated for life, so you, Princess," he pointed his finger at her. "Better get your shit together and deal with it before tonight."

"I don't have to deal with dick and I don't give a fuck about tonight," she answered through her teeth. "I don't believe this bullshit that you all have been telling me about the full moon. You want to fuck, find someone else or use your hand, because I'm not laying down for you ever again."

Kane chuckled, but it wasn't in humor. "It doesn't work like that, babe. You think I was a hard ass our first time, you just wait and see what I do to you tonight."

"There isn't going to be a tonight." Again, she spoke through her teeth, glaring at him.

He took a threatening step towards her, a low deadly growl slipping past his lips. "Wanna bet?"

They had a stare off, and Kane refused to back down. All his life when he stood up for himself or Sasha, either he was beaten back down, or she was used against him. This time, neither was in affect.

Her chin went up, clearly stating that she was challenging him, and being so close to his heat with the full moon hours away, there was no way in *hell* he was going to be able to let it go unchecked.

Kane couldn't stop himself from lunging at her, grabbing hold of her arms, forcing her to walk back to the bedroom where he pushed her up against the wall. She didn't try to stop him, just held onto the blanket, her eyes wide, but that damn chin of hers was still up defiantly. She also wasn't backing down from *his* challenge.

"For. Get. It." She spoke slow, emphasizing each word.

The control that he had tight rein over snapped and he felt his heat hit. He growled, yanked her around with more force than was necessary, and pushed her face up against the wall. He jerked the blanket away. When she started to fight him, Kane grabbed both wrists, pinning them over her head, holding them with one hand. He tried like hell to be gentle since she bumped her head, but damn if it wasn't hard to do.

"I forget nothing," he said low in her ear.

He pulled her hair away from her shoulder and bit the mark, getting a hiss from her. *His* mark. Kane didn't hold back a thing from her. He was pissed and horny, not the best combination for a shifter in early heat.

She struggled against him, tried to twist her body and pull away from his mouth on her shoulder, but holding her still was easy.

Keeping hold of her shoulder with his teeth, Kane raised her left leg up and impaled her deeply. He growled against her shoulder at the feel of her tight pussy parting for his dick.

Jada gasped, "You bastard," and strained against him, pushing back, taking him deeper inside her.

"That I am." His voice vibrated when he spoke, and his skin started itching. He felt tiny hairs sprout over his body, but it didn't distract him from what he needed right now.

But he kept his change at bay. Kane wasn't going to become the animal that was inside of him when he took her. He was going to claim her as a man, not a beast.

He pulled out slow and plunged back into her, bringing Jada up on her toes. Several more times he did this until he began a steady rhythm inside her. Each thrust felt like it wasn't enough, that the next was better, but the ultimate goal was very far away and he felt as if he wasn't going to reach it.

It was the position.

Kane stopped, yanked Jada from the wall staying inside her, and turned her towards the bed. Two steps, forcing her to bend, and he slid into her and started the rhythmic pounding again, eyes closed in bliss. This position the first time was the best for him. He was deeper inside her; her pussy gripped him tighter, milking him.

"Damn it, Kane." Jada panted when he forward thrust inside of her. "I'm going to...I'm going—coming."

Kane growled loudly, closing his eyes. She contracted around him, making it feel like the first time he was inside her body. She being so tight around him it was slightly painful for him, but he didn't stop or slow down. He felt more hair cover his body and this time he couldn't hold it back. He wanted to take her in one more position, but with her contracting and pushing back, even a few nips to his wrist, it was impossible. He couldn't hold any of it back.

His cock swelled inside her, mouth sucked on her shoulder right before he sank his teeth back in and came hard. Each spurt of his seed that shot out of him left him weak at the knees. Pleasure like this only came with her. In his past when his captors forced him to have sex, he never came like this. The one time he did, but it sure as hell didn't feel like it did now.

Kane collapsed on top of her, crushing her small body under him into the thick mattress. He breathed hard, gulping as much air into his lungs as he could while he held onto her shoulder.

He thought it was over, until he finally rolled over to his back and felt the burning pain start up again.

The heat wasn't over.

Drake explained to him that each shifter was different, and until you were with your mate, you never knew how yours was going to be. Some would have many orgasms before they were done, others could go many different times in different positions but only come once. Kane had a feeling, by the way he was feeling, that he was going to be the kind that had several before he was done.

Jada moved, and Kane took it as her trying to leave him. He quickly moved, getting his hands back on her before she could leave the bed.

"Don't," she whimpered.

He sat up quickly, placing her on his lap, holding her tight. "I have this hunger for you that never goes away. It only gets stronger," he purred in her ear.

Jada squirmed on his lap. She had no clue that when she moved like that it killed him with the need to have her again. Her ass moving, teasing the throbbing erection was murder to his senses.

"You're out of your mind," she huffed, pulling on his arms. "This is over."

"Who says?" he kept purring in her ear and rubbed her bottom against his cock. "Give me one good reason why I shouldn't take what belongs to me? Why I shouldn't have you all night long."

"I don't belong to you, damn it!" He heard the anger in her voice and smiled, even though she couldn't see it.

Kane held her easily with only one arm around her. With his other, he picked her up and dropped her down onto his cock. He hissed in her ear at the pleasure that gripped him—nothing he could put into words as to how it felt having her wrap around his flesh in the way she was doing right now.

"Do you feel that?" he murmured in her ear. "Do you feel how right this is, how perfectly I fit inside you, and how you stretch just right for me?"

Jada shook her head. "It isn't right."

She was breathing hard, her nails dug into his wrists. Kane moved his hands up to her breasts, cupping and squeezing the mounds. "Even your breasts fit perfectly in my hands. We are right for each other. You just have to open your eyes and see it."

"Since when did you become Mr. Analysis?" she was grunting, breathing hard and fast.

By the way her sweet cunt tightened on him and how she shook in his arms, he could tell that she was close. It wasn't going to take too much to push her over the edge, and when she went, he hoped like hell she went screaming.

Kane moved his hands down to her legs, went under the thighs, picked her up, and began to bounce her on him, fast. Jada whimpered, clawed at his arms, reached back and pulled at his hair or tried to scratch his shoulders. She became instantly wild and he loved every second of it.

She clamped down on her muscles, contracted, and squeezed his dick to a point that he groaned, but didn't stop the bouncing. Now Kane was very determined to hear her scream this time no matter what.

"Give it to me, Jada," he breathed into her ear. "Scream."

She shook her head and he grunted. Defiant to the absolute end. "Never!"

"Never?" he growled the word. "I bet you will before I'm done with you tonight."

Kane picked up the pace bounced her even harder onto him. He fought within himself to not come, to not end this until he had the one thing he wanted from her.

"Oh, oh, oh, oh," Jada cried out.

Within seconds, he had what he wanted. Jada screamed, her pussy clamped down so hard on his cock and she yanked brutally on his hair that he hissed in pain, but he didn't stop. He couldn't stop, not until he had every ounce of her orgasm out.

He came with her, and it burned. Kane could feel his heat pour out of him with the seed that left his body. With each bounce or thrust, his pleasure was heightened and for the first time ever he understood why sex became something additive; if it felt this good all the time, it was no mystery why everyone wanted to do it so often.

One more slam down and he hugged her tightly. Out of nowhere, Jada began to cry. Her body shook in his arms and the sniffling, the way she tried to hide it from him touched Kane right in the chest. He pressed his face into the crook of her neck, turned and lay down with her still in his arms.

"Shh," he soothed. He brushed the hair from her face, hugged her, and closed his eyes. "Don't cry."

He felt a tenderness towards her that he'd never felt before. All his life it was take what you could. Giving only involved his sister. Now Kane wanted to give and comfort another. He wanted to hold Jada close, never letting her go.

When she quieted down, he let himself relax as well. He took a deep breath, brought the covers over their bodies, and waited for sleep to take him. The heat was over. He knew that. It wasn't as brutal as it had been in the past, but still miserable enough. And over. He finally had someone to help him take the pain away, and he wasn't going to let that go, no matter what she said or might do.

* * * *

She wasn't even healed completely from the wreck and her grandfather was already shipping her off. Jada sat next to the door of the limo, staring out at the scenery going by, feeling numb inside. James Leonard sat next to her, his cane between his knees, hands clasped on top of it, and his mouth set in a stern line like always.

He picked her up right from the hospital, demanding they let her out. Everything she owned was packed up, in the back of the limo and her destination was unknown. She didn't even want to know or talk to him. She just didn't care where she was going this time. Without Chris, things just didn't matter to her.

The limo stopped in front of a private plane. Her grandfather said nothing to her, just opened the door and got out. Like a trained dog, Jada did the same. Her things were taken from the back, handed over to others as she stood there staring at the plane.

"Get in girl," her grandfather said to her.

"So this is my punishment." She turned, faced the man who treated her no better than dirt under his shoe. Her ribs hurt, but she held the pain at bay. "For Chris."

"You have been nothing but a burden to me," he spit out, the hate no longer held in by his cold eyes. "Why in the hell your mother had to go out and have you is beyond me!"

"Maybe to show the world just how much of a bastard you really are."

She didn't get a chance to brace herself from the slap that landed across her face. Chris had always put himself between her and their grandfather's wrath. For the simple fact of not upsetting Chris, James didn't beat Jada. Now Chris was gone, leaving her completely alone.

"You are dead to me," he hissed out in hate.

"When was I ever alive?"

Jada woke with a jolt. Between her legs, she was tender and felt a heavy arm draped over her waist and deep breathing at her neck. She was breathing hard, sweat covered her forehead, and a reminder gripped her ribs. Each time she had one of those dreams her ribs would ache slightly. And as much as she would love to forget it, this time every damn year, she had the same dream. The one where her grandfather shipped her off, never to see her again. He paid for her to finish school, but college she got all on her own. The day she graduated she was gone, never to look back at the old cold life she used to have.

Slow as she could, she turned to look at Kane. He was sleeping deeply. Carefully she moved his arm and slipped from the bed. Biting her lower lip she looked around for something to wear, finding only one of his large shirts. It sucked, but she put it on and left the bedroom for the bathroom to do a quick clean up before heading to the fireplace.

She tossed two thick logs onto the dying fire and watched it come back to life before curling up on the sofa. She couldn't sleep with him, couldn't act as if everything was all right when it wasn't and couldn't shake off the depression of the dream. *God I miss you Chris!*

She was tired and sore. Kane wore her out pretty good with his heat crap. She yawned and leaned to the left, laying down, staring at the fire. She didn't have a clue as to what she was going to do now. She knew what needed to be done, but didn't know how to do it. She had to get away from Kane, plain and simple, before she hurt him to a point that he would never recover from it. Everyone who was around her for too long got hurt. Look at Chase! He came looking for her that one time and got shot.

"Anything you ever touch or love will die, just like Chris," Her grandfather yelled before he backhanded her so hard she fell to the ground. "You disgust me!"

"Can't sleep?"

She didn't jump or move when he spoke, only closed her eyes and tried to act as if she was sleeping. He crawled onto the sofa, lying right down behind her, wrapping his arm around her waist. Jada wanted to lean back against him, but didn't. Instead, she sat back up, keeping her back to him, staring at the fire.

"I can't love you, Kane," she said softly, breaking the silence in the room. "Don't ask or expect it, because it won't happen."

He reached for her and she quickly stood up, moving away from him. "Why do I get this nagging feeling like you're about to start another fight," he sighed.

"There wouldn't be any fights if you'd leave me the hell alone," she snapped back, rubbing her forehead. "You're reaching out for something that can never be. Don't you understand that? I can't give you what you want. I can't give anyone what they want!"

"What I see right now is a girl who is used to running away from anything and anyone that gets close to her. Always running." He stood up also to face her. "When does that stop?"

"It keeps me alive."

"It keeps you lonely," he stated.

"What do you know about it? You've spent your whole life in a cage."

"Yeah, and I was very alone," he stated. "I don't want that loneliness again," he thumbed his chest.

"I like being alone, don't you understand that?" She faced him and frowned. Kane had a look in his eyes, a look that told her he was holding out some kind of hope for them. "Why are you staring at me like that?"

Kane frowned too, "I'm trying to figure you out. Figure out what you're so afraid of."

"There isn't anything to figure out," she snapped, crossing her arms over her chest and stood her ground. "And I'm not afraid of anything, so mind your own damn business."

"Come on, Jada," he sighed. "Don't you think it's time we be honest with each other by now?"

"I'm honest with you, Kane." She met his eyes, chin raised. "You just don't like it."

"No. What I don't like is the lying and your secrets." He crossed his arms over his massive chest. It was hard having a conversation with someone who stood before you naked. "I've had to deal with that shit all my life. Not anymore."

"Well, get used to it with me, because I never change. Everyone has secrets." He growled at her before going over to the small fridge. He yanked a beer out and twisted the cap. Then he took a long drink right before tossing the cap across the room. "Bullshit."

"I don't need this shit." She shook her head and moved to pass him. She was going to the bathroom, but he stopped her.

Kane grabbed hold of her arm and said, "Chris Leonard isn't the only one who cares about you." She slowly turned and stared at him as if he'd lost his mind. "I care."

"H—how?"

"I saw the scrap book," he said.

She jerked her arm free. "How could you read that after I told you to mind your own damn business?" Her voice broke as she backed away from him. She shook her head fighting the tears that quickly came. "My life has nothing to do with you!" she yelled, the tears falling. "Or my past."

Kane shook his head also. "Sorry, Princess, but you're wrong there. Your life is my life." She opened her mouth to argue with him but stopped when his phone went off. "Saved before you could start another fight."

"Oh I'm going to start a fight, you can count on it." She brushed past him and went back into the bathroom, slamming the door.

* * * *

Kane grabbed his phone, but his eyes were on Jada all the way into the bathroom. "Yeah," he answered harshly.

"Kane, are you alright?" It was Sasha.

"Hey, Pumpkin!" Kane had to close his eyes and bite his lower lip. He brought himself under control, not wanting to upset his sister. "You okay?"

"Yeah, I wanted to check on you," she said. "Drake told me that you found Jada and this storm is going to last for another night. I know you and Jada have been at each other's throats so it kind of worries me that you're going to be there alone. Was your heat okay?"

A vision of Jada standing under the spray in the shower with water trailing down her body hit Kane. His cock grew thick and the hunger to have her under him, his tongue tasting her as she came, made him groan inside. "Don't worry about us. I promise I won't kill her when she gets too lippy, and yeah it went okay."

She giggled. "I like her. I'm glad it went okay for you. Did you, um, you know with her?"

Kane smiled. "Isn't that a bit personal?"

"You've never kept anything from me before."

Kane rubbed his face. He was tired, still horny as hell, but he needed answers also. Jada had too much built up inside and if she didn't let some of it come out soon she was going to blow.

"I know I do," he sighed. "But maybe I should keep this to myself."

"What's wrong?"

He heard the concern in her voice, just like he heard how much she'd grown up in the few years they had been free. Sasha wasn't a baby any longer. At least not the kind of baby who needed him. No, Drake was right and he just now saw it. One day someone was going to come into her life and do all the things he was doing to Jada. Someone was going to love her and he wasn't sure if he could handle it.

"I guess I haven't seen how much you've grown up until I heard your voice just now," he answered.

Sasha chuckled, "I'm not that grown up. I'm only eighteen."

"Hey, you're not eighteen for another two months." He held up his finger, even though she couldn't see it. "Don't rush it."

"Do you think I'll have someone like you?"

The question had him closing his eyes and slumping down in the chair. He jumped at the coldness, which reminded him that he was still naked.

"Sasha, please!"

"I'm only asking," she said and laughed.

"I can't believe you're messing with me like this! Of all the times to have this conversation." He never heard her talk like this and didn't have a clue as to where it was coming from. "What the hell are you guys talking about over there?"

"I've just been asking some questions is all. No big deal."

Kane snorted. "Sounds like a major deal to me."

"Kane? I'm afraid to be with anyone." Her voice lowered and once more, he heard that fear that she always had when she first started to talk more. "I've read that it hurts so badly the first time, and, and, and..."

"Shh," he quickly soothed her, standing back up. "Sasha don't think about that okay. No one is going to hurt you. I promised you then, and I'm promising you now. I won't let anyone touch you or cause you pain."

"But if I'm someone's mate, like Jada is yours, how are you going to stop it?"

Now he heard the tears coming and wished like hell he was with her, holding her. "Sasha you're too young to be thinking about any of that crap right now. I'll say it again. No one will hurt you, or I'll hurt them."

"Big bad brother," Jada snorted, causing Kane to jump. He didn't hear the shower turn off or her come out. "Too bad I didn't have one when you came into my life."

"Sasha, I need to let you go," Kane said into the phone, his eyes on Jada. He didn't wait for her to answer, only hung the phone up, and put it down on the table. "I know that look all too well."

"Do you now?" She cocked her head to the side, long wet hair falling over her shoulders. "And what look is that?"

"The kind that tells me the shit is about to hit the fan."

She crossed her arms over her chest, leaned to one side and one eyebrow went up. Yep, she was starting it right off with a nice little defiant stance. Bad move.

"You do remember the last time you stood like that with me, don't you?" He tapped a finger on his lips before pointing at her. "You ended up on your back."

"No, I was pushed up against the wall," she said. "And a repeat of that isn't going to happen."

"If we're going to fight, I'm going to get something on." He flashed her a quick smile when he walked past her to go into the bedroom. "Like to have some protection in case you try to kick me or something."

He grabbed a pair of sweats put them on and when he came back out of the bedroom Jada was standing in front of the window, hugging herself, staring at the snow. He just watched her. There was something about Jada, something he felt he had to find out, no matter how much she might hate him or fight it.

"So who was he?" he asked, causing her to jump. "Your brother?"

"I don't have any brothers or sisters, Kane," she sighed, sounding like she didn't want to be bothered. Tough!

"Then who's Chris?"

She turned around fast, "Listen, it's none of your damn business who he is or what he was to me. So mind your own damn business."

"You *are* my business, Princess."

"That's where you have it very wrong, wolf boy."

They had a short stare off. Neither, it seemed wanted to back down or give that one inch.

"We can do this all night long, Jada, but you know you'll lose," he told her, crossing his arms over his bare chest. "Who is he?"

"Careful, Kane, you almost sound like you're jealous." She turned her back on him, which had that inner alpha inside growl.

He snapped a little, rushed up to her, grabbed her arm, and forced her back around to face him. "Don't turn your back on me," he told her through his teeth, his voice vibrating with a growl. "Who is he?"

"You're hurting me!" That damn chin of hers went up and he shook her. "Kane, stop it!"

"Then answer my damn question."

"My cousin!" she yelled. He stilled and she twisted out of his hold. "Happy now?"

Kane let her go, and Jada brushed past him, going right back to the window. He took several deep breaths before he turned around. He felt guilty at how he just treated her and yet he was still angry with her. She loved Chris, but couldn't love him. He didn't know it until right now that he wanted her to love him, because he knew for a fact what he felt towards her was a hell of a lot stronger than what he felt for Sasha.

But she made it very clear that she wouldn't love him, and that hurt.

"Jada, I'm—"

"He died in a car crash taking me out for my birthday," she said, her voice sounding detached. "He wasn't supposed to. Our grandfather wanted him to stay away from me, but Chris didn't listen."

Kane was shocked that she was opening up to him. He also held his breath with the fear that she was going to stop and didn't move a muscle because of that fear.

"I'm the bastard of the family," she went on. "My mother got pregnant just to get his attention. My grandfather only valued his son, not his daughter, and then his grandson. When my mother died and he was forced to take me in, he made damn sure that I knew my place in the family. Chris was the only one who treated me like I was a person, not a disgrace," her voice softened as if she was remembering her past. Kane could tell that it hurt her lot to talk about it.

"I was in a coma for a week." She took a deep breath and turned around. Not one tear was in her eye. It almost seemed as if she forgot how to cry or something. "The day I woke up he died and that bastard who called himself my grandfather blamed it all on me and shipped me off to a boarding school the moment I was out of the hospital. So there you have it." She extended her arms out and quickly brought them back down to her sides. "My dirty little quick history. Now can you drop it?"

Kane cocked his head to the side and frowned, "You've never cried for him?"

Jada snorted and gave him her back again. "Don't try to act like you give a shit or know anything Kane."

Kane came up to her, took her arm, and swung her back around. He didn't let her go, not even when she tried to twist away again. "I know by looking into your eyes that you've never cried for him or anyone. It's still eating away at you. His death."

"Stop it."

"I can see it."

"I said stop it."

"What are you afraid of?" He grabbed her by both arms, giving her a shake.

"Let me go!" For the first time he heard her voice shake.

"Haven't you figured it out by now? I'm never letting you go."

She stilled in his arms, relaxed enough that he let his guard down long enough for her to slap him across the face so hard and unexpectedly he took a step to the side. She didn't say anything, only began to hit him and slap at him until he turned her around and wrapped his arms around her body, restraining her.

Out of nowhere, she broke down and started to cry. "Damn you!" she sobbed. "Why can't you just let me go like the rest?"

She cried hard and slumped against him. Together they lowered to the floor, him holding her as she cried, what he was guessing was for the first time in many years.

"Because whether you want to believe it or hear it, I care about you," he said with his face pressed against her head. "Maybe even love you." He sighed.

"No, no, no, no," she cried, shaking her head. She tried to get out of his hold, but he only tightened it. "You do that, and you're dead. I'm toxic."

"Shh." He was able to hold her with one arm, and with a free hand brushed hair from her face. "You're not toxic, only lonely like me. One day you'll realize we're perfect for each other. No matter what you say or do, Jada, my heart belongs to you and only you."

A fresh wave of tears started and he held her through them,

rocking her gently. Kane didn't know much, but his gut was telling him that she needed this cry. He didn't know how long it had been since this Chris held her or gave her the comfort that she so needed. What he did know was that he was going to take the man's place. Jada was his now, and he was going to do everything he could to fix what was broken inside. What ever her grandfather did, he was going to pay for it. No one should ever treat a child who lost everything, like she was dirt. And no one was going to treat his Jada like that ever again. If they did, they were going to die.

What Drake had given him, and Sasha, in the short three years ended up making up for most of his life. What Jada had now, could seal the rest of his bad past.

They were like two peas in a pod. Both wanted to be loved so bad when they were younger, getting it only from one person. Where Kane had Sasha in his mind to give him that small amount of comfort, Jada lost hers when this Chris died. She needed him, just as he needed her and his new family.

Chapter Eight

Josh Stan stepped out of his limo with Jason Spencer on his heels in front of one of the largest mansions he'd ever seen in his life. The house surpassed the one Conner Martin gave him not only in size but also in design. This place spoke of old money, which was just what he wanted and needed. He adjusted his jacket and walked right up the steps and through the door without knocking. Inside was just as impressive as the outside. White marble graced the floors, antique tables, and top of the line paintings lined the foyer and when he got to the middle of the room, he was greeted with a grand staircase.

"Damn," Jason whistled. "This place is impressive."

"And just what we need." Josh headed towards the stairs and went up, taking a right.

He'd sent a man ahead of him who took over the place. Guards were stationed throughout the house for his protection, some even stood on the second floor leaning against the walls. And the second floor was just as impressive as the first. Dark, blood red carpet covered the floor, more paintings and some family pictures hung on the walls as well as tables in corners and near doors. Even the light fixtures on the walls had an old money feel to them.

Josh stopped at the end of the hall at the last door on the left. A guard opened the door for him and he went inside. The bedroom was very spacious. To the left a desk in front of the window, to the right a sitting area. In the center of the room there was a large king size bed with a frail old man resting in the center, blankets on his lap and a tank of oxygen next to the bed with a canella in his nose.

"So you're the bastard that has taken over my home," the old man panted, having trouble catching his breath when he spoke.

Josh smiled. "You have no protection and I fear that you may be at risk."

"Bullshit," he coughed. "Piss up someone else's leg and get out of my house!"

Josh grabbed the chair at the desk and dragged it over to the side of the bed. He sat down, crossed his legs, and smoothed out his jacket sleeves. "Now that isn't polite."

"And neither is walking in my house without being invited," his voice raised, but had a strained sound to it. He was sick, maybe dying and it showed.

Josh extended his hand and Jason handed him the file that they brought. He opened it up to look at the photo before he tossed it to the old man. He waited until he also opened it and saw the wrinkled eyes widen.

"We have something in common, you and I," Josh sighed. "But where you can't get it back I can." He sat forward, watching each and every reaction the old man had to the photo in that file. "I need your help to get your granddaughter, Mr. Leonard, and in exchange I'm at your service."

James Leonard looked up at Josh and out of nowhere, he began to laugh until he started coughing. When Josh was about to get up to help him James waved him off. He took hold of a mask and put it over his face, taking several deep breaths.

"I'll do one better," James snickered with a strain in his voice. "You find the bastard of my daughter and I'll set you up for life." He pointed an old finger at Josh and struggled to take several deep breaths. "You bring her here first, and I'll line your pockets until they overflow. She and I have something to settle, something of great importance."

* * * *

"You're too quiet."

And she was. Jada was sitting on the sofa, legs drawn up to her chest, chin on knees staring into the fire. She couldn't get over the simple fact that she broke down and told Kane about Chris and cried. She fucking cried! She never cried.

"Jada?" He knelt down in front of her, resting his chin on his hands next to her feet. "Talk to me," he sighed.

She closed her eyes and moved away from him, off the sofa. Hugging herself, she went back over to the window and sighed. "God I hate the snow," she moaned.

"The snow or being locked away with me?"

She rubbed her face and closed her eyes. She couldn't do this. Couldn't face him after she broke down in front of him. "I can't do this," she whispered.

"Do what?"

"I can't stand here acting like I didn't just have one hell of a meltdown in front of you!" she whined, not meaning to sound like a child.

"You mean you can't show me that you're human," he stated.

"Yes!"

"Jada..." he sighed.

"Don't Jada me," she snapped at him. "You don't know what it was like living in that house."

"And you don't know what it was like living in a damn cage," he growled back. "Don't act like you are the only one to break down and cry. You don't think I broke down in front of Drake?"

"This isn't the same thing."

"Sure it is!"

Jada took several deep breaths. "My family lives by a very strict tradition." She licked her lips, trying to find the right words to explain this to him. "Having children without being married is sinful." She rushed out, "My grandfather drilled it in my head that I was a bastard, unworthy of everything and that the best thing for me would be to be alone. To die."

Kane wore a puzzled expression. "I don't understand. I thought with Chris dead, you don't have family now."

"I still have a grandfather," she mumbled. "If that's what I can call him."

"So you have family then?"

"No, I share a last name with someone," she lowered her voice. "Nothing more."

"What are you trying to tell me?"

She took another deep breath and let it out slowly. "My grandfather is a hard man. My mother was a mistake, one that he made sure she knew about all her life. He had his son and that was all he cared about. It crushed her when she learned that he never wanted my mother and demanded my grandmother abort her, but she didn't. Everything he had went to my uncle, even what little love my grandfather had."

"And this is why you can't love anyone?" She heard the doubt and shook her head.

"At a party years ago, when my mother was a teen, she went to the gardens with one of the waiters and had sex with him. She was sixteen and got pregnant with me on purpose. Once he found out, he shipped her off to a boarding school. I was five when I met him. She refused to give me up, left school, and tried to raise me on her own. My uncle talked my grandfather into letting her come home. At eight my mother, aunt, and Uncle were killed in a car crash and Chris came to live with us. I got my grandfather's hate, Chris got his love."

She smiled and pressed her hand to her forehead. "I've never told anyone this before." She turned away from Kane and pushed her tears back. Tears that she never let fall over her family.

"Then why are you telling me this now?"

She felt him behind her and closed her eyes. Jada wanted nothing more than to be wrapped up in his arms and sheltered from the pain of her memories. She wanted to be held the way Chris held her when she was young. When the monsters of the night came to frighten a young girl who wanted nothing more in the world than to be loved. She'd fought Kane, every time he touched her, every time he forced himself on her—because she didn't trust him—didn't trust or believe the fact that it was possible someone loved her in this world. She wanted to believe in his love, wanted to believe she could spend a happy life with him, after having had little joy in her life. She didn't want to spend her life alone.

"We are two dysfunctional people, Kane." She couldn't face him. If she did, the tears were going to fall and she was going to crumble into a million pieces. "And once this lust that you feel goes away then there isn't going to be anything left but—"

He turned her around fast, grabbing her arms tight and bringing his face down in front of hers. "This isn't lust, Jada, and you know it." His voice was low, lips thinned out. "I've only cared about one person my whole life until now. Only Sasha has mattered to me until you. When I have you in my arms and am so deep inside you, I feel like a complete man. And the moment you suck the life out of me when I come I only want to start over again. Don't you understand that?"

"You need someone who can love you and that isn't me." She tried to twist out of his hold, but he stopped her by kissing her, and stealing her breath away.

Kane pulled her closer and deepened the kiss, plunging his tongue into her mouth to mate with hers. "What I need is you," he sighed, lips touching hers.

The phone rang and Jada was relieved by the sound. She pulled out of his arms and went into the bathroom, leaving him to talk. By the way his voice softened after he said hello she knew it was Sasha.

She splashed some water on her face, took a few deep breaths, and went back out. Kane was still talking on the phone, a grin on his face while he walked around. Jada went over to the bed and slipped under the covers. She was tired, in more ways than one.

* * * *

Kane stood in front of the window, the same spot where Jada had stood, staring at the snow. It was his third snowstorm, and it still fascinated him. Amazed him in fact, with how the sky could bring something so cold down upon their heads. But the snow wasn't what was on his mind. He was thinking about his past, and how much he and Jada had in common. He was missing the love as a child like her. Now she had it, just like him, if she would only open up and take it. She was tough; he'd give her that one. But as he'd learned over the last few years, one could be tough as stone and underneath it scared as a babe. Jada was very scared, and he couldn't blame her.

"I can see it."

Kane smiled and hung his head down. Sasha. "You're snooping again."

"Why are you so sad? I thought you were happy."

"I am happy."

"I don't see it. You're sad."

He took a deep breath, letting it out slowly. Kane turned to the sofa, sitting down with a sigh. "I don't know what to do to make her see that's she not alone."

"But she isn't alone, she has you."

Again, he smiled. Sasha was still pretty innocent when it came to this stuff, just like him. It had him wondering what he would do or how he would act once her time came.

"Why are you thinking about me?"

Kane shook his head. "You really need to stop reading my mind, Sash. I don't read yours anymore." Silence. "Sasha?" He frowned. She just left him, without one more word.

"Was it something I said?" he mumbled before standing up.

He walked into the bedroom. Jada was sleeping on her side covered to her waist his shirt on. She looked so good in his bed, in his shirt, so good in fact that it hurt. When she turned over to her back—the blankets going down her legs even more—the need to taste her hit Kane. He pushed his sweats down his legs then went up to the bed, getting in next to her slow and easy.

He turned her towards him, moving a leg up over his hip. It didn't take much for him to get hard, not when he had Jada not only close, but in his arms. He worked as easy as he could to get the shirt up and off. When he had it over her head, Jada woke up, her arms crossing over her breasts. Kane stopped her from moving around by grabbing her leg on his hips.

"What the hell are you doing?" she gasped, squinting at him through tired eyes.

He didn't answer her, only kissed her. Kane wrapped his arms around her body, rolled to his back, taking her with him. He felt her relax on top of him and took full advantage of it. He kissed her deep, hands cupping her rear, squeezing the flesh, grinding her closer. She rubbed against him and he growled low at the back of her neck.

Kissing her was only a part of what he wanted. Kane desired and hungered to taste all of her. He moved his hands from her ass to under her arms. Holding her over him, he moved her body up, bringing her breasts right up to his face. He sucked a nipple into his mouth, rolling it with his tongue. Jada sucked her breath in quickly, her nails dug into his shoulders when he pulled on it. With a popping sound, he released one so he could suck on the other.

"What're you doing?" she sighed.

Kane glanced up while he used his tongue on her other nipple. She had her eyes closed, head back. He could smell her wetness and it caused pain in his groin. But as much as he wanted to be inside her, he wanted to taste her again. He wanted to taste everything!

He moved them both on the bed, turning her and placing her on her hands and knees. He was a bit surprised that she wasn't fighting him, and wasn't about to slap a gift horse in the mouth. He brushed her hair from her back and his mark, going right to the back of her neck, kissing. One hand he used to hold his weight from her, the other he grabbed a breast, kneading the mound, pinching a nipple. He played with both while he kissed her back, moving his way down.

"Kane—"

"Shh," he soothed, silencing her. He sat back on his knees, right behind her. "Stay just like this, Jada. Don't move."

He rubbed her back, moving his hands in large circular motions down her back to her ass. When he got to the curves, to the flesh of her rear he squeezed then kissed each cheek before parting them and licking the crevice. Damn, she tasted good.

"Not a good idea," she panted.

"Don't think, just feel," he purred.

* * * *

She was shaking with the need for an orgasm that she didn't have a clue as to why. He wasn't doing anything really to her, but touching and kissing her lightly, so why did her body feel ready to explode? Because you want him to make you scream. You're craving him as much as he craves you, you dumb ass! Jada was helpless to do anything but wait. Kane took hold of the cheeks of her ass, squeezing them and parting them for fingers that probed and pushed into her pussy, which was very wet, then back to her rear. She moaned. There was no way in hell she could hold the sound back.

She tossed her head back, welcoming the slight burn from his fingers, shaking with the need to come. She almost came when his tongue touched the small ring of her ass. Jada lost her breath in the pleasure, and was powerless to stop her hips from bucking, or from stopping at pushing back into his face, wanting a stronger contact.

"I want your ass, Jada." His voice was so thick and low it sent chills down her spine. It didn't help when he touched her straining clit. "I want to sink my dick into your tight ass and fuck you so hard you will feel it tomorrow all day long." He slid his finger out, teased around her pussy only to push her juices back, lubricating her up this time with two fingers. "That's all I want tonight. I want to lick this sweet pussy, and fuck that tight ass. And I guarantee, after you get used to it, you'll love it and beg me for it."

He moved behind her, but she had her eyes closed, trying to push it back, to will her climax away. When he sucked her clit into his mouth and rolled it with his tongue, she was lost. Jada screamed her climax, dropping her hips down, pressing her pussy into his face, riding out the pleasure. Three fingers slid into her rear easily, intensifying the orgasm, and this time she didn't give a fuck.

"Stop, please!" she screamed when her clit became too sensitive from the rapid flickering of his tongue. "I can't handle it anymore."

He stopped, but his fingers didn't. Kane kept moving them in and out of her ass, getting more of her juices from her pussy, spreading them back. She grabbed onto the sheets and held her breath as she waited to see what he was going to do next.

Kane moved again, coming behind her once more. He never gave her any warning. He shoved his whole length into her pussy, causing Jada to arch her back. He pushed into her several times before pulling out and placing the head against the tiny ring.

"Slow and easy this time," he said, his breath brushing against her shoulder over the mark he'd left. "I'm going to take my time. I'm going to push my dick in slowly, and feel each stretch, each throb we both have."

He pushed and she held her breath. Jada could barely think from the feelings of being stretched from behind. Yes, this time was different. This time it felt like Kane had some control and was trying to be easy with her. It was something she really wasn't expecting, not after that first time he took her anally.

"Breathe, Jada."

She did and it almost shattered her sanity. Jada never felt such an intense need to be taken, filled, and fucked to screaming completion. She took gulps of air into her lungs, holding onto the blankets and sheets until her knuckles turned white. It burned, it thrilled, and turned her on unlike anything she ever experienced with him. This slower, tender side of him felt different, but the fullness that she felt in her ass was the same, the tenderness drove her crazy.

"I can't stand this." She shook her head, panting. The pressure was so intense, she felt on the verge of tears, so great was her passion.

"Neither can I," he groaned. "You're so fucking tight. It's taking all my willpower to not come right now."

"Kane, please!" she was begging now and didn't give a damn.

His fingers dug into her hips painfully, but she welcomed the discomfort, knowing he was readying himself to give her what she craved—what she needed. "Get ready then."

She nodded, held onto the bed, took a few deep breaths, but wasn't prepared for what she got. Kane shoved it all into her. He stretched her ass, burning her from the inside out with his thick cock. She screamed, pushed back, and gulped as much air into her lungs as she could get. He moved, stroking her with enough force and power that his balls slapped against her pussy. Jada knew that right now she was dying. The pleasure became too intense and, to make it worse, Kane moved one hand to her pussy and rolled her clit. The climax hit unexpectedly. She screamed until she was hoarse and couldn't scream anymore. Kane kept moving, and he thrust his cock into her ass, slapped into her enough that she rocked forward.

Before she came down from the first orgasm, she was hit with another. "I'm...I'm..." Kane panted behind her. "Oh, fuck!"

He swelled inside her. She could feel the throbbing release of his climax deep inside her. Kane jerked against her, slammed into her hard twice before stilling and leaned over her. He didn't bite her shoulder, which surprised her. With the lax feeling she had at the moment she really didn't give a damn.

"I love you, Jada," he breathed hard. "Even if you don't, I do."

Jada stilled. Of all the things for him to say to her, that was definitely not one of them. She was sore and tender when he left her body and very tired, since he woke her up. He pulled out, causing her to whimper.

"Take a shower. I'll clean up and put some more wood on the fire," he said as he kissed her back. "Think its going to get very cold tonight. Perfect snuggle weather."

She couldn't answer him. Hell, she couldn't even look at him. Before Kane could reach her, she scooted from the bed and went into the bathroom, closing the door slowly. She was shaking. Jada couldn't steady her hands while she turned the water on and stepped into the hot water. The water felt good, and washed away the mess but it couldn't wash away the dreaded feelings she had. "I love you, Jada. Even if you don't, I do."

She closed her eyes and slid down to the floor, the water beating over her head. Covering her face with her hands she cried as silently as she could, not wanting him to hear. Then memories assailed her.

"Why is it so hard for you to say it?" Chris asked her. He found her sitting alone in the garden, staring at nothing. She ran from him, after he told her he loved her and tried to give her a hug.

"I'm sinful," she answered him. "If you love me, then you'll die."

"Who told you that crap? Grandpa?"

She nodded. "My mother loved me, look what happened to her."

"Jada, there's nothing wrong with being loved, or loving someone else."

"I can't love you, Chris. I can't love anyone."

"Yes, you can." He sat down next to her, placing his arm over her shoulders. "Just because he doesn't love, doesn't mean you have to follow. One day someone is going to come into your life and love you terribly and there won't be a damn thing you can do about it."

She shrugged off his arm, standing up. "No, Chris. No one loves me. And it's best that way."

He frowned. "Why?"

"Because I won't get hurt when they leave me." Before he could say more, she ran away from him.

"I told you," she whispered, hugging and rocking herself under the water. "I told you that loving me would get you killed. And I won't let that happen to Kane."

Chapter Nine

"She arranged for something to be stored in a freezing unit at a research facility." Jason strolled into the library where Josh Stan had set up his office in Leonard's home. He was drinking coffee and reading a paper when Jason walked in. "If she doesn't come back by the end of the month they have instructions to destroy whatever it is they are holding for her."

Josh lowered his paper slowly. Jason never took his eyes off the man. He watched Josh pick up his cup and take a sip. For years now, Jason had been taking orders from him. For the most part everything was going well, except for now. Now Jason wanted to play and he wanted to play his way.

"I know that look, Jason," Josh sighed, crossing a leg over his knee. "You want to play."

"I want the girl," Jason told him. "I owe her and she's going to pay my way."

Josh smiled, linked his fingers together, and rested his chin on top of them, tapping his lip with both index fingers. Jason almost held his breath waiting for the man to say something. In the years that they had worked together, Jason had noticed that Josh was a very cold-hearted man. A lot more so than Martin ever had been.

"We get what we want, you can have the girl." Josh nodded. "And we keep this between us. I don't want the old man to back out of our deal if he thinks that harm might come to his granddaughter."

Jason laughed. He couldn't help himself, "Are you kidding me? You didn't pick up the hate that bastard has for her. I bet I could bend her over his bed and fuck her in front of him and the old fart would eat popcorn and watch."

Josh snickered as he picked up his paper, "You're probably right, but I don't want to take the chance. Blood is always thicker than water. Remember that."

Jason turned to leave, but stopped. "Do you really think he's going to go with her?"

"You've seen the test." Josh snapped the paper, turning a page. "She was there the night he went nuts. Those things mate only once and she is his. When she goes to retrieve our goods, Kane will follow. It's just a matter of when she goes."

"And if she doesn't go for it, what then?"

"You let me worry about that. I have something special in mind for you and Ms. Leonard. Something I know for a fact you'll enjoy."

* * * *

"I thought I was supposed to be the one with a lot on my mind."

Jada jumped when Kane came up behind her, wrapped his arms around her waist, and spoke in her ear. She didn't hear him come out of the shower, didn't hear him talk, and sure as hell didn't hear him come up on her.

"What?"

Kane chuckled, "You were definitely a mile away. What were you thinking about?"

"Nothing." She stepped out of his arms, walking away from the fire towards the front window. She pulled the curtain back. "Looks like the snow's letting up."

"What's wrong?"

What's wrong? Now that was a question she had been asking herself since the moment her eyes opened this morning. Something had changed in her, something she wasn't prepared to face. Not now.

Where's this going?" she turned around, facing him. "What happens after we leave and go back to the real world?"

Kane frowned, "I don't understand."

"What happens after it's all over Kane? Where do you think this is leading to?"

"What are you afraid of?" he asked, hands on his hips. "Because it isn't me. You haven't been scared of me since day one. So what is it?"

She couldn't tell him what she had. Couldn't tell him what scared her at night and had her worried about everyone around her. "Kane, I have a target on my head. You know that. You stay with me, then that target—"

He held up his hand, stopping her. "You don't think that son-of-a-bitch is after me? We both are marked, so if you're using this as your excuse..."

"This isn't an excuse!" she yelled. "You want someone to love you and I've already told you that isn't me. I'm poison, plain, and simple."

Kane shook his head, "No, you're scared." He turned his back on her and started to pace the small bedroom while she stayed in the front part of the cabin. He stopped, rubbed his chin, and stormed back towards her, rushing up and boxing her against the wall. "I've never needed anyone in my life, Jada, the way I need you."

"You only need me to take care of an itch you have!" She pushed him away, and surprisingly Kane backed off.

His eyes narrowed on her, causing Jada to lower her own and turn back to the window. She stared at the falling snow, wishing like hell that she were out there falling with it.

You make the ball in your hand first, then put it in the snow and finish rolling it until it's huge. And when you can't push anymore, that is where we're going to build your snowman."

Jada took the ball from Chris's hand. His green eyes sparkled down at her, his smile warmed her, but it all came crashing down with the yelling of their grandfather. She didn't get out of the way fast enough. James Leonard pushed her out of the way, knocking her to the ground in the snow. She watched helplessly when her grandfather backhanded Chris.

"I told you no!" James Leonard said between his teeth angrily. "You have work to do, not time to play with the bastard." Their grandfather grabbed Chris's arm and pulled him away, leaving Jada to sit in the cold snow alone, tears falling.

"Jada?"

Kane's voice snapped her out of her childhood, another memory she worked hard to block. She didn't want to remember her past. It hurt too much.

"My cousin tried to show me once how to build a snowman, but my grandfather stopped him." She touched the cold window, a single tear falling free. "He didn't want Chris to play with the family bastard," she mumbled.

"Then let's do it now."

She turned around just in time to catch her coat. "What?"

"I think we can get out of here for a bit to play in the snow." Smiling, he added, "Never really played before, and I'm dying to try a snowball fight."

"You're serious? She couldn't believe what he said. Kane wanted to go out in the cold to play in the snow. "It's freezing out there."

He zipped up his coat, pulled gloves from the pockets. "Not going to stay out all day, just for a little bit." He cocked his head to one side, and added, "Not scared that I'll beat you, are you?"

Jada narrowed her eyes on him and quickly put her own coat on. "Oh, I'm going to enjoy pelting you with snow balls, canine."

* * * *

Kane pulled the collar of his coat closer to his neck, looked up at the falling snow, and figured that this fun outing wasn't going to be very long. The snow was still coming down thick and the cold was bitter as when he found Jada, unconscious.

"So what're the rules to this—" he didn't finish his question because a big, fat, slushy snowball smacked him in the face.

"Not every game has rules, wolf boy." Jada was rolling another ball out of snow, a wicked grin on her lips.

"So I'm learning."

She hit him with two more before he was able to get one off himself. She got him good too. Jada hit him several times in the head; he got her back in the ass and back. By the time he called it quits, thanks to the damn temperature dropping again, they both were soaked.

Back inside, they changed, Kane giving her another shirt of his. Jada fixed something to eat, but sitting down he noticed that she was quiet again. It had him worried, but he kept it to himself. He didn't want to disturb the peace they seemed to have.

When they went to bed Kane was content with just holding her and it seemed that she was okay with it.

* * * *

Jada waited until Kane was deep asleep before she slipped from the bed. She eased from under his arm. As quietly as she could she hunted for her clothes and dressed. She packed everything of hers, slipped into her coat and biting her lip turned the lock on the door.

She needed to leave. It was a decision she had come to and in time. Kane would come to see that it was the best one.

It was still cold when she went outside, but the snow had stopped. Instead of taking off right away, she worked her way back to Drake's place. It was night, so she was hoping that everyone would still be in bed when she slipped inside to get the rest of her things.

Both the front and back doors were locked. Biting the inside of her cheek, Jada walked around to the side where her bedroom window was located. Climbing out was a hell of a lot easier than going in, but she managed it, and was thankful that the window wasn't locked.

She was as quiet as a mouse, smiling at how easy it ended up being, sneaking in. Everything was as she'd left it and she wasted no time in changing into her own clothes before packing up some stuff in one backpack. Once finished she was about to start out the window, but stopped. A note. She needed to leave a note, or he was going to come looking for her and that would be trouble. What was she going to say to him? Was she going to come back?

She didn't have that answer, so all she wrote on a piece of paper was, 'Please forgive me, but I have to do this on my own. Jada.'

* * * *

Kane came awake with a jolt, rising up on his hands since he was sleeping on his belly. He gulped air into his lungs turned his head and felt his heat drop. Jada was gone. He turned to his back, got out of bed and looked in the bathroom. When he didn't see her there, he knew without a doubt she was gone from the cabin.

Dressing quickly, tugging his coat on, Kane left the cabin and followed her tracks in the snow back to Drake's. The sun was coming up and the fear that she was gone was overpowering him.

He reached the porch just as Drake opened the door. Without saying a word to him, he rushed inside, going right to the stairs, taking them two at a time. For the first time in three years, he went past Sasha's room without checking on her. He was bent on getting to Jada's room.

He rushed in and stopped. The room was dark, cold feeling and very empty. Clothes were still on the floor in a pile. He was just about to turn away when he caught sight of a piece of paper on the desk.

Please forgive me, but I have to do this on my own. Jada.

His heart dropped and his fist closed on the paper, crushing it in his hand.

"Kane?" Drake came up behind him, but he didn't turn around. "What's going on? I was just about to get you guys to tell you the storm is over, but—"

"She's gone," he stated calmly.

"What? Who?"

"Jada." Kane could hear the coldness in his voice. He turned, brushed past Drake, and went back down stairs.

"Kane, wait!" Drake yelled.

"I'm going after her," he stated.

"Damn it, will you wait!" Drake caught him at the front door. He slammed it shut when Kane opened it. "Calm down for a second please."

"I am calm." Kane looked him in the eyes. "Can't you tell?"

"Yeah, and that's what has me very worried at the moment." Drake sighed, rubbing his face. "What's going on?" Kane handed him the note, which Drake read quickly, frowning. "I don't understand. Do what?"

"She's going back there." Kane couldn't keep the growl from slipping as he spoke. "I have to go after her or she's going to get herself killed."

"You don't know if that's where she's heading or not."

"Then where the hell else could she be going?"

"I don't know, maybe the cemetery for Christ sakes. Didn't you say she was close to her cousin?"

Kane growled, pushed away from the door, and rubbed his face quickly with both hands. "This is so damn crazy. Why the hell would she run?"

"Because it's who she is," Drake stated. "Cole told me that Chase had explained that Jada has been running all her life. And I bet she's just running from the memories of her past."

Kane shook his head. "I can't let her go, Drake. I can't just stand here and let her run away."

"And we won't. The first thing we need to do is find out where she might go. Do you have any idea where he might have been buried?"

Kane shook his head again. "I didn't really get to read the thing. She took it out of my hand and hid it."

"Never mind. I'll call my Uncle Adrian. He can find out while we head back to the city."

"We?" One eyebrow went up as he watched Drake start back up stairs.

"Yeah," Drake nodded. "If you think I'm going to let you go alone, then you're crazy." He went up, taking the steps two at a time. "No way in hell you're going anywhere alone."

Kane smirked and went to the kitchen to grab a quick bite to eat before they left.

* * * *

Jada took the cab to the cemetery and went right up to Chris's grave. Chris Leonard, her first cousin, the first guy to ever show her not only love but respect. It had been years since she came here. As soon as she was able to get enough money together, she left school for the weekend to come here. It was also the first time she ever saw her grandfather weak.

He was there, kneeling in front of the headstone, crying into his silk handkerchief. Everything he cared for was gone with Chris. He loved Chris and hated her, and when he died, she was blamed for it and shipped off like a dirty secret. It wasn't until that moment, seeing him cry for Chris that Jada understood that the man felt nothing towards her. She could die and he wouldn't give a shit. It wouldn't matter to him.

That was why she stayed alone. Getting close to anyone was painful. She refused to go through the loss again, as she had when Chris died. Refused to be close enough to anyone to hurt when they walked away. Chase was her only friend and she even kept him at a distance. One day he would leave, just as the rest of them did. One day Chase would find himself someone and she would be nothing but a memory.

A single tear fell and she slowly went down on her knees in front of the tombstone. As always, only one tear fell for Chris. One tear of pain and loneliness. Like always, when she thought of him, memories of the past hit. Painful memories that she couldn't stop from coming and needed in order to remind her why she needed to stay alone. Why even now, as much as she wanted to go back and let Kane into her heart she couldn't. Everyone she loved died. She hadn't lied about that.

She woke up with a tube down her throat. She couldn't stop the panicking or trying to get the thing out. Nurses had to come over and hold her down as a doctor came to take it out. Once gone she sucked air into her lungs and looked around.

"Where am I?" she rasped out. "What happened?"

"You don't remember anything?" the doctor asked, shining a light in her eyes. "You've been in a deep coma for two weeks. You and your cousin."

Jada looked over and there was Chris in a bed with tubes everywhere on his body and their grandfather sitting in a chair. His cold eyes glared at her, but it didn't bother her this time as it normally did.

"Chris," she whispered.

The heart monitor went off and the doctor who had been checking her over turned to Chris. "We have a code blue!" he yelled.

They all went over to Chris, doing something to him while her grandfather strolled over to her. "You killed him. It should be you dying."

"We're losing him!"

Jada snapped out of the memory and wiped her eyes.

"He said you would come here, but I really didn't believe him." Jada looked up at a man standing not five feet away from her. He was dressed in a very nice suit, long coat, gloves and had the coldest eyes she ever saw in her life. "Guess he was right."

"Who are you?" She stood up, keeping her eyes on him.

The corner of his lip curved up, "A family friend."

"I don't have them." Two more guys came out from behind the trees, and her heart pounded in fear, but Jada didn't show it.

"Where's Kane?"

Jada turned and ran, but she didn't get far. She slammed into a body and arms wrapped around her tightly. When she looked up at the one who grabbed her, her mouth went dry. It was the same guy who she watched torture Kane.

"Hello, little girl." He smiled. "Remember me, because I haven't forgotten about you."

She was turned and forced to face the other one. He came up to her in a lazy manner with a cell phone in his hand. "Call him."

She shook her head and then winced when her hair was yanked on brutally.

"Last time," the one in front of her said. "Call him to come."

"Fuck you," she said thought her teeth. She should have seen the backhand that came, but didn't. But she sure as hell did feel the cut on her lip and taste the blood. "Beat me all you want. I'm not calling him for you. So you can just go straight to hell!"

He grabbed her by her throat, cutting her air off. "Oh, I promise you by the time Jason is finished with you, you will be calling him. One can only stand so much pain after all."

Jada laughed then spit blood in his face. "Have you met my grandfather?"

"I can see, Jason, why you were in such a hurry to get your hands on her." He brought out a hankie and wiped his face. "She is a delight."

"Then you have no objection to how I do things?" Jason asked.

"Not if it gets my pet back." He grabbed her chin, forcing Jada to look up at him. To the left, then the right he moved her head. "Going to be a shame to mark a face like this up. You are a pretty thing."

She smirked. "And you're an asshole."

"Have fun, Jason. I'll make sure James knows we have her."

The creep jerked to the left, and forced her to walk away. She only went willingly because of the shock. Her grandfather was involved in this. That son-of-a-bitch!

When they got close to a car, Jada snapped out of her shock and began to struggle with the hands on her arms. She dropped down, twisted her body back and forth. Jason slammed her up against the back; she turned and with her fist hit him across the jaw. It forced him to take a step back and gave her a split second to make a run for it.

She didn't get far.

He grabbed her around the legs and she went down. Jada turned on her back and kicked at him, aiming for his face, but landing a blow to his chest. She kept kicking as she scooted back, but it didn't work.

Jason grabbed her legs, dragged her close, and landed one hell of a blow to her jaw, putting her in complete darkness.

* * * *

"Wakey-wakey!" Cold water splashed onto Jada's face, jolting her awake. She groaned, opening her eyes, feeling this dull pain in her jaw on the right side. "Wouldn't want you to miss out on our fun now. Would we?"

She stiffened when her eyes focused on Jason bent over in front of her face, smiling at her. He tapped her nose, straightened up and walked over to a desk. Then he sat on the edge. She tried to move her hands but they wouldn't budge. Looking down, Jada saw that she was tied down to a chair. Not good.

"Found your stash." He shook a small vial in his hands. "I will say I'm impressed. It wasn't easy getting this back."

She smiled. "Pity you were too damned stupid to test it." He frowned, looking at it closer. "Animal. Or better yet, horse."

She laughed, when he threw the vial towards the wall, breaking it, then rushed up to her and slapped her hard on the left side of her face. It was about as hard as a fist, and drew blood. From her nose.

"That's going to leave a mark," she mumbled to herself, taking several deep breaths.

He grabbed her hair, yanking her head back. "Where is it?"

Jada hissed with the pain. She licked her lips, looking him right in the eye. "Gone."

He released her hair and slapped her again, same side. "Where is it?"

"I told you. Gone." Again, he slapped her and this time she couldn't hold back a whimper of pain.

He grabbed her throat, cutting off her air. "I don't believe that you would get rid of the one thing you have for leverage. So why don't you save yourself a lot of pain and tell me where it is."

"How about up your ass if you don't let me go."

He jerked her hair, took one-step back, and slapped her this time on both sides of her face. The backhand was the hardest, splitting her lip open again.

* * * *

"I'll break her, if that's what you came down here to wonder," Josh remarked when he heard the tapping sound of James Leonard's cane on the cement floor.

The old man chuckled, then jabbed Josh in the stomach with his cane when Josh turned around to face him. "You have a lot to learn with her," he rasped out. "The beatings never seemed to faze her that much. Not like the cane."

Josh raised one eyebrow at the old man. "Is that so?"

Jada yelled out. It was the first time he heard her yell since he left Jason alone with her. He turned his head towards the door, thinking over what he was going to do next.

She was tough, he'd give her that. From the impression he just got of her grandfather, he would bet it was because the old man used to beat her himself. Why, he didn't know or care. All he wanted now was the information she took and his pet back. He didn't give a shit on how he was going to get it from her.

Josh nodded and was about to say something when Jason came out of the room. It was a storage room that wasn't being used. Perfect for him to 'question' Jada without the staff getting involved. In fact, Josh was setting up a special place to have a talk with Kane once he was back.

Jason's hand was bloody but a smile spread over his face.

"Have fun?" Josh asked him.

"A little," Jason answered. He flexed his hand, taking the towel that Josh handed him to wipe off the blood. "She says its horse, not the real sample."

Josh took a deep breath, letting it out slowly. He had a feeling that getting his sample back had been too easy. "How bad did you work her over?"

"She can still talk."

"Good." Josh nodded.

He walked over to the closed door and opened it. Jada was slumped over, sitting in a chair with her hands tied down to the legs. Her hair was in her face, and there was a small amount of blood on the floor and on her jeans.

"Think you might have gone a little overboard, Jason," Josh stated, going up to Jada, kneeling down in front of her and raising her head with one finger.

She was a mess. The entire right side of her face was turning dark shades of black and blue. She had blood drying under her nose, a lip busted and bleeding, swelling on her cheekbone and her eye was even blood shot and swollen. All she had on the other side of her face was one large bruise.

"Are you ready to call him, or should I let Jason spend some more time with you?" he asked. She looked him in the eye before she nodded. Josh smiled. "Good." He brought out his cell and dialed the number. "Hello, Drake. I have someone here who would love to speak with Kane." He put the phone up to her ear. "Tell him."

She didn't say anything, so Jason went up to her and yanked her head back.

"Jada!" Kane was yelling on the phone.

She hissed, glaring from Jason to Josh. "Kane." Her voice rasped when she spoke. "Shut up." She looked around the room, and Josh instantly knew that she wasn't going to do what he told her to do. "Don't you come here!" she screamed. "They'll kill you!"

Jason acted fast, hitting her so hard she fell over in the chair. He brought out his pocketknife and cut the ropes on her wrists, yanking her up by her hair, his arm going around her throat. Josh took another deep breath before he brought the phone up to his ear.

"I hope you don't plan on being stupid. I would hate to see her take your place in the cage," Josh said. "I don't think she could handle the breeding."

"You motherfucker," Kane growled. "Hurt her and I'll kill you."

"At the moment, Kane, you are not in any position to make demands." Josh sighed. He snapped his fingers and Jason dragged Jada away. "If you want the girl back, you're going to have to come home. Think about it, and then make your decision and be at the Hathron Cemetery in one hour." He hung up, pocketed his phone, and went in the direction where Jason took Jada.

Jason was struggling with her. Jada was twisting her body to escape the restraints that he was working to get onto her wrists. When Josh was exploring the house, he found a soundproof room. There were whips, a cane, and a few straps. When he questioned James about it, Josh learned that when she was younger, James brought Jada to this room for punishment. Only when his grandson discovered them did they stop, but James beat Jada for every little mistake she made.

Josh put a few of his own touches to the room. One being, he had Jason put chains with metal cuffs into the walls, the ones he currently tried locking onto Jada's wrists. His gut was telling him that she was used to pain, or at least had a high tolerance for it, so he was going to see just how much she could stand.

"That was foolish of you, Ms. Leonard."

"So sue me."

Josh chuckled. "You're quick."

"And you're still two steps behind."

Josh picked up her hair and placed it over her shoulder. Holding out his hand, Jason handed him the knife, and he cut her shirt straight down her back. He brushed the pieces to the side then touched her bare back. Jada jumped.

"I get the impression that you have a high tolerance for pain," he stated, running the back of his hand up and down her back. "But how high I wonder?" He turned to Jason. "Try not to break the skin too much. She does have a very pretty back."

He walked away, closing the door behind him. He waited for the first sound. A slap he heard, cry out he didn't. Locking his eyes with James, Josh waited. Three more hits he heard before Jada made a sound.

"Time for me to get ready to bring my pet home." He grinned when Jada yelled. "And I'm sure she will corporate very soon."

James laughed, which turned into a cough. He took several deep breaths from his oxygen before he could speak. "You have a lot to learn with that bastard." He wheezed. "She's just like her tramp mother. She won't break."

"Then you should spend some time with Jason." Jada was screaming now. "He can break anyone."

Chapter Ten

"Argh!" Kane yelled at the top of his lungs, which turned into a very loud growl. He took Drake's cell phone, got out of the truck, at the cemetery and threw it at a tree, smashing it. He then started pacing.

"You know, the more I spend time with you two, the more I can see the resemblance between you." Cole tapped a finger on his lips before pointing it at Drake. "Didn't you break a phone like that?"

"Shove it," Drake grumbled. "What'd he say?"

"He's hurting her and I'm going to kill him," Kane said. He was boiling. Not since they threatened to kill Sasha when she was a baby, after they discovered she wasn't anything shifter did he want to kill.

"Kane—" Drake had a warning tone in his voice, but wasn't able to get out what he was going to say.

Kane shouted when a dart tore into his neck. He went down to his knees, his vision blurry, and an all too familiar weakness taking over his body. He reached out for Drake, but stopped when automatic gunfire rang out at them.

They made it to the cemetery and knew without a doubt that Jada made it here. They were going to leave when they got the call. Neither thought that Josh would be on his ass within minutes of calling him, but the shots that rang out were proof that he was.

"This is not what I agreed to when I said I'd come help!" Cole yelled.

"Kane!" Drake yelled.

Kane couldn't yell back to ask for help. He was down, the drugs taking hold of him so fast that he couldn't do anything. Not even stay awake.

* * * *

"Cole, here!" Drake tossed a handgun to Cole then he stood up and shot off a few rounds before kneeling back down behind a headstone. "Kane, talk to me!"

"He's down!" Cole yelled over the shooting.

Drake looked around the headstone he was hiding behind, glancing in the direction where Kane was. Sure enough, he was down. Face down in fact on the ground. He made a move to go get him, but a bullet ricocheted off the headstone, forcing him back around.

"Fuckers," he mumbled. "I can't get to him!" he yelled at Cole.

Drake shot a few more rounds off before he had to reload. Cole stood up then, shooting away, and trying to get to Kane. Drake couldn't do a damn thing to provide cover for him.

"Argh!" Cole yelled.

When Drake shoved a new clip into his gun, he stood up to give Cole the backup he needed but instead he watched Cole get hit in the shoulder by a round. Cole dropped backwards, down to the ground, yelling the whole time.

"Cole!" Drake yelled.

He fired off another round, dashed out for Cole and managed to drag him back behind the headstone without getting his own ass shot off.

"You stupid bastard!" Drake growled.

"Tell me something I don't already know," Cole panted.

Drake quickly looked over his shoulder wound. The bullet had gone right though and when he pressed to see if anything copper might be inside, Cole yelled. "I thought you might have shattered your collarbone."

"Celine is going to kill me," Cole groaned.

"Yep, but on the bright side, no copper."

"You're just full of good news."

Drake patted his arm and looked around to see what was happening now. The shooting had stopped and he knew why. Kane was gone.

"Shit," Drake sighed.

"What's wrong?"

"They took Kane." Drake rubbed his face and groaned. "Damn it!"

"That's what they planned." Cole struggled to sit up. He held his arm to his chest and winced when he moved. "Shot at us to get at him."

"Where do you think they've taken him?"

"Wherever they have Jada. Come on," Drake grunted, helping Cole to his feet. "Need to get you patched up. Oh, and can I, um, borrow your phone. Need to let Carrick know what's going on and have Brock meet us at Dad's."

"Now I'm definitely going to be in trouble," Cole moaned. "Dedrick's going to rip me one before Celine."

"How do you like being in the family?" Drake asked with a grin.

* * * *

Kane slowly woke to a pounding head and a cold floor. He had a hard time opening his eyes and couldn't seem to shake the chill that gripped his body. He heard everything around him and smelled cleanness instead of the rancid stench of the lab.

Forcing his eyes to open, he found that his worst nightmare had come to life. He was back in a torture room, chained to a floor stripped of all his clothing. He looked around, trying to figure out where the hell he was and what the fuck was going on. What he saw was the last person Kane ever wanted to come face to face with again.

Kane snarled while his eyes followed Jason Spencer, right hand man of Josh Stan, around the room. Hate filled him and for some strange reason the colors in the room flashed from normal to red.

Kane's neck was chained to his wrists, which were shackled to the floor, forcing him down on his knees. Chained and with the drugs still in his system, but leaving his body, Kane didn't feel like he was as weak as he used to be in the same room with Jason. Kane was not the same man that Jason used to torture for his sick pleasure. He could control his animal just as he could focus his rage.

"Good, you're awake." Jason smiled. "I've got a nice surprise for you. One you're going to love."

"Kane!" Sasha screamed so loud in his head that he grimaced. Her panic added to his pounding head.

"I'm fine," he sent back. *"Calm down."*

"No!" she sounded like she was crying. *"Not you."*

Kane shook his head, trying to clear it. He looked up when Jason came back into the room, struggling to hold someone. He thought he was going to be sick as he watched Jason toss Jada to the ground before him.

Her back was to him, and she was a mess. Her shirt was split down the back. What he saw on her skin had him almost throwing up. Jason had beaten her, just as he used to beat him. She had bruising and blood on her back, mostly on her lower back as if she had been caned or something. Jason turned her over with the toe of his boot, giving Kane a view of what her face looked like.

Kane growled and strained against the chains. Her face, her beautiful face was swollen, bruised, and cut. That motherfucker had beaten her so bad that her eye on the left side looked like it was swollen shut.

"I figured you might want to see her one last time," Jason said with his cocky smile in place. "It's the least I can do." Jason turned his back on Kane and walked away.

"Jada!" Kane tried to keep his voice down and speak loud enough to get her attention.

She kept her eyes closed, moving her head back and forth. "I told you to stay away."

Her voice rasped, strained when she spoke. Kane let out a breath of relieve at just hearing it.

"Never listen to shit, you damn animal," she went on.

He smiled. "Guess your just going to have to try to train me, huh?" Kane flinched when Jason slammed a chair down next to a metal table.

"Get ready," Jada groaned, opening her eyes, or one eye, staring up at the ceiling.

"For what?" Kane frowned.

"For, whatever."

Jason walked back over to Jada, grabbing her by her hair, pulling her up to her feet. "The show's not over yet, Kane." He wrapped one arm around Jada's throat, holding her close.

"What're you going to do, Jason?" Kane asked, locking his eyes on the man he itched to kill.

"Oh, I'm thinking of enjoying myself with your little whore here." Jason smiled.

Jada chuckled while she hung onto his arm around her throat. "Don't hold your breath, dickhead. I would rather fuck a bum on the street than you."

Jason rubbed his face into her hair. He rubbed with his eyes closed as a cat would against a leg. "I am the bum on the street."

"Knock it off, Jason!" Kane growled. He snarled at Jason to get him his full attention. "This is between you and me."

Jason glared at Kane. He tapped a finger on his lips with a cruel grin on his face. "You know, you're right. This is between us. However..." he grinned. "I find that I just can't let this treat go, until I have a sample." Kane lunged at him and Jason laughed. "But that is going to have to wait for later. Someone else wants to spend some time with this sweet thing."

Jason jerked Jada around, forcing her to walk to the table. Kane kept his mouth shut as two men came into the room with another chair. They handed one to Jason who put it down at the end of the table and shoved Jada down into it. The other one was placed at the other end.

"Now be a good little girl," Jason said.

The door opened again and Kane tensed up, waiting for the worst. An elderly man came inside, leaning on a cane, making a taping noise with each step and a tank of oxygen right behind him. He sat down in the other chair with a sigh.

"So the bastard has come home," the old man wheezed.

"This was never my home," Jada said, her eyes down on the table.

"You took my boy away, and now it's time to pay the price."

Kane watched Jada slowly raise her head up, eyes locked on the old man. He saw the hate and pain on her face and he strained against his chains. He wanted to go to her, protect her but couldn't. As much as he hated to admit it, this was a battle that she needed to face without him. Just as he needed to deal with Jason alone.

"You rotten old bastard!" Jada lunged on the table at him, but Jason was right there to stop her. He grabbed hold of her arms, yanking her back to her chair. "You killed Chris!" she yelled. "You!"

"He would be here now if the likes of you had never crossed his path." He wiggled a wrinkled finger at her. "It should've been you, not him. Only tainted blood like yours kills things."

"And what about you?" Jada crossed her arms over her chest, glaring at him. "What good has ever come from you? Your own children left your pitiful home. Did you beat them or just my mother?"

"You mother was a whore!" he yelled, his voice straining. "Just like you."

Kane couldn't keep quiet any longer. He growled, getting the old man's attention.

"Animals." He stood up with his cane, spitting on the floor, walking slowly towards Kane. "What kind of person would fornicate with animals?" He raised his cane and hit Kane on the side of the face, cutting him right next to his left eye.

"Be careful, old man," Kane growled low at him, blood sliding down the side of his face. "You fuck with me, and I'll fuck back."

He laughed at Kane, walked right up behind him, raised his hand, and brought his cane down across his back. The pain that Kane felt was a new one. All these years he had been beaten with whips, never with a cane.

"Stop it!" Jada screamed, standing up again only to be held in place by Jason grabbing hold of her arms.

Jason smiled. "Not just yet. I'm finding I like the show."

"You would, you sick freak." She twisted and turned in Jason's' grip, but he didn't let her go. Whack! "Kane!" she screamed.

He glanced up at her to see Jason toss her over to the side. Jada sort of went flying across the floor, landing hard on the ground and skidded to a stop. Jason came up to the old man and stopped another blow from landing on Kane's back. Blood trickled down his back, as well as a nice throbbing, but Kane ignored it. His eyes were on Jada.

"Don't want to kill him," Jason said. "At least not yet."

Jada crawled over to one of the chairs, unnoticed by either man. Kane held his breath as he watched her stand up, grip the chair, pick it up, and walk right up behind the men. She swung and came down hard behind the old man. He went down. Jason looked at her with shock and she swung around, hitting him as well, knocking him down also.

Dropping the chair, she dropped down next to Kane, working to release one of his wrists.

"You're nuts, you know that?" Kane said.

"Lecture me later."

Jason lunged from behind. He grabbed her hair at the same moment Jada got Kane's wrist free. Jason yanked her back, pinning her to the ground.

"Feisty little bitch." Jason smiled. "I like that."

Kane lunged for Jason, but the chains stopped him. "Hurt her again, and I'll rip your fucking throat out!" Kane snarled.

"She is a cute little thing." Jason chuckled. "Does she taste as good as she looks? I bet she's a great fuck with all this fight in her."

Again, Kane tried to lunge at Jason, but Jason laughed at Kane when the chains held him off. Jason pinned her wrists over her head before reaching out to run one finger down her cheek. Jada moved her head away.

"Ah, don't worry. Soon you will be very used to my touch." He got closer and licked her lips.

"Yeah, well not today."

Kane flinched when her knee came up and nailed Jason right in the crotch. Jason grunted and Kane chuckled.

"You fucking bitch!" Jason sat up and hit Jada with a closed fixed, knocking her out. Kane growled again low when Jason moved his hand down on Jada, cupping one of her breasts. "Nice handful."

Kane snarled and let his animal side out enough to show Jason that he wasn't afraid of him any longer. Hair sprouted over his body, fingers got longer and he began to grow bigger.

"I don't think so, mutt." Jason pushed off Jada, walked right up to Kane, and kicked him hard in the chest. "You've forgotten your manners."

Kane felt something crack. A rib maybe. He gasped for air, and each breath he took gave him excruciating pain.

"Maybe its time I reminded you," Jason turned his back, and left the room. Kane wanted to call out to Jada but he couldn't catch his breath. He hung his head, working to steady his breathing and the pain. "Brought something just for you."

Kane looked up. Jason had the whip that he used on Kane so many times in the lab in his hand.

The first crack of the whip landed with a sting on Kane's back to join the throbbing from the cane. Another one, harder had him hissing. After the fifth hit he lost count and wasn't able to hold back from yelling any longer either. His breathing was coming fast and hard as he kept his eyes closed to block out the pain.

"That's enough, Jason." Josh walked up next to him, but Kane was too weak to look up at the man. "Don't want him unable to perform later."

"I'll never fuck for you," Kane panted, shaking his head.

Josh knelt down grabbed his hair and yanked his head back. "Sure you will, Kane. Because I really don't think she can take the pain like you do."

"The old man doesn't look too good," Jason stated.

"Have someone take him to the hospital, and put her up on the table." Josh said.

Kane stiffened and watched. Jason picked Jada up and tossed her on the table. She was so limp that her arm hung off the side, as did her legs, and she didn't make a sound being laid down on her bruised back. She was out cold.

Josh jerked Kane's hair and then let it go, stood up and slipped out of his suit jacket. He nodded to Jason who picked up the old man and took him out of the room. Kane kept his mouth shut as Josh pulled on his tie then released it from his neck, walking up to Jada.

"I don't think I've ever considered that you might have good taste in women before, Kane." He stood at the end of the table and parted Jada's legs, standing between them.

"Don't do it, Josh," Kane huffed, breathing through the pain.

"She is a very pretty girl Kane," Josh's voice lowered, becoming husky sounding. When he touched her, Kane jerked, testing the chains again. The one that Jada started working on was loosening up. He was almost free. "And so soft." Josh's hand moved her ripped shirt up, exposing her belly.

The growl that came from the back of his throat was a deep rumble. Josh tugged on her jeans, unsnapping them, and yanking them down her legs roughly, tossing them behind his shoulder. She was in her panties, completely at Josh's mercy and out cold.

When he took the back of his hand, skimmed it up her leg, over her mound, and hooked his thumb inside her panties as if to start to pull them down, Kane lost it.

With no drugs in his system, Kane was powerful, pissed, and the control that Drake worked so hard at teaching him snapped. He snarled, along with growling in a pure animal manner. Kane changed once more.

Hair sprouted all over his body and hands, wrists, legs, feet, everything on him became larger. The chains that were holding Kane by his wrists snapped in two. The thick collar around his neck broke into two pieces as Kane slowly stood up on his feet. Color in the room turned to dark red. A bloody red as he stared at Josh Stan.

Kane felt his face change. A large snout replaced his nose, sharp and deadly teeth filled his mouth, and in his anger, foam and spit came out of his mouth. Kane was now completely changed and pissed was a mild word to describe how he felt right this minute.

Looking at Josh, Kane released an ear-shattering growl at the man, showing him each and every one of his sharp teeth. The growl was pure animal. Nothing on Kane at this moment was human, and mercy was something he knew nothing about, not after the bastard threatened to rape his mate.

Josh made a move towards the door. The moment his hand touched the knob, Kane was right behind him. He jumped up and landed hard on the ground. The whole floor shook from the force and weight of his jump.

Josh turned around and Kane grabbed him by the throat, picking him up, pressing him against the door. Kane squeezed, watching the life slowly slip from the bulging eyes. How many times had this man watched him suffer? How many times had Kane begged as a child for one ounce of mercy when he was being beaten? When did Josh Stan ever give an ounce of shit about anyone but himself and what Kane could bring him? Never!

He brought Josh close to his large mouth, making sure that the man knew the anger and danger he was in. He snarled in his face, enjoying how Josh shook under his hand.

"Jason won't let you leave this house," Josh strained when he spoke. "You're dead."

Kane's only response was to snarl at him again. With all this power and all his anger over the years he spent under this man's hand, Kane twisted Josh's neck and pushed him through the thick oak door with all his power.

He turned and went over to the table. Jada was still out cold. He reached out with his paw like hand and touched the side of her face—the one that was bruised so bad he cringed for her when he touched it.

He was still in wolf from when he scooped her limp body up in his arms. Kane turned and left the room, walking out into a basement. He snarled at Josh's limp, dead body, heading right for the stairs.

Kane made it to the kitchen where Jason was waiting for him, gun pointed at his chest. Kane snarled at him, right before he placed Jada on the wide island countertop.

"You're not walking out of here, dog," Jason spit on the floor, glaring at Kane. "At least not alive."

Kane lunged at him and the gun went off. He wrapped both of his hands around Jason's throat, squeezing. The gun exploded again and this time Kane felt the raw burning pain from the gunshot.

His grip loosened and Jason rolled him off. Kane panted, his change slowly receding back to normal. Once he was a man again, he was covered in sweat and felt the pain in his stomach, where he'd been shot.

Jason smiled. "Always did have to bring you down the hard way."

Kane lay on the cool tile floor, holding his stomach, watching Jason walk around. He put his gun into the waistband of his jeans while he went to the back door. Kane said nothing and moved very little.

Jason went outside briefly and when he came back in, he had two canisters of gas in his hand. Kane just watched him pour the gas around the room. He was breathing hard from the pain and didn't want to move much for fear that he would bleed to death.

"You know, I told Josh keeping you as a pet was a mistake." Jason splashed gas over the counters and up the walls, walking around slowly. "But no, he thought he could train your sorry ass." He finished with another splash before tossing the can off to the side. "Guess it's left for me to do what he didn't have the balls to do."

Kane growled again the second Jason brought out a match and lit it. A fire broke out in the kitchen. Heat engulfed the whole room, but still Kane didn't take his eyes off Jason.

Jason extended his hands out and laughed, "I do have to say, Kane, that I'm enjoying watching you bleeding on the floor. I'm really hoping you don't die. I want to hear you burn."

"You're a sick fuck, Jason."

"Not until I have your pretty sister I ain't," Jason snickered. "I can hardly wait to taste her."

Somehow, Kane got a second wind of strength. He moved fast, reaching up and grabbing Jason by his throat. Slowly, pushing the pain back, Kane stood up, holding onto Jason.

"That's the last threat you will ever make towards my sister," Kane said through his teeth. "Now you can go straight to hell!" He pushed Jason with the last amount of his strength he had towards the burning fire.

Breathing hard, Kane watched as Jason bounced off the burning wall, his body catching on fire. The man screamed, flapping his arms around, twisting his body. Holding his stomach, Kane glared, saying nothing as Jason ran from the kitchen into another part of the house, spreading flames throughout as he went.

* * * *

"Are you sure this is the place?" Drake asked Brock. They pulled into a gravel drive that appeared very deserted.

"This is the address Uncle Adrian gave me." Brock sighed.

"Yeah, well we both know how great you are with directions." Drake grumbled.

"Hey, that was one time. One time! Get over it."

"Boys!" Stefan snapped from the driver seat. "Don't make me pull over like you're five again."

"It's on fire!" Drake pointed straight ahead towards a house that was burning.

Stefan stopped the truck parked it and quickly got out with them. They all stared at a once grand home engulfed by huge orange flames.

"Kane!" Drake yelled. He was about to run towards the fire, but

Stefan stopped him.

"You can't go in there." Stefan grunted as he held Drake back. "It's too late."

"Dad!" Brock raised his voice enough to be heard. Both Stefan and Drake looked in the direction in which Brock was staring.

Kane was coming around from the back of the house, in his arms a limp Jada. He was practically naked, dirty, and if Drake was mistaken, bloody. Stefan let Drake go and the three of them ran towards Kane.

They reached Kane just as he dropped to the ground on his knees. Brock got a hold of Jada and Drake grabbed onto Kane before he could fall to his face. He took hold of him by his shoulders, but Kane still dropped down face first to his lap.

"Jesus," Stefan gasped in a whisper, "He's been beaten, and shot."

"So has Jada," Brock stated, "But take out the shot. What the hell happened in there?"

"Kane?" Drake took his face in his hands, moving his head up to look at him. "What happened? Where's Stan?"

"Dead." Kane panted, shaking his head. "Both dead." He strained in Drake's arms. "Jada."

"She's safe," Drake told him. "Brock has her."

Kane nodded, and then slumped in Drake's lap. He passed out. Drake stared down at him and gently brushed the back of his hand, sighing. He promised Kane that he wouldn't be hurt ever again, and here he was beaten and shot.

"He's going to be fine." Stefan grabbed Drake by the shoulder, squeezing him. "His threat is over. He's completely free, just like the rest of us."

Drake nodded, but said nothing. He fisted his hand into Kane's hair, lowered his own head down, resting it on top of Kane's. When he had himself collected, Drake looked up where Stefan was standing, staring at the burning house.

"Dad?" Drake said, frowning.

"It's a bit ironic," Stefan said.

"What is?" Brock asked.

"This whole war started with a fire. Now it ends with one." Stefan sighed. "It's finally over."

Brock stepped up next to him, Jada in his arms. Somehow, Drake was able to pick Kane up, slinging him over his shoulder. He grunted with the extra weight, but also stood next to Stefan, watching the house burn.

"I couldn't think of a better ending," Drake said. He grinned at Stefan when Stefan turned his head to look at him. "Started with you, ended with us. Just like I said years ago. I was going to end this shit." Brock cleared his throated. Drake smiled, hung his head down for a second, and took a deep breath. He straightened up as much as he could with Kane over his shoulder and said, "Okay, we did it."

"Thank you." Brock turned, heading back to the truck. "Is it too damn much to get some appreciation around here? Damn!"

Stefan chuckled and reached for Kane. Drake took a step back, shaking his head. "No. I have him."

"He's heavy." Stefan pointed out.

"Yeah," Drake nodded. "But for once I want to hold him. Just once."

Stefan nodded. "Let's go home before the cops show up and he bleeds to death."

* * * *

"I swear I could quit the hospital and take up private practice with just you Draegers." Doctor Sager came into the kitchen of the Draeger home, wiping her hands on a rag. She took a deep breath as she sat down at the table.

Stefan was leaning up against the counter, Dedrick at the table with Drake and Cole, who had his arm up in a sling. Brock was in the study making calls to Heather and Carrick, while Sidney and Jaclyn were upstairs helping with Kane and Jada. Celine was on her way home.

"The girl has a concussion. She's been beaten pretty badly, and I think she's in a state of shock. She didn't say one word to me as I checked her out and I know some of those bruises have to hurt like hell."

"And Kane?" Drake asked. He almost held his breath, fearing the worst.

"He's lost some blood. Luckily, for him they didn't use copper. Bullet didn't nick anything, it's out, and he's sewn up. He has one cracked rib and lots of bruising from the beating he took. I gave him a heavy sedative. He'll be out of it until late tomorrow. He kept trying to get up to go check on the girl."

"Thanks, Doc," Dedrick sighed. "You've been a life saver."

"Don't say that until after you've seen my bill," She snorted, standing back up. "I've given your wife the instructions," she said to Stefan. "If that wound begins to bleed get him to the hospital ASAP."

"You got it," Stefan said.

"Night." Sager walked out, leaving them alone.

"So when does CeeCee get here?" Drake asked.

Dedrick groaned, rubbing his face then the back of his neck. "I called Chase. He's stopping to pick her up on his way here."

"*You* got Chase to come home?" Cole asked with both of his eyebrows raised in shock.

"You make it sound like it was hard." Dedrick leaned back in his chair, tipped it back and reached for the fridge. He pulled out a few beers, sliding them on the table.

"I couldn't get him home for Christmas last year, and you got him to come home for this shit," Cole snorted. "Not fair."

"Stop acting like a baby." Brock walked back into the kitchen, leaned over Cole and grabbed the beer that Cole was about to drink. "Carrick and Sasha got to the house just fine. Heather said that Sasha sort of freaked her out. Said that Kane was fine, just hurt a bit. How the hell would she know that?"

"Because she's telepathic," Stefan said, getting everyone's attention.

"What?" Drake frowned.

Stefan shrugged. "She's telepathic. She can see into each one of our minds. Sort of like what we do when we seduce our mates." Dedrick grunted. "Okay, some of us."

"I don't understand." Drake rubbed his forehead.

And he didn't. Sasha was the quiet one. She didn't have anything shifter. Nothing at all, besides a birthmark on her shoulder that looked just like the bite mark males left on their mates. But the more he thought about it the more it sort of made sense.

Sasha seemed to always know what they were thinking and was gone when he wanted alone time with Carrick. She rarely talked. So yeah, it was possible. But how?

Drake was about to ask that question. He even had his mouth opened when Stefan went on. "I did some research and talked to a few of the Council members. Twins of our race have very unique talents. When the egg splits, you never know which one will get what. Most of the time, they are equal in everything. But when one gets nada," he shook his head. "Only ever heard of once before."

"What's it got to do with what ever it's called?" Drake frowned.

"Wait a sec." Cole held up his good hand.

"It's the birthmark," Dedrick said. He sounded tired, just like everyone. "That twin your father is talking about had the same mark."

"Sasha can see into our minds. Everything?"

"You know, Kane did say that the two of them communicated with their minds in the lab growing up," Brock said. Drake gave him a dirty look. "Hey, didn't you just even *talk* to him about his past?"

"Can't forget it, Drake, no matter how much you try," Stefan stated.

"I didn't want him to remember the pain." Drake sighed, feeling the weight of the world on his shoulders. "Kane has enough going on that I just didn't want him to think about the cage or the beatings."

"But it's who he is," Stefan said. "His past is what's made him the man he is now. All we've done, Drake, is show him how to be the man he can be. And we need to help Sasha with this gift of hers."

Drake nodded in agreement, and kept his mouth shut.

"Well it sure is going to make Christmas interesting," Brock stated with a smile. "Could've used her when we were younger."

"Dedrick," Stefan sighed.

Dedrick leaned over and slapped Brock on the back of the head.

"Now this is why I don't want you living up there alone." Cole groaned when Celine came in from the back, slightly yelling at him, "They shot you!"

"She's taken up the roll of mate very well," Stefan said to Dedrick.

Dedrick nodded. "Just like her mother.'"

Celine dropped her bags and rushed up to Cole, hugging him. He grimaced but said nothing, only hugged her back with his good arm.

"Look, he's still alive," Drake stated.

"Yeah, just peachy." Celine stepped out of Cole's embrace so he could get a good view of Chase. "Shot with a broken collar bone. You win bro."

Cole stood up and faced Chase. Drake waited, almost holding his breath, thinking that they were going to start fighting any second. Chase had been gone for three years. He called, but didn't come home for the holidays or anything. Each time Drake tried to get him home, Chase had an excuse of some kind. After the first couple of years, Drake was beginning to get an idea as to why Chase was staying away, but shrugged it off. Shifters didn't stay away from their mates as long as Chase has been gone. So that thought he tossed out.

Cole came over to Chase and hugged him. Chase hugged him back and Drake let the breath he was holding out. No fight. Good. He really didn't need to break one up at the moment.

"You look like shit." Cole smiled, holding onto Chase by his leather jacket.

"Have you seen yourself?" Chase teased back. "You're not a top model either."

"Hey!" Stefan pushed off the counter when Sidney walked into the kitchen. "How're they doing?"

"Jacy is still with Kane," Sidney answered. "I'm worried about Jada though. She's just sitting there, staring out the window. I helped her get dressed, and she didn't make a sound. Only went through the motions."

"I'll go talk to her." Chase said.

"I don't think it's going to do any good," Sidney said, shaking her head.

"Yeah, it will." Chase pulled out of Cole's arms and left the kitchen.

"Think he can get through to her?" Sidney asked.

"He's her only friend," Cole stated. "He'll get her out of it."

Chapter Eleven

Jada sat at the edge of the bed staring out the window. The guilt was eating her up inside. She was stupid for leaving and even dumber for being caught. She should never have gone to visit Chris's grave, but she needed to go and say her good-byes. She needed to put her own demons to rest finally.

"Jada?" she closed her eyes. Chase. He was here.

She heard the door close. Heard his steps walk closer and could even feel him kneeling down in front of her. She couldn't look at him.

"You're a mess, girl." She could hear the teasing in his voice and would have smiled if she could. She'd known Chase long enough to know when he was trying to cheer her up.

She also knew she was a mess. Jason did a nice number on her. After Sidney left her, she went into the bathroom to look at herself. The whole left side of her face was one big ass bruise. Cheek swollen, lip cut, and her eye made a raccoon look sexy. She just hoped like hell that Kane wasn't in even worse shape than she was. But then, he had to be didn't he? If he weren't then he would be in here with her. Unless he figured out that she was trouble as if she'd been trying to tell him since the moment they met.

"Where's Kane?" she whispered.

"He's down the hall." Chase touched her legs, rubbing her knees gently. "Resting. Guess he fought pretty hard with that Jason guy. At least, that's what Celine told me on the way here."

"I fucked up," she said, her voice shaking. When she opened her one eye, a tear fell down her face. "He could have died because of me."

"Jada—"

"How—how could he do that?" She couldn't stop herself. The words started to come forth before she could push them back where they belonged. More tears came and fell.

"How could my own grandfather...okay, that sh—"

Chase wrapped his arm quickly around her neck came up on his knees and hugged her tight. "Sh."

Jada fisted her hands into his jacket and let it out. She cried, well maybe screamed the pain into his chest. The harder she cried, the tighter Chase held her.

* * * *

Chase held Jada as tightly as he dared, being she was hurt. In all the years that he had known her, he never once saw her break down. Hell, he never even saw a tear fall from her eyes and now she was holding onto him. Crying and screaming against him and he took it.

He felt bad for her and didn't know what to say that might help to ease her pain. All he could do was hold her. When he glanced up Drake was standing in the doorway staring at them both. Chase saw the concern in Drake's eyes.

It took some time, but Chase got Jada calmed down and resting in the bed. He left her, meeting up with Drake in the hallway. Drake was leaning back against the wall, both hands in his pockets. He looked like a man beaten down to Chase.

"How's she doing?" Drake asked.

"I've never seen her like this before," Chase answered. "Jada has always been so strong, and feisty." He shrugged. "This isn't the Jada I know."

"She's been through a lot."

"I think everyone has." A few seconds went by before Chase scratched the side of his head. "So how's Kane doing?"

"Why'd you leave, Chase?"

"What?" Drake's question caught Chase off guard. He wasn't expecting it and wasn't sure just how to answer it.

"You heard me."

Chase shrugged, trying to put on a carefree attitude. "Needed to do my own thing, I guess."

"Bullshit." Drake snorted, pushing off the wall. "When you decide to tell me the truth, you know where to find me."

He was halfway down the stairs when Chase started to follow. "You know, don't you?"

Drake nodded as he kept walking down. "Yep."

"Damn it!" Chase sighed. "Drake." He grabbed Drake by the arm, stopping him. "Don't do this. Don't put me in this kind of position like you did Cole."

"And what position might that be?" Drake frowned.

"There's a reason for everything we do. Trust me when I say that my reason is for the good of everyone here."

"You sure it isn't you running away like your brother?"

"Hell no!" Chase took a step back. "She needs time and you know it."

"And just how much time are you planning on giving her?"

"As much as she needs." Chase brushed past Drake to the kitchen. "Trust me, I'll know when the time's right to make my move. You just keep that boy of yours civilized."

* * * *

Jada woke up glanced out the window and sighed. It was four in the morning and the house was very quiet. She had cried in Chase's arms until she fell asleep. That much she remembered.

Wincing, she sat up, flinging the covers off her legs. She was shaky when she stood up, weak, but determined. She walked to the bathroom, flicked the light on, and went right up to the mirror. She stared at herself, seeing a stranger looking back.

Hanging her head, she turned and left, looking for her clothes. In a chair was her bag of cameras and another with some clothes in it. She was so sore that it hurt too much to move. Jada wanted to crawl back into the bed and just sleep, but she had to move, had to see for herself that Kane was okay.

It took her longer to get her jeans on, and by the time she had her shirt over her head she was panting and sweaty but she was dressed. The shoes were a whole other matter since she could barely bend over. She would have sworn it took her an hour to get dressed instead of twenty minutes.

Grabbing her camera bag, Jada slipped from the room. She wasn't too sure which room was his and went all the way down the hall to the last room. It was a good enough place to start as any. Luck was on her side. It was Kane's room.

She went inside, closing the door quietly. Kane was on his back, in the middle of the bed. The covers were up to his waist, a bandage over his stomach. Slowly Jada walked up to him, her bag slipping from her fingers to the floor, where she went down to her knees. She took his hand, slipping her own under it. Silent tears fell down.

"You just couldn't listen, could you?" Jada dropped his hand and stood back up. She paced the room, shaking her head. "If you had, then you wouldn't be in that bed—hurt. You'd be in the woods where you belong." She stopped, covered her mouth as more tears fell. "Why'd you have to be so damn stubborn?" she whispered. "Why the hell did you have to come for me?"

She went back over to the bed, sitting down on the side. Gently she touched his forehead, brushing a long lock of his hair to the side. "You stupid son-of-a-bitch," she breathed out. "You did what no one has been able to do for years. You made me feel." She leaned close, lips mere inches from his. "I miss you already you damn animal, and that isn't fair. Just like I can't stay here and have only a damn photo of you like Chris. I'm sorry."

Jada brushed her lips against his, pulled back, and reached for her bag. She dug inside, finding the one camera that had her secret. She brought out one single film container and set it down on the nightstand next to the bed. Sniffing back the tears, wiping her sore face, Jada stood up and went to the door. She opened it, peeked out to make sure no one was around.

She slipped out, but stopped. Jada looked once more at Kane, her heart breaking. But she had to do this. It was right. Deep down she knew it was the right thing to do. If she stayed with him any longer then he would die. Everyone she ever cared for did.

"I lied to you, Kane," she said, taking a deep breath. "I do love you."

* * * *

Kane fought to come out of the haze his body was in the moment he picked up Jada's scent. But he couldn't. What ever it was the doctor injected him with was keeping him under, drugged and weak. Just like when he was in the lab, only he knew this time it was for him and not for others. He understood that he needed to rest, to give his body time to heal. When she walked into the room all he wanted to do was hold her, to feel her breath on his face and know that she was all right.

Somehow, Kane was able to turn over in the bed, and for his effort, he was slapped with excruciating pain.

"Hey, what're you trying to do, rip the stitches open?" he heard Drake's voice, but couldn't open his eyes.

Kane opened his mouth to speak and nothing came out. When Drake touched his arms, pushing him back onto his back he gripped his shirt, fisting it. By this time, he was panting with the effort to get something to come out.

"Ja...Ja," he tried to say.

"What? I don't understand," Drake said.

Kane took a deep, big breath and said in a rush, "Jada!"

"She's okay." Again, Drake pushed him down in the bed. "She's down the hall resting. In the morning, I'll let her come down and see you."

Kane shook his head. "No."

"Drake, Jada's outside...leaving." Cole stuck his head into the door.

"Shit. Stay with him!" Drake yelled, running out the door.

* * * *

Drake ran from the bedroom, almost knocked Chase over and took the stairs two, or three at a time. It was still very early in the morning, so everyone else in the house was still sleeping. Perfect time for her to try to run again.

He yanked the door open, looked around quickly, and saw her walking with her head lowered down the drive.

"Jada!" he yelled.

She looked over her shoulder, but didn't stop walking. In fact, when she saw him she took off running.

"Fuck," Drake mumbled, running after her.

She had a good lead on him, which wasn't good. When she made it to the fence and started to climb, Drake's heart dropped in his gut.

He slammed up against the bars just as she dropped down, landing on her rear, breathing hard.

"Jada, please don't do this," he said. "Please don't do this to him!"

"I'm sorry, Drake." She slowly stood up. "I can't stay to watch him get hurt because of me."

"Damn it, you still don't understand." He rattled the fence, praying that Cole or Chase would open it up for him. "You leave, it will kill him."

"But he'll be alive." She started backing away from the fence. "Take care of him, Drake."

"Jada," he gave a warning growl when she turned her back on him. "Jada!" Drake yelled the second she ran away, disappearing into the night. "Argh!"

"Drake!" Chase skidded to a stop next to him. "Look at this."

Drake took the small canister popped the lid open and tipped it over. A key fell out onto his hand along with a small piece of paper.

You'll find everything at 425 Brooklyn, basement frozen storage. Jada.

"What the hell is that?" Chase took the key and Drake glanced once more down the street where Jada had disappeared. "I don't get it."

"Come on." Drake slapped him on the back and jogged back up to the house.

"She's gone, isn't she?" Cole asked the moment they were inside.

"Yeah." Drake opened the hall closet and grabbed his and Chase's jackets. "Stay with him. We'll be back later."

"What's going on?" Stefan asked. He stood at the top of the stairs, in his robe.

"Jada left," Drake answered. "And she left something. I'm taking Chase with me to see what the hell it is. Try to keep Kane down. Have the doctor give him another shot if you have to. Come on."

Drake was out the front door before Stefan could say another word.

"Are we going to find Jada?" Chase asked.

Drake wanted to. He really did want to drag her ass back, but his gut was screaming that what she left was too damn important. This was what Stan was willing to kill her for.

They reached the city by six. At a quarter to eight, they found the storage building that was on the note, but had to wait until nine to go inside. The place was a medical unit and the basement was where all frozen specimens were kept.

"May I help you?" A man in a white doctor's coat came out from a glass office.

Drake looked around before he showed the man the key. "I'm here to collect Jada Leonard's box."

"Ah, yes." He smiled. "She said you might be showing up today. Follow me, please." The man showed them to a room, took the key from Drake and left. Seconds later, he came in with a large yellow envelope and a small cooler.

Drake opened the envelope first, dumping another white envelope on the table. Chase picked it up and Drake looked at the information before him.

Jada took everything. There were the experiments that were done on him as a baby, each stage of development of Kane, when Sasha was born and what they did to them. Drake sat there, reading it, unable to believe the tortures his children had endured. Even Sasha had a few experiments done on her and was to be soon bred because of her birthmark. Once it was known that Kane would do anything to protect her it stopped. For her that is. Still they probed her, took eggs, and tested on them. Drake feared now that she wouldn't be stable for a mate and didn't think either would be able to have children ever.

"Drake, listen to this," Chase said, getting his full attention. "This is the information that was worth killing for. I also took each sample Stan ever had on Kane and Sasha." Drake reached for the box, opening it up. He pulled out three vials. One had sperm, another eggs, and the third was dated back thirty years. His sperm! "It's a letter from Jada. She goes on to say that you have your sample back and the ones that were taken from Kane and Sasha." Chase's head came up fast. "Sasha?" He dropped the letter, snatching up the file that Drake had in his hand. "That fucking bastard!" he growled.

"She's right." Drake stated. "This shit is worth killing for." He slumped back in the chair with a sigh. "How could she have pulled this off alone the way she has?"

"How am I supposed to go forward now?" Chase asked, tossing the information back on the table. "I can't go through with this now, Drake. I can't traumatize her again." He shook his head and Drake watched him. "I've—I've got to get out of here."

When he made a move to leave, Drake lunged; grabbing Chase by the front of his jacket. "Get it together, Chase." Drake lowered his voice, vibrating it with a low growl. "Given time I understand, but you walk away there isn't going to be a walk back in. Understand?"

Chase took several deep breaths before nodding. Drake let him go fixed his jacket and then ran a hand through his hair.

"What are you going to do?" Chase asked.

"First thing I'm going to do is destroy all of this shit," Drake told him, packing up the information. "No one is going to use me or them ever again. Then after that, I don't know."

* * * *

Six weeks later

Kane sat on the side of the bed, trying to get his shirt on but having very little luck. His rib was killing him, which went right along with his back and the hole in his stomach. He was so damn sick of being in that bed that he could scream. Speaking of screaming, Sasha was doing a nice little number inside his head.

"Hey what are you doing?" Drake came over to the bed, a glass of water in one hand, and some pills in the other. He put them down, taking the shirt from Kane's hand. "You trying to bust something open?"

"I'm doing okay." He sighed when Drake held the shirt up over his head, stretching the hole for his head. "Come on, man, this is embarrassing."

"Humor me."

Kane growled at the back of his throat and let Drake help him get dressed. By the time he was done, he was breathing hard and sweating. When Drake handed him the pain meds Kane didn't hesitate in taking them like he normally would.

"You still haven't found her, have you?" Kane asked.

"No."

"Do you think you will?"

"We did last time." Kane winced, pinching the bridge of his nose. "Sasha again?"

Kane nodded, "She's worried, freaking out. It's the first time we've been away from each other."

Drake grabbed the chair dragged it over to the bed and straddled it. "We need to talk about Sasha some." He rubbed around his mouth, then stroked longer on his chin. "There's some stuff you need to know and things you need to come to terms with starting now."

Kane frowned. "Why do I get this feeling I'm not going to like any of it?"

Drake snickered, "Probably because you're not. But you need to know that she isn't alone either." He got serious and that put Kane on edge. He was the only one who ever took care of Sasha, and as far as he knew he was going to be the only one. "So I'm going to start you off easy by telling you that she's a telepathic."

"Huh?"

"Her gift for communicating with you is extra special. Twins of our kind can do that, and males do the mind seduction, as I told you before. Well, with her, and it has been proven with our kind, that when a twin is born with the mark Sasha has on her shoulder and no shifter traits, well the telepathic thing comes into play."

"I'm not getting you."

"She can read everyone's mind," Drake said. "But can only *talk* with you, using it."

"Wow," Kane breathed out.

"Yeah, well that's not all." Drake took a deep breath and Kane got uncomfortable. "She also has a mate."

"No." Kane shook his head. "No mate." He was about to get up, but the sudden move had him wincing. "Shit," he hissed.

"Kane—"

"No, you don't understand." Kane strained to talk with the pain. He twisted the wrong way, pulling at his rib that was still very tender. "She can't handle this, us! She's, she's. . ."

"I know, Kane." He stilled, looking Drake dead on. "Jada left us all of the stuff she took. Everything that Stan was willing to kill her to get back. I know, and so does he about what happened to Sasha before you were able to protect her."

Kane gritted his teeth together in frustration. "Who is he?" He hated asking the question, but at the same time needed to know. He didn't want to think about the things someone would do to her. The same kind of things that he had done to Jada, but couldn't stop his mind from going there.

"Kane," Drake sighed.

"I want to know." Kane said through his teeth.

Drake took a deep breath and let it out slow. "Chase."

Holding his side, and his stomach, Kane stood up. He walked away from Drake to the window, staring down at the pool, which was empty. "Is that why he left? Because of us?"

"I think partly, yes."

"Partly?"

"Chase hasn't even stood on his own. By leaving he can figure out who he is and what he wants." Drake also stood up, coming to stand next to Kane, leaning against the wall next to the window with his arms crossed. "He was prepared to walk away after seeing what they did to her. He doesn't want to hurt her or you."

"When will he do this then?"

"Whenever he feels it's time. Kane, why haven't you asked me what you really want to ask?"

Kane turned away from the window. He didn't look at Drake as he headed for the bathroom. "I want to go home, Drake. Tomorrow please." He went in, closing the door. He leaned back against it, closing his eyes with a sigh.

"I lied to you, Kane," she said, taking a deep breath. "I do love you."

He heard her say it, and still she left him. Kane couldn't shake the feeling of being abandoned by Jada leaving after she said she loved him. It hurt, but what hurt even worse was deciding when he woke up this morning that he was going to let her go. He just hadn't told Drake yet. He didn't want them to go looking for her.

In the morning, they left. Drake called Carrick to tell her they were heading back. She already went home with Sasha and told them both she had everything ready. Kane was going to stay at the house until he was completely healed. He didn't complain. The entire trip home he sat in his seat, staring out the window saying nothing. When

Drake stopped to eat, Kane ate. It was almost as if he was going through the motions of life, but not really living it.

Sasha was very excited to see them both. She hugged Kane tightly, and he in turn hugged her quickly, then he let her go to head up to his room. There he stayed for a couple of days, only coming out for the bathroom. He didn't even eat much. *So this is what depression feels like. It sucks!*

* * * *

Three weeks later

Sasha woke early, went to Kane to check on him only to find an empty room. She sighed, resting her head on the doorframe, staring at the bed then the tray of food she brought up. The bed was a mess and the food untouched.

"You're up early." Drake came up behind her, kissing the top of her head as he did every morning.

"He's been home for three weeks now and hasn't come out of it." She looked up at Drake with a frown. "I'm worried about him. All I hear is this sadness in him."

"I know," Drake sighed.

"He needs Jada," she stated, letting Drake pull her away from Kane's door. He wrapped his arm around her shoulders as they went downstairs. "This isn't like Kane, Drake. It's like he's just given up or something."

"He has."

She stopped; he took another step before stopping also. "Then we have to fix it. I want my brother back."

"Sasha, it isn't that simple."

"Yes, it is. We find her and everything will go back the way it was."

"Honey, things never go back the way they were. He has made the choice not to go after her and we have to respect that."

She shook her head. "I can't do that."

Sasha brushed past him out the front door. The first days of spring were here, flowers were blooming, the trees were getting their new leaves, and the air was so fresh smelling. But the air still held a bitter coldness.

Taking off at a run, she went into the woods, following the sadness that was in her head. Each step she took it got stronger. Kane hadn't been back to his cabin since coming home. But he did spend a lot of time in the woods just sitting and staring out at nothing. It made her feel bad for him, but she didn't know what to do.

She stopped when she saw the freshly worn path that her brother had made. For weeks now, he kept coming to this hot spring and just sat there. Sasha knew it was a place that Kane had watched Jada swim. It was a memory he often relived in his mind. At first, it made her blush seeing it, then she became curious as to why it was so special or if the emotion she was picking up right now was sexy. She didn't understand how one person could feel that by looking at another without clothes. It didn't make much sense to her, until Carrick had the sex talk with her. Now that was something she hadn't seen or noticed. She didn't understand the whole thing. How could one get pleasure doing that? Kane did with Jada, and he was missing that contact now.

She went up to him. He was sitting on a rock, his back towards her, but he knew she was there. She saw that.

Sasha wrapped her arms around him from behind, resting her head on his shoulder. "Please don't give up." She whispered. "It's going to be all right."

Kane moved his head so his cheek rested on her arm. "I'm lost, Sasha, and can't find my way out this time."

She walked around to the front of him. She took his face in her hands, tilted his head up to look at her. There were tears on his face. For the first time in her young life, she watched her brother cry.

"You're not alone this time, Kane. We have family to help."

"I...I...I." he broke down and she wrapped her arms around him, holding him tight and close.

Kane held onto her tightly also, crying into her stomach when he fell from the rock to his knees. He fisted his hands into her sweater, and she fisted her hands into his hair. She felt his pain and hurt inside her head, but Sasha took it. This time she was going to be the one to fix things. She couldn't let Kane hurt like this for a moment longer.

"It's going be all right," she soothed.

* * * *

Sasha stood at the top of the stairs, biting her lip, straining to pick up where Drake and Carrick were, and what they were doing. So far, they were in the kitchen talking and Kane was in his room, resting.

Once she was sure they were busy, she walked as softly as she could down the hall to their room. Drake's cell was on the nightstand, which was just what she wanted. She sat down on the bed, picked the phone up and tried to figure out how to get the contacts to come up. It took some time, but she was able to get the one she wanted to show. Cole.

"Hey, Drake what's up?" Cole said after a few rings.

"Cole, its Sasha."

"What's wrong?" She heard the concern in his voice, and even on the phone, she could feel it.

She smiled. "Nothing. I need to ask you for help. You're the only one I could think of to ask, who is still in the city."

"What do you need?"

She licked her lips, glanced at the door to make sure she was still alone before going on. If Kane knew what she was doing he might get upset, but then again he might not care. "I know you found her last time. I want you to find Jada again." Silence. "Cole?"

"Sasha, I don't think that would be a good idea." He sighed.

She frowned. "He's dying inside, Cole. All I feel is this sadness in him. We need to fix it!"

"Honey, its something he's going to have to do on his own if he wants that."

"No. That's not acceptable." She shook her head.

"Sasha we can't interfere here. I know you don't understand, and I do get it that you want to help Kane. But his shifter pride won't let us help him this time."

She didn't want to hear anymore of it and hung up on it. Tears of frustration came to her eyes, but she refused to let them fall. She needed to help Kane. Someone had to!

Taking a deep breath, she flipped through the contacts again. One name stood out. A name she had heard, but hadn't really ever seen or met. She knew he was at the house when they got Kane home. He brought Celine home to be with Cole. And he was friends with Jada.

Sasha placed the call to the name Chase. Her nerves started to scream at her as she waited for him to answer the phone.

"Drake, you sure do know how to call when I'm busy as hell."

Her mouth went dry and hands started to shake. His voice was so deep that it made her feel funny. What really had her scared to talk was that she didn't pick anything up from him. There was no feeling, no sound in her head. Nothing! Everything around her seemed to go quiet.

"Drake! You there."

"This isn't Drake," she had to force herself to speak, and her voice shook when she did. It went quiet on the phone and Sasha almost feared that he had hung up. "Hello? Are you still there?"

"Sasha?" he sighed her name and it sent chills down her spine.

"Yes," she answered. Swallowing hard and taking a deep breath she went on: "I need help to find Jada. Can you find her, please? Kane really needs her."

Time seemed to stand still. She couldn't pick up a thing from him. She was afraid that he was going to tell her no like Cole had. It was so strange not being able to read him or see what he was thinking like the others. Even before Cole answered her, she knew he wouldn't. She just hopped that he might change his mind when he talked to her. With Chase, she didn't know a thing.

"Are you still there?" she asked tenderly, fearing that he was going to say no and hang up on her. He sounded so strange.

"Okay." He sighed again. "I'll find her for you and let Cole know so he can have Drake bring him."

She smiled, even though he couldn't see it. "Thanks! How long do you think it will take for you to find her?"

"It won't take me too long."

"Thank you so much. I owe you one."

She heard him take a deep breath. It almost sounded like he was trying to get control or something. "No, you don't. You don't owe me anything. Take care."

The phone went dead. She put it back down and left the room wondering why she couldn't read him or pick up anything at all. For the moment she didn't care. Someone was going to help her help Kane and that's all that mattered.

Chapter Twelve

Jada walked down the clean, sterile halls of one of the fanciest and most expensive private hospital/nursing homes around. Only a few people had large enough bank accounts to be able to stay here for treatment and James Leonard was one of them.

She stopped at the nurses' desk and put on her best smile. "Hi, James Leonard, please."

The nurses stopped talking and looked at her with a shocked look on their faces. "Are you a relative?"

"Unfortunately, yes."

"Down the hall," one pointed, "Last room on the left."

"Thanks." Jada pushed away from the desk whistled and headed for the room knowing that the nurses were still looking at her in shock.

She didn't bother with knocking on the door. Jada opened it, walked in, and kicked it closed, grinning at the way it seemed to echo in the room.

"Who's there? Nurse!"

"Nope, not the nurse." She strolled into the room, which was set up like a hospital room. A few feet away from the door, behind a half wall was a bed with an old man. "Hello, Grandfather."

He had a tray of food sitting in front of him. Jada grabbed the croissant roll, sat down in the overstuffed chair at the foot of the bed, and crossed one leg over the other. She tore off a piece, put it in her mouth, and chewed with a smile.

They had a stare off, but which one was going to give in first, she couldn't say at the moment. She kept eating the croissant, waiting.

"What the hell are you doing here?" he strained when he talked. In his hand, he had an oxygen mask and it shook. "You were supposed to die in the fire."

"Would that have made you happy?" She rubbed her hands together, brushing the crumbs off and then cleaned off her jeans. "I mean, isn't that what everyone is supposed to do? Keep you happy?"

He took a few deep breaths, his cold eyes narrowing on her. "Yes," he breathed out.

Slowly she smiled and sat forward, fingers linked together over her knee. "Ah, that's right. I know your dirty little secret. And so did

Chris."

He started coughing and she just sat there. Jada wasn't going to get up and help him, not this time. This time she was going to let him sit there and suffer, just as she'd suffered.

"You know, you really got lucky. You just don't know it." She stood up, walking around the bed to the built in heater, leaning back. "We discovered your dirty little deeds," she said and waved her hands in the air in front of her. "It's what he used to stop the beatings, isn't it?"

"You don't know what you're talking about." He huffed, taking more deep breaths.

"But what I want to know is did it bother you at all, her screams, or is that what you used to get off?"

"You listen here—"

Jada came over to the bed, yanked the mask away, and took hold of his face, making him look her in the eyes. "No you listen to me, you sick bastard. I know what you did to her. I know all the sick things you forced my mother to do, just like I have never forgotten the beatings you dished out to me because I locked you out!" She spoke low and right in his face. "You don't scare me any longer. You're not that monster under the bed any more. You took away her youth, and you beat mine out of me. But if you think you're going to get away with it think again. I'm going to bring you down, you fuck!" She shoved his face away and stood back up. She jerked her jacket down and took a deep breath then put her smile back on her face.

"The board of your company already knows about your wrinkled ass." She went back to the chair, sitting down. "I told them everything." She smiled at him. "I even showed them the proof that my mother had and what Chris put together. You know, the DNA test showing who Chris's father really is. Come morning you'll be as broke as I am."

He pointed a finger at her. The hate coming from his eyes would have been enough to have Jada backing down in the past. Not this time. He didn't get a word out. The monitor next to his bed went off and he grabbed his chest. Jada stood up, turned, and walked out of the room.

She went right past the nurses who were quickly coming to their feet. "I think he's having a heart attack," she mentioned stopping in front of the elevator and pressing the down button. "Funny. Never thought the old bastard had a heart."

* * * *

She walked down the sidewalk, head down, and pack slung over her shoulder making her way through the crowd of people. After spending any amount of time with her grandfather, Jada need a stiff drink. Nothing changed between them. She was the mistake, the sin, and he was the saint. Hah! Well the world was soon going to learn that was one hell of a lie.

Jada walked into the nearest bar. She pushed through the people, planted her ass on a barstool, and pulled out a twenty, slapping it on the counter.

"Shot of whiskey, beer kicker please."

"Sure thing, honey," the bartender said, taking her money, and putting a shot glass in front of her. He poured, left her change, and Jada downed it before the top of her beer was off.

"I don't think I've ever seen you drink like that before."

Jada closed her eyes, hung her head down, and took a deep breath before turning to the left of her stool. "Hi, Chase. How're you doing?"

Chase smiled. It had been six months since she had last seen him, and he still had the rough look going on. His face still had the four-day beard look, hair still appearing like it was trying to grow out, and the clothes he was wearing could've looked better.

"Because you look like shit still," she added, turning back in her seat, taking a drink of her beer.

"Yeah, but I bet I'm doing a hell of a lot better than you." He sighed. She glanced at him, said nothing as he raised his finger up to the bartender, and ordered a beer. "Talked to Sasha the other day."

"Yeah?"

"Yeah. Kane isn't doing too good. Went through a depression or something, and now I hear he's going nuts over you. Drake's about ready to let him loose on your ass I hear."

She turned in her seat again, facing him. "And what makes you think he can find me?"

"I did." Chase took a big drink of his beer before turning to face her. "What are you running from?" She opened her mouth and he raised his hand up. "I mean the truth this time. I think I'm entitled to know. I mean, Sasha figured out how to call me and drag me back into this shit. I swear I thought I was done doing the match making shit with Cole and Celine."

"What're you running from, or should I say who?" She cocked her head to the side with a smile. "Does Cole even know?"

Chase groaned, rubbed his face before pointing a finger at her. "I'm not here to talk about me. So don't change the subject."

"You can't save me, Chase." She took another drink, grabbed her bag, and hopped from the stool. "So don't try to."

"I'm not trying to save you." He shook his head, taking another drink. "I only want to understand better."

Jada turned back around on the stool, facing the bar. She thought long and hard about her past; the secrets that her grandfather worked so damn hard to hide from the world. He was dying now, in a hospital, wallowing in his family sins with no one by his side to tell him he could die peaceful and without guilt. She lied to him about telling, mostly because she wanted him to suffer some before he died, like she had suffered. Maybe it was time for someone to let those secrets come out. Maybe that someone was her and by telling Chase that guilt over Chris would be lifted from her shoulders.

She should tell Kane, but she couldn't face him. When she left, it was, as she said, to give him a chance at a normal life. He didn't need her sins on his shoulders. He had enough baggage of his own, didn't need hers as well.

After all this time, Jada felt like she really did need to talk to someone. To say aloud what was hidden behind those burnt down doors.

"You know every family has their own set of secrets right? I mean, look at what you hid from the world," she chuckled.

"Yeah, we all have something to hide, that's for sure," Chase sighed.

She glanced at him. Something in Chase changed and she wasn't just thinking about his appearance over the past three years. Something deeper inside him was different and she would bet it had to do with a girl.

"Well my family secrets go on the dark side." She took another drink, a deep breath and turned once more in her seat, facing him. "My grandfather raped my mother when she was around thirteen or fourteen. It was to teach her a lesson about the sins of the flesh after she was caught making out with some boy."

Chase's mouth dropped open. "Son-of-a-bitch," he gasped softly.

"Yeah, well that sin cost them both. She got pregnant and he shipped her off to have the baby. My good old Uncle didn't do shit to help her either. See, my grandfather would twist this Bible crap whenever it suited him, and my Uncle followed like a dog on a leash.

Since dear old James Leonard didn't love much, and he thought his only son was a weakling, well he kept the baby and made my Uncle raise it as his son."

"Chris," Chase stated.

"Yeah, and for whatever twisted reason, my grandfather treated Chris like gold. I found out later on that it killed my mother to have to watch her son being raised by her brother and his wife, none of them would stand up to my grandfather for anything. But it seemed that wasn't the only torture my grandfather hid. He beat my mother all the time, preached to her, and just treated her like shit."

"But he isn't you—"

Jada quickly shook her head. "Lord no! She got pregnant again when she was sixteen at the party I told you about. When that happened, she stood up to him for the first time in her life. She wasn't going to give me up for anything, so he once more shipped her off. The first time I met him was when she died. Later on I found out that the reason they were all together that night was she was demanding Chris back and going to file charges for kidnapping and rape if they didn't agree."

"And then they got in the car wreck."

"And I was shipped off to my closest living relative, as was Chris. It was the first time I'd ever met him." She took another deep drink, feeling like some of the weight of her past was being lifted after all. "We were teenagers before we found out that we were more than cousins."

"Bet your grandfather didn't like that," Chase snorted. She watched him finish off his beer and order another. She ordered another shot.

Jada took the shot, hissing with the burn. She shook her head. "No, he didn't. It was the leverage Chris needed to get him to stop beating me."

"What, he beat you too?" Chase sounded shocked.

She nodded. "For the sins of my mother. Never really understood why he didn't try any shit with me either."

"You know, I think you're right. Kane shouldn't know this shit." He downed half of his fresh beer. "He'd kill the bastard I think," he said with a tight sounding voice.

"What can I say, Chase," she finished her beer, slamming the bottle down. "I give a new meaning to the word dysfunctional." She stood up, grabbing her bag.

"Where are you going now?" he turned in his seat, facing her.

"Well I'm not stupid, and pretty sure you let them know where I'm at. So it's time to move." She smiled.

"You can't keep running from him, Jada." He smiled back. "He'll only find you."

"But can he catch me?"

Chase laughed, "Oh I think he can."

She slung her bag over her shoulder, and leaned against the bar close to him, between the stools. "You're a good friend, Chase. The only one I've ever had." Jada brought him down and kissed him on his whiskered cheek. "Don't keep her waiting too long." She whispered.

Jada walked away, not looking back. She never looked back. It was the last thing Chris had said to her. The one thing she'd never forgotten all these years later.

"How could he do this to her?" Jada cried, reading the letter her mother had left her. It was hidden away in a safety deposit box, which she had the key hidden in a locket her mother gave Chris to give to her for her sixteenth birthday, but instead he gave it to her for her thirteenth.

"How could my father keep it hidden?" Chris added.

"He hurt her so much." Jada couldn't stop the tears from falling down her face. Crying was a weakness, one her grandfather tried like hell to beat out of her.

Chris grabbed her face, making Jada look him in the eye, the tears falling fast. "But he is never going to hurt you again. I promise you."

"You can't stop him."

"Yes I can," he pulled her into his arms, holding her tightly as she cried. "He'll never hurt you. Never put one finger on you again as long as I live, and we'll never look back." He pulled her back, staring her in the face, wiping her tears away. "Understand me? From this day on, we are brother and sister, not cousins. No matter what he says or does. You are my sister. We never go back to the past and what we were. We only go forward." Jada nodded and Chris pulled her back into his arms. "Never look back, Jada. No matter what happens."

The place she was staying was a rent a room for a night. Jada didn't have a lot with her, since she was staying on the move. It was mostly out of habit. She stayed on the go because one didn't get hurt that way. If you stayed in one place too long, you always got attached, then it would be taken away.

Her room had two rooms in it or three if you counted the tiny bathroom. You walked into a small front room that was closed off by a curtain to hide the kitchen. In the back was the bedroom and bath. Already had a sofa, table and chair, and bed, so Jada didn't need to worry or bother with any of that. All she had to keep track of was her cameras and her few clothes.

She unlocked the door, kicked it closed, tossed the keys to the table, and stopped in her tracks. Something wasn't right. Her first clue, the new scrapbook she owned was open and Kane's face was looking back at her.

It was the photo she took of him in the cabin, where he wasn't smiling. She caught him off guard then, and he in turn kissed her.

Jada stilled, her back to her bedroom. Closing her eyes, she sighed. She felt him, didn't need to see him, and just knew he was there. For six months, she'd dreamed of him holding her at night. She even woke up a few times and thought about going back, but stopped. They both needed time to heal away from each other, or so she thought. She knew that she needed to stand on her own once more. She needed to face her past alone for the last time and bury it where it belonged.

"What are you doing here?" she asked, keeping her back to her room.

"Waiting for you."

Opening her eyes, Jada swung around. Kane was standing in her bedroom doorway. Arms crossed over his massive chest, and his loose hair that was covering his shoulders, was lighter. He looked bigger, or she was just in a very tiny room, because he definitely took up most of the space.

"You know, I'm definitely going to kill Chase." She put one hand on her hip, the other up to her forehead. "I *knew* he was going to tell you where I was at."

"He didn't tell me you were here," Kane sighed. "Just what town I could find you in. He figured I needed to get off my ass and do the rest of the hunt."

"Hunt?" she frowned. "Look, cave boy."

Kane growled and rushed over to her. He backed her right up to the one counter she had in the kitchen, picked her up, and sat her down, standing between her legs. He pinned her in, fisting her hair in his hand, pulling it until her head was back far enough to look up at him.

"Six months, Jada. Six fucking months I've been dying inside for you. Do you have any idea what it's done to me?"

"Given you one hell of a hard-on that won't go away?"

He growled again, pushed away from her, and paced the room. Jada didn't move. She didn't dare. In the short amount of time she'd lived with all of them she had learned something after all. Don't push too much. It never ends pretty. Her first time was proof of that, but then there were parts of that memory which was enjoyable. As much as she hated to admit it, she did like the feel of his hands and mouth on her then.

"For the first time in my life, Jada, I go to sleep and I don't wake up panting from a damn nightmare." He stopped pacing and looked at her. His blue eyes were darker, his body tense. "I dream about you."

"Yeah, sexual frustrations can do that." He growled again and she jumped down from the counter. "What do you want from me?" she yelled. "Okay, I left, but deep down you know it was for the better."

"Says who?"

"We both needed to heal and there was no way in hell that was going to happen staying together." She cut through the air at her waist with her hand. "Period. All you would have tried to do is fuck me instead of healing."

"Bullshit!" he snapped.

"Bullshit?" She crossed her arms over her chest, leaning to one side. "Let me tell you what is bullshit."

She didn't get to finish. He rushed up on her again, picked her up, placed her back on the counter none too gently, fisted his hand into her hair and kissed her hard and deep. "You still have a mouth on you," he breathed out against her lips.

She couldn't control her breathing. Jada stared at his mouth, her lips tingling from the kiss, her body quickly waking up with memories.

"And I love that about you," he went on.

She shook her head. "I hate you," she whispered.

His mouth curved slightly. He licked her bottom lip, sucking it. "No, you don't. You love me. You said so yourself."

"Argh!" She pushed at his chest and he took a step back. Jada hopped down again from the counter, putting space between them. "I did not."

"Still going to lie to yourself?" She glanced over her shoulder and he shrugged. "Fine, but don't try to lie to me. Not anymore."

"Go home, Kane," she snapped. "I can't give you what you want. I've told you that before."

"And I say that is a load of crap!" he yelled. She flinched when he yelled, but stood her ground with him. "You're afraid of being happy!"

"Go to hell." She gave him her back and headed for the bedroom. The one thing she wasn't expecting, but should have, was Kane to follow.

"Not this time," he growled when she tried to close the door on him. "I'm not going to be shut out anymore!"

She got the door closed, locked in fact. But it didn't stay that way. Kane kicked it open and Jada jumped. "Are you out of your damn mind?"

"As a matter of fact, I am right now." He went up to her, backing her up to the wall, boxing her in with his arms over her head and his body pressed close. "I'm tired of you shutting me out, running away. It all ends right now or so help me I'll hog tie your ass home and keep you tied to my bed until you come to reason."

"You wouldn't." On purpose, Jada raised her chin up and challenged him. Why? She couldn't say.

And Kane took the bait. He pushed himself from the wall, grabbed both of her arms, jerking her off it as well. They had a small stare off before he turned them and shoved her down on the bed.

She fought with herself not to show any interest when Kane pulled his shirt over his head, tossing it behind him. Each move he made the thick muscles on his chest and arms moved. It was mouth watering to watch him move, but even though she wanted him like she needed to breathe, she wasn't going to give in to her desires.

"What the fuck do you think you're doing, wolf boy?" she asked, rising up on her elbows.

Kane had kicked his shoes off and opened his belt. His hands stilled at the snap of his jeans and those sexy blue eyes of his gave her the chills when he met hers.

"Showing you reason," he told her. "Take them off."

Both eyebrows went up. Jada tried to put on the innocent look. "Take what off, my shoes?"

"I'll rip them all off if I have to." He sounded on edge. His voice so thick and deep she felt it all the way to her clit.

"I thought I told you last time you tried to pull this shit that I don't like being told what to do." Jada spoke through her teeth, hoping like hell she was putting on a good front with him.

"I smell different," he snickered back.

Her breath left her when he pulled his jeans open and pushed them down his legs. Kane wasn't wearing anything under them and stood before her naked as the day he was born. And he was very hard.

Jada rolled her eyes, "I don't think so." She put her foot up, pressing against his chest, stopping him when he made an advance towards her.

Kane looked down at her foot on his chest. He wrapped one hand around her ankle, moved it up her leg to the knee, back down then, out of nowhere, and flipped her over to her stomach. Jada cried out. Kane grabbed the back of her shirt and ripped it down her back.

"Are you out of your damn mind!" she yelled. He didn't answer, just pulled the ripped shirt from under her, then both hands went to her waist, gripping her jeans. "Don't you fucking do it you shit!" He pulled to the sides and her jeans made a very loud ripping sound, parting to the side. "I can't believe you did that!"

He chuckled behind her. "You should. Done it once, why not again."

He grabbed her hips, pulling her up to her knees. Jada was about to tell him off when he did the unexpected. "Ouch! You bit me." He did. Right on her ass.

Kane licked the same spot and purred. "Damn I love it when you wear this kind of panties. Almost makes it a shame to rip them off."

"I'll show you rip." She rose up on her knees, reached back, and fisted both of her hands into his hair.

He hissed and bit her again, on the shoulder. Jada almost climaxed from the pleasure of the bite. She didn't fight him as he pulled her panties down her legs. Jada was half expecting him to rip them off as he did her other clothes.

Both of his hands closed around her breasts, squeezing the mounds before pulling her bra up to release them. He wrapped one arm around her, over her chest and his other hand slid down her body, cupping her throbbing pussy. Jada moaned and Kane sucked on her shoulder, sliding his hips, pressing his hot cock between her legs.

She parted her legs as much as the panties on her knees would allow. The feel of the head of his cock teasing her clit was pure torture, but one she'd missed terribly. When the change in her happened, she couldn't answer. And when the hell she started craving his touch, she would never know.

It felt like he was using his body only to push her back down to her hands and knees. She hung her head down, he let go of her shoulder. He pushed her hair to the side, leaving the mark available for him. One swift motion and Kane was embedded deeply inside her. Jada gasped. He stretched her, burned her in more places than one. And she loved it. With his hands planted on the bed next to her, chest touching her back, and his mouth kissing around the mark, Kane moved. It felt like he wasn't holding anything back with her, and wasn't doing gentle. He pulled out, thrust in hard and powerful. It took her breath away, and left her panting to catch it back.

The bed rocked with his motions. Jada fisted her hands into the bedding, pushing back against his thrust, praying for it to end, yet, at the same time, hoping like hell it wouldn't.

She heard the rip and knew her panties were gone as well. But she didn't care. Kane stopped, turned over with her in his arms, and slammed her down onto his lap. The position, her facing away from him, had a deeper, thicker feel. He yanked her bra from her body and both hands cupped her breasts. She grabbed his arms and moved, rocked her hips. It wasn't enough.

This time Jada stopped, only so she could turn around and face him. With his help, his cock stayed inside her as she straddled his lap.

Jada took hold of his face kissed him deep and loved the man before her with her body. She slapped into him just as he had done to her many times, and Kane helped her. His hands grabbed her ass, giving her an extra push each time she took him back into her body.

Tears formed in her eyes with the pressure that was slowly building up inside her. The orgasm that was coming was going to be different. She knew it. She didn't fight it. She moved faster, harder, reaching out for the release as she kissed him deeply.

Jada broke the kiss with an, "Oh, God!"

Her climax hit, as did the tears. The sob that slipped past her lips matched the release in her body. She couldn't stop either. She cried and moaned at the same time, and Kane kept pushing her. He slammed her hard onto him, making the orgasm seem to last longer. When she rested her head on his shoulder his lips closed on the mark, biting her. One climax turned into another and all she could do was wrap her arms around his neck and ride it out.

She felt him swell inside her, heard the moaning growl against her shoulder, and even felt his seed fill her up. But she couldn't stop crying, even when his arms held her tight against him, she couldn't stop.

"Shh," he soothed. "It's okay."

Jada slapped him on the back. "You damn animal," she cried into his shoulder. "Why'd you have to do that?"

"Do what?"

She sniffed back the tears and moved back to face him. "Come back into my life?"

He wiped the tears from her cheek, taking a deep breath. "Because as much as you want to fight it, I love you." He kissed her. "There isn't anyone else out there for me."

Jada lost it and cried fresh tears that had nothing to do with the great sex they had just had. Once more, she wrapped her arms around him, holding him as tight as she could. "Don't leave me," she whispered. "Everybody I care about leaves me."

Kane tightened his arms around her, resting his head on her shoulder. "Never. You're stuck with me for life, princess. That's a promise."

* * * *

"Now, aren't you glad I made you go find her?"

Kane smiled. *"Yes, Sasha, I'm glad you made me go find her.* Now can we go home," he said against Jada's shoulder." Sasha is busting a gut to see you again. She's been taking pictures like you wouldn't believe."

Jada laughed against his shoulder, sniffed again, and sat back. Just having her in his arms again made him a walking hard-on.

"Later." She smiled. "I'm not done with you yet."

He glanced at the clock next to the bed. "Well we only have about fifteen minutes before Drake picks us up." She moved, or more like grinded herself on him. That had him raising one eyebrow at her. "I'll call him."

She smiled, cupped his face, and brought her lips very close, nodding. "You do that." She kissed him, teasing her tongue on his lips. "I have a few positions of my own I want to try right now."

Kane growled, kissed her deep, and slid his arms under her legs, picking them up. "So do I."

Epilogue

It was her third Christmas, but Sasha still felt like a little girl. She was so excited she felt like she was going to bust any second waiting to get to the packages under the tree. Kane and Drake went out the week before to get the perfect tree. Like the past, they tended to argue some about what one was the best.

Carrick took her shopping, and Cole went to Celine's family for the holiday. He told her that when Chase decided to get home, he was going to have a big holiday party at his place, just like Carrick and Drake put on here. The day after Christmas, they went to the house and had another Christmas with Stefan and Dedrick's family. It was the best! Now she was dying for everyone to get up so she could see what was under the tree!

Drake told her on their first Christmas, when she got up at four in the morning, that it was something young kids did. He and his brother always got up early and snooped under the tree, and like always their mother caught them. He told them stories of growing up and what each holiday was like. She thought it was something of a dream, until he started doing all of those things for them. Not being able to stand it any longer, she left her room to go down to Drake's and wake him up.

"About time you got up!" She stopped at the top of the stairs. Drake was smiling up at her. "We've been waiting for you."

Everyone was already there. Sasha couldn't stop the childish smile that spread across her face as she bounced down the stairs. She jumped into Kane's arms first. He kissed and hugged her, and then she went to Drake who also hugged her tightly.

"Merry Christmas," he said into her hair. "Now let's get this party started!" He slapped his hands together and everyone sat down.

Sasha went right to the floor, next to the tree. Carrick began to hand out the presents and Sasha didn't hesitate ripping them open. She got clothes, music, and a stereo to play it, and many books. Drake knelt down next to her and handed her a strange long box.

"Okay I know you are pretty old for this, but every girl in our family has to have one of these. It's a must." Drake said.

"The only other girl in the family is Celine," Carrick stated.

"Yep, and I still send her one, too," Drake said to her.

Sasha frowned and ripped into the paper. Inside the box was a porcelain doll with long blond hair, big blue eyes and dressed in a white lace gown.

"She's beautiful," Sasha breathed out.

"I saw her when I was getting Celine hers," Drake stated. "She reminded me of you."

Sasha turned and wrapped her arms around his neck, hugging him tightly. "Thank you."

"Okay, I'm *not* cleaning up this mess," Jada said, breaking the silence.

Sasha looked over at Kane and the two of them tossed tons of paper at Jada. She laughed.

"Hey, we forgot one," Kane said. He brought out a small box wrapped in shinny pink paper. "Has Sasha's name on it."

"Who's it from?" Carrick asked.

"Don't know." Kane shook his head. "No name on it."

He handed it to Sasha. She opened it up to a black velvet box. Inside the box was a gold, open heart necklace with a solid heart diamond in the middle of it and a note. Two hearts beating as one, Always! C.

Sasha held the necklace up for everyone to see. "It's beautiful," she whispered. There was something about it that held her attention. It made her feel safe, and she didn't understand why.

"Why don't you like it?" she asked Kane.

Kane was staring at Drake when she spoke. He blinked a few times at her. "In my head again."

"Sorry." She felt her face heat up. Sasha held the heart in her hand, touching it with her fingers. "But why don't you like it? It's very pretty."

"Kane's just being an over protective brother," Drake said. He took the necklace from her hand and put it around her neck.

"I need a leash," Jada snorted.

Sasha smiled when Kane threw a rolled up paper at her again.

"Come on you two," Carrick sighed. "Let's get the food going before Drake starts whining about how he's starving."

Sasha looked down at the heart resting on her chest. Drake stayed with her, kneeling down in front of her. She could hear whispers only from Drake, but always had a hard time understanding them.

"Someone like you is going to want me," she said. "Right?"

"What do you mean?"

She looked up and frowned. "Someone is going to claim me as

their mate one day. That's what Kane doesn't like."

"Yes."

"Is it really that bad?" She couldn't stop the fear from gripping her or her voice from shaking with the question.

Drake reached out and touched her check. "It's not that bad, but we can be frightening at times, when the need becomes too strong."

"What need?" she whispered, holding her breath.

"The need to be with our mate." He smiled. "But hey, don't think about that now." He smiled, stood up, and helped her up as well. "It's Christmas. There is a shitload of cookies in there and if we don't get our butts in the kitchen," he put his arm around her, giving her a squeeze, "then your brother is going to eat them all."

"How many of these do we have to save for Cole and them?" Kane asked with a mouth full and more in his hands.

Sasha giggled, resting her head on Drake. "I think I'm going to have to bake more," she whispered.

"I think you're right." Drake whispered back.

* * * *

"Are you sure you won't change your mind?" Celine asked Chase for about the fifth time on the phone.

He called to let the family know he wasn't going to make it for Christmas after all. He wasn't ready yet to face the family or her. It wasn't time. It killed him to have to hold out for another year, maybe even two. He made a deal with Drake that he wouldn't stay away for another three years. Cole guilted him into calling once a week. If they all knew where he was now, they would be kicking his ass.

Chase stood in the woods, a nice distance away from Drake's house so that Sasha wouldn't pick him up. She could hear thoughts and see into their minds, not good, if you wanted to be sneaky, which he did. But he wanted to see her. Needed to see her face as she opened the gift he left for her. And it was magical. Her face lit up like the lights on the tree.

"No, I can't Celine," he sighed into the phone. "I just wanted to tell you and wish you all a Merry Christmas."

"Cole's going to be so disappointed. He was really hoping you'd be home this time."

"Maybe next year." He turned away from the scene and got back into his truck. "I've got to go, Celine. Tell Cole I'll call him later tonight."

"Chase—"

He hung up, cutting her off. Feeling the dread of leaving again, Chase started his truck, put it in park, and drove away. How long he was going to stay away this time, he didn't know. He only hoped that it wasn't much longer.

He was dying inside.

Dying for her.

* * * *

www.jadensinclair.com

Also by Jaden Sinclair at www.melange-books.com:

Interplanetary Passions
Outerplanetary Sensations
S.E.T.H.
S.H.I.L.O.
Lucifer's Lust, with Mae Powers

In the Shifter Series:
Book 1: Stefan's Mark
Book 2: Claiming Skyler
Book 3: Dedrick's Taming
Book 4: The Prowling
Book 5: Cole's Awakening
Book 6: The New Breed
Book 7: Seducing Sasha

Seducing Sasha
By Jaden Sinclair

Chase Sexton has watched Sasha from afar for years. He has longed to touch and hold her at night and take away all the pain and bad memories from her past. The only problem is that Sasha doesn't trust any man but her brother. How does one man show the one woman who is right for him that all men are not created equal? That in the arms of the right man, his arms, all bad memories can and will disappear. Can he replace them with something special, or will all his longings be for nothing?

Lightning Source UK Ltd.
Milton Keynes UK
UKOW08f1432010517
300253UK00002BA/557/P